Wherever the tides take you . . .

Guided by the winds of fate, Henry 'Ric' Robbins arrives on a hot June day in Port Royal. But the moment he sets foot on what should be a pirate's paradise, he's driven to steal a woman destined for slavery, survives the worst natural disaster to ever hit the isle of Jamaica, and answers the call to be captain of the *Scarlet Night*.

Jocelyn Beauchamp's life is one of privilege—until she is rudely thrown into the hands of pirates. Freed from the chains of her cloistered society, Jocelyn is drawn to her newfound life at sea—reckless, thrilling, and utterly unpredictable. And the man who saved her life not once, but twice—why not do it all over again?

WITHIN A CAPTAIN'S Fate
A Captains of the Scarlet Night Novel

Visit us at www.kensingtonbooks.com

Books by Lisa A. Olech

Captains of the Scarlet Night
Within A Captain's Hold
Within A Captain's Treasure
Within a Captain's Fate

Published by Kensington Publishing Corporation

Within A Captain's Fate

A Captains of the Scarlet Night Novel

Lisa A. Olech

LYRICAL PRESS
Kensington Publishing Corp.
www.kensingtonbooks.com

To the strong, formidable, and beautiful women who have influenced my life.

Acknowledgements

Again, I have to thank Kensington/Lyrical for believing in this series, my editor, Amanda; my agent Dawn, and all the wonderful hands that have lovingly touched this story.

Thanks to NHRWA for their endless support, Kathy and Christyne for their brilliance, and the Plot Bunnies for their wisdom.

A special thank you to Professor Matthew Hornbach of Southern Methodist University for his wealth of knowledge and information regarding the earthquake of 1692.
(Me thinks ye'd made a fine pirate!)

A huge thank you to my "RUM RUNNERS" — Ben, Jenny, Nick, and Robyn. You took my research of this book to a whole new level of amazing!

And last, but certainly not least, I want to thank my readers. Without you, my wonderful characters would simply be words on a page. Your dedication to this series has given them life and furled the sails of the Scarlet Night. I'm forever grateful.

Chapter 1

June 7, 1692
Port Royal, Jamaica

A wicked grin tugged across Henry "Ricochet" Robbins's face. The *Scarlet Night* sat secure at the dock, and he was the first one off the ship after the captain dismissed the crew. His boots hit the wide, weathered boards of the pier and he set his sights on spending the next twenty-four hours drinking as much sweet rum as he could hold while enjoying the lusty pleasures of Port Royal

The last time he was here was over the winter's careening of the *Night.* He'd filled his pockets with winnings from the billiards tables and caught the eye of a dark-skinned beauty who worked as a bar wench at the Rogue Wave Tavern.

Ah, Teja.

Did she have a last name? Didn't matter. They'd spent four wild days followed by four incredible nights in her bed. She was the kind of woman a man could lose himself in then take a month finding his way out. Silken hair the color of midnight, whiskey-colored eyes, the sweetest mouth that could do the dirtiest things, and ample curves.

More than ample. Just the way Ric like his ladies. Soft, round, plentiful.

After being aboard ship for months, regaining his land legs put an extra swag in Ric's swagger. The noise, heat, and smells of Port Royal welcomed him home. This was his town.

The *Scarlet Night* and Captain Quinn were on top of the heap, and he was the best swivel gunner there was. He could thread a six-pounder through a knothole at two hundred yards. He'd earned his nickname by cushioning a cannon shot of a rocky shoal to take out a British mast--that, and he was in the habit of bouncing from woman to woman.

The day had dawned sultry. After the constant breeze aboard ship, the airless swelter of Port Royal lay steamy upon his skin. Pushing his way through the crowds loitering about the docks, he headed straight for the Rogue Wave.

Port Royal had become an interesting mix of humanity. A pirate haven, it teemed with society's dregs. Thieves and murderers. Whores and connivers. Lately, it was also seeing an influx of English influence. Beyond the city, the British hold was gaining strength. Plantations and colonies were becoming more established. Of course, you'd never catch a proper British gentleman wandering these fermented streets, not without good reason, and certainly not at night.

Ric pushed into the dim tavern. The reek of stale ale and rank bodies met him head on. It took a moment for his eyes to adjust after the brightness of the morning. Time was irrelevant here. Patrons from last night lay passed out in their chairs and littered upon the floor. Others played cards. The billiard tables were active and revelers still crowded the bar.

He sidled up then ordered a rum. "Make it a double."

"Ric Robbins." A cluster of men at the far end of the bar recognized him. "Ye bastard. Back to take more of me gold at the tables?"

"No time to fleece ye again, I'm afraid, I've a mind to spend my shore leave in the arms of my luscious Teja." Ric downed his drink and dropped a coin in payment.

The men burst into laughter, jostling one another. The bartender snatched the coin, snapped off what was owed him, then shoved the remainder of the gold back across the bar.

"Ye be a mite too late there, Ric. Teja done hooked herself a captain."

The group laughed louder. One of them leaned toward him grinning like a toothless loon. "Captain Black." He gestured to the back corner of the tavern.

It took Ric a second to register what he was seeing. A couple kissed. The deep, long, wet kisses of lovers. Captain Black had a hand pushed under Teja's skirts and had bared one of her full breasts.

"Captain Black?" Ric choked. "*Pandora* Black?"

Roars of laughter erupted around him. "Guess the great Ricochet Robbins done bounced her right over te the other side."

At the commotion, Teja and Black ended their kiss. Seeing Rick over Pandora's shoulder, Teja adjusted the neckline of her blouse to cover the dark peak of her nipple and smoothed down the front of her skirts.

Pandora Black turned a lazy look over her shoulder. Dressed as a man, Rick wouldn't have guessed she was a woman had he not known her by name. A fierce captain, she would fight any man who made the mistake of underestimating her. And she only took women into her bed.

She pierced Ric with an icy blue stare and hauled Teja back against her body. Holding Ric's gaze, she lifted her hand and licked her fingers.

Hoots, catcalls, and uproarious laughter followed Ric out of the tavern.

"Son of a bitch," he growled. "I should 'ave known. She was wearing the same britches as me."

"Someone's in your trousers again, Robbins?" Captain Gavin Quinn laughed as he and Bump approached him. Bump was another crewmate from the *Night*. A lad of less than a dozen years, Bump had been like a little brother to Ric since they brought the lad aboard. Sharp as a honed blade, the boy had become a first-rate seaman. The fact he was stone deaf only made his accomplishments more impressive.

"Damn women in my pants," Ric grumbled to Bump. "Story of my life." He shook his head and gathered what was left of his pride. "Nothing, Capt'n. Rum in the Rogue Wave leavin' a bitter taste in my mouth."

"Forget the rum, stick with Bump while I meet with Fin Willy. I'm heading to The Barnacle now to seal our deal. Soon we'll be sailing the *Scarlet Night* and the *White Witch*. Add that to the *Raven Wing;* more ships, more bounty to share."

The trio maneuvered their way past the array of taverns and brothels lining the docks. Urchin children picked the pockets of the unaware.

"Congratulations, Capt'n. Gonna give Tupper a chance at the helm of her own ship?" Robbins asked. Tupper Quinn was the former Alice Tupper. She and Gavin had married and spend the last six years pirating their way back and forth across the Atlantic.

"Doubt it." Gavin dodged a puddle of filth. "Wouldn't care to be apart from her. Not now that I've grown so used to her being at my side."

Ric jostled past a group spilling out of a doorway. "Ye could always make me captain."

Gavin chuckled. "Another year or two under your belt and maybe the crew'd be ready to vote you in."

A crowd had formed into a tight knot of bodies surrounding the town's auction block. Gavin stopped. A fierce defender of the abolishment of the African slave trade, he hated these auctions. Men, women, and children being sold as property was abhorrent to him. Ric had been with him long enough to see him hunt down and track slave haulers to deliver their human cargo back to the safety of their own shores. The number of those he'd saved must have reached a thousand in all these years.

By the look, today's auction wasn't for Africans. A line of women, chained together like dogs, was being dragged before the crowd. Young, old, weak, strong. The mob jeered and shouted lewd comments as the chained group was towed up onto the block.

Sex slaves.

Bought and sold into prostitution, life as concubines, some into harems, or simply to satisfy the lust of the owner. The youngest and prettiest went to the highest bidder.

Quinn scowled before turning away. "It's a good thing Tupper loathes Port Royal and is still aboard the *Scarlet Night*. She'd be drawing her sword, taking on this whole crowd to set those women free." He slapped Robbins on the back. "I've kept Fin Willy waiting long enough. I'll meet you and Bump back on board. Tonight we celebrate the new addition to our fleet."

Quinn made a few hand gestures to Bump who nodded in agreement before the captain headed off to his negotiation for the *White Witch*.

Ric barely noticed. Over the heads of the pack of bystanders, he caught the panicked gaze of one of the women up for sale. She'd been scanning the throng before her, her face ashen beneath a tangled mop of dark curls. Dirt and scratches marred her face and neck, one sleeve of her blouse torn from its seam at the shoulder.

He moved closer to the block. The noise and energy of the crowd seemed to make the ground tremble. Bump gave a sharp tug on Ric's arm. He paid him little notice, as he was too absorbed in the scene before him. The raven-haired captive held his gaze. It was as if she were reaching out to him alone. Looking for some tether. Perhaps a sympathetic face in the mob to keep her from tipping into the abyss of insanity.

Whatever the reason, she had found him amongst the dozens of faces and held onto him. Pale frightened eyes seemed to silently plead with him to stop this madness as the bidding began.

Ric's world narrowed to a pinhole. A buzzing sounded in his ears. His brain screamed at the insanity of his thoughts.

Save her.

Her tenuous bond was broken when she was jerked to the forward edge and became the next victim to be auctioned off.

"That one be mine," slobbered the fat man standing next to Ric. He smacked his thick lips and opened a sack of coins.

"Who among ya will start us off at ten gold pieces fer this comely wench?" The auctioneer scanned the crowd for any takers. Rick shoved his hand into his pockets and curled his fingers around the rough coins held there.

"Ten," he shouted. His gaze never leaving her.

The man next to him bid fifteen, another yelled eighteen. Soon the bidding passed twenty-five gold pieces.

"Thirty," Ric shouted, knowing full well he didn't have more than twenty on him.

"Thirty-five," yelled the fat man, narrowing his eyes at Ric before scratching at his crotch.

"Fifty," Ric countered. In his mind he knew he couldn't keep this up. Even if he managed to scrape together that many gold pieces, what would he do with this girl? He couldn't leave her here unprotected, and he sure as hell couldn't take her with him when the *Scarlet Night* sailed.

The auctioneer smiled an oily grin as if he could sense a bidding war commencing. Turning back, he tore at the woman's blouse exposing her breasts to the fevered audience. "Show 'em what they be buyin', Frenchie."

A black rage flooded Ric as the beast next to him frantically counted coins then raised the bid to seventy-five.

"Eighty."

"Ninety."

Blood rushed in Ric's ears. He shook with anger and a rush of indignation. His stomach turned at the thought of this man laying his fat, filthy hands on her.

Bump tugged on him once more trying to pull him away. Ric scowled at the boy's imploring gaze and shook his head.

No, he wasn't leaving. He wasn't going to back down. There was no way he was going to lose her.

"Three hundred!"

Chapter 2

The heat of the day weighed down upon her like the breath of the devil. Appropriate, as Jocelyn Beauchamp was sure to be standing at the gates of hell. Before her, a crush of vile-looking, leering men pushed and shoved to get closer.

She pressed back into the cluster of panicked women behind her. Several wept silently. Next to her stood the once-imposing figure of Sister Bernadette. Stripped of her vestments, wimple, and veil, she was just another woman awaiting a hideous fate. Hair cropped to renounce vanity and worldly ways, her fervent prayers to the Virgin falling from trembling lips.

Dazed, red-rimmed eyes met Jocelyn's while her lips moved over the prayer again and again, *"Je vous salue, Marie pleine de grace, le Seigneur est avec toi…"*

How many times had Jocelyn lifted that prayer during her years at the abbey? *"Hail Mary, full of grace…"*

Boarding a ship bound for Port Saint Maria should have gained the Blessed Virgin's favor, but it was obvious as Jocelyn scanned the crowd before her, the moment their feet left French soil, the voyage was doomed.

Weeks of storms rocked the passenger ship bringing colonists and pilgrims to the island. For Jocelyn it had been a journey filled with a mix of emotions. Anxiety, dread, fear, but also liberation and a thread of excitement. Riding away from the Abbey of Sainte-Genevieve after years of their strict discipline had been exhilarating. She was free. For at least as long as the voyage lasted.

Sister Bernadette was delivering her to her father. A high ranking officer in the French Navy, he was gathering the western fleet in Port St.

Maria before joining King Louis's war in Tripoli. He sent for her with the message he had secured a marriage contract for her, and she was to join him immediately.

In Jocelyn's mind, she was being taken from one cage only to be locked within another. Father insisted this time, her refusal would not be tolerated. He was through with her petulant behavior, and was prepared to leave her permanently in the care of the Sisters. At two and twenty, if she did not agree to marry, she would be forced to don the veil of the calling herself and live out the rest of her life in service to the Lord.

But the Lord was likely busy having tea with the Virgin, because no amount of grace could be found in having their ship captured by the depraved men who now held them. Sister Bernadette would have taken the rod to her if she knew the blasphemy of her thoughts.

Scanning the crowd, Jocelyn stood straight and defiant. She pushed down the panic threatening to crash over her.

Then she saw him.

He was staring at her. Not like the others running their lascivious gazes down the length of her body. He was looking straight into her eyes. Seeing her.

Sunlight shown in the wave of his hair like a beacon. His light eyes capturing hers. She couldn't make out their color at this distance, but the intensity of them caused a shiver to run through her. And not one of fear.

"Saint Michael," she murmured. His resemblance to Raphael's painting of the great Archangel was astounding. The golden man before her carried no great sweeping sword, but a fine polished pistol sat at the ready in his baldric against the white of his billowing shirt. He fairly glowed. Perhaps the Lord had sent her a savior after all.

The man leading the auction grabbed at her arm and dragged her to the edge of the platform. He lifted her hair before forcing her chin to one side, showing her off as if she were a prize horse. Next he'd be showing them her teeth. She jerked out of his grasp as he called for the bidding to begin.

Frantic, she sought out her savior, only to have her hopes shattered. He made the first bid. Her brain slowed after that. The scene before her moving in measured agonizing beats while a deafening buzz filled her mind.

Shock of the man tearing at her chemise jerked her back into the nightmare. Before her, a frenzy of bidding occurred until the final shout of "Sold!" reached deep into her belly.

Behind her Sister Bernadette choked out her name. Jocelyn turned in time to see her collapsed in a faint. Shouts and chaos erupted in the crowd. Before she could reach the good Sister, strong arms grabbed for her and pulled her into the fray.

Jocelyn screamed. Around her men fought one another with crushing swings of their fists. She ducked as she was dragged through the mêlée. When she stumbled, she was hoisted like a sack of wheat and unceremoniously tossed over someone's shoulder.

With her hands still shackled, she pounded her fists upon their back and kicked at their crotch. After a satisfying "Ooof," her abductor dropped her to her feet.

Saint Michael?

"Dammit, woman, I'm tryin…shit…this way." He pushed her ahead of him, dodging people, animals, and carts, until he veered right, pulling her into a dark alley.

He was no Archangel. The scruff of a beard decorated his rigid jaw. A dark scowl drew his brows together. A ragged scar marred the top of one cheek.

When Jocelyn tried to scream, he clamped a hand over her mouth and pressed her against the rough boards of the building behind her. "Quiet," he hissed then shot a glance over his shoulder.

She jerked her chin to one side and demanded he release her. *"Je demande que vous me libérer, à la fois!"*

In broken French he told her to relax. "I'm trying to save both our necks." He continued to cover her body with his own. The strength and power of him surrounded her. She could smell the alcohol on his breath. The spice upon his skin. "I won't hurt you. Play along."

With another quick glance toward the main street, he lowered his head as if to kiss her. In the dim light of the narrow alley, he held her gaze. The rush of his breathing tickled across the bare skin of her shoulder. "If we're lucky, they'll run right by," he whispered.

He reached down and lifted the side of her skirts to expose her leg clear to her thigh. She gasped and pushed against him. When she once again demanded he release her, he covered her lips with his fingertips. His pale gaze never leaving hers as he captured her knee, boldly raising it to rest upon his hip.

She would have screamed and fought him save for two things. At that moment, a loud, angry mob rushed past the end of the alley. And the sensation of his fingers at the back of her knee and the press of his heat against her body had robbed her of any sane thought.

Jocelyn followed his glance when he next looked back toward the street. A boy with thick ropes of dark hair stood near the entrance. She'd seen him standing with her rescuer at the auction. It was as if he guarded them. At the shake of his head, the man holding her shifted his head and raised her knee another inch. Anyone looking into the alley would assume they were random lovers tucked away from prying eyes.

She met his gaze once more, her breath racing. Surely he could feel her heart beating its way out of her chest.

He lowered his fingertips from her lips and released her leg. Jocelyn braced herself against him to keep from toppling over. The wall of his chest solid beneath her cheek.

"Are you well?" His French was terrible. She could only nod. "Good. Follow me."

On the way past the young man, he grabbed his hat and shoved it down upon her head. He pulled the brim down forcing her to look at her feet. "Head down. Stay close."

Jocelyn clutched at her torn chemise, and did as she was bid. Perhaps it was foolish to trust this complete stranger, but what choice did she have? Running to keep up, she found herself rushed along the hollow-sounding wood planks of the docks. Soon thereafter, he stopped to scoop her about the waist and swung her down onto the deck of a wide, three-masted sloop.

Her fair-haired savior then returned the hat to its rightful owner before catching her elbow and guiding her toward the bow of the ship. She had to run to keep pace with his long strides.

"Where the hell do you think you're going?"

He stopped on the spot.

"Shit," he mumbled under his breath and made a slow turn.

Jocelyn followed. A woman strode toward them unlike any woman she had ever seen.

There was no mistaking her sex, but dressed as a man with her long legs encased in tight breeches and tall boots that rose higher than her knees, she made quite the impression. Long dark hair reached toward her waist. She wore a man's waistcoat over a wide-sleeved shirt the color of cabernet. A wide belt crossed over one shoulder. Its delicate tooling in the leather was traced in silver and ended below her hip with the cage of her sword hilt.

A pirate. Jocelyn tipped her chin to sneak a stealthy glimpse above to confirm it. The black flag flew off the tip of the ship's center mast.

When Jocelyn lowered her gaze, she met the woman's scowl. In one hand, she held a pipe. A ribbon of smoke curling up from the bowl. Her other hand was planted at her waist.

"Tupper," her companion muttered.

"Robbins." She bit back in reply. "That doesn't answer my question. Who is this and why is she aboard?"

"I don't rightly know," he replied glibly. Turning to Jocelyn, he began to ask her name until the woman called Tupper saved her from his butchered French and asked herself. Her French was flawless.

"Jocelyn Angelique Beauchamp," she answered.

"Parlez vous anglais?" Tupper questioned.

Jocelyn nodded, *"Oui."*

"You do?" The man she now knew as Robbins gaped at her.

"Yes, I speak English. And Latin, Spanish, and a bit of German."

Tupper raised an eyebrow. "Impressive, and yet, I still don't know why you're here."

Robbins blurted, "Slave auction."

"You *bought* her?" Tupper's hand moved to the hilt of her sword.

"Yes," Jocelyn replied as Robbins insisted, "No."

He raised his hands in surrender and rushed to explain. "I only bid to rescue her." He lifted a shoulder. "Came a bit short in coin, but my intentions are honorable. I give ye me word." Robbins checked the dock again. "It might be safer for all of us if she gets below, if ye gather my meaning."

Tupper jerked her chin. "MacTavish can rid her of those shackles. Fetch him and bring him to the Captain's cabin."

Robbins hesitated a moment before acquiescing. His gaze swept Jocelyn as if he were only now realizing the full extent of his predicament. He gave a slow shake of his head and smirked. *"Oui."*

Jocelyn followed the slender back of the woman down a dark galley way into the lower deck of the ship. She was ushered into a richly appointed room.

The entire back wall was a gentle curve of windows. Panes of leaded diamonds sparkled in the morning sun. Fine oak furnishings filled the room, a large carved desk, and trimmed sleeping nook. Chests of every description were piled neatly along the walls. There was even an oak cabinet built into the corner filled with beautiful leather-bound books.

Not that she'd been on many pirate ships in her lifetime--none actually, but this room was nothing as she would have imagined. Before this moment, she would have told you pirates were all like that throng of vile men ogling her less than an hour ago. Filthy and crude, representing the lowest of all humankind. Barbarians.

"You look surprised." Tupper appeared amused.

Jocelyn once more observed the woman before her. "I am, frankly. You are a pirate, no?"

Tupper relit her pipe. "Have you never seen a woman pirate?"

"Until yesterday, I'd never seen any kind of pirate. Male or female."

"Well, look around." Tupper swept an arm. "You're in Port Royal. You can't swing a dead cat without hitting a pirate here."

"But you…"

Tupper notched her chin. "What about me?"

Jocelyn indicated the richness of the surroundings. "You are the captain?"

"No. The captain is my husband."

"Ah, I see. So you do not participate."

"Oh, I participate. I've been a full member of this crew for more than half a dozen years." Tupper dropped into a chair and raised her knee to rest her boot heel on a rung of the chair. The pose was most unladylike. "It just so happens I also greatly enjoy bedding the captain."

Jocelyn's ears burned. She wasn't embarrassed by the improper turn of the conversation, quite the opposite, she found it fascinating. Flustered at her puritanical assumptions, of course a woman could plunder and pillage as well as a man.

"Have you ever…" She stopped herself from asking such a rude question.

"Killed a man?" Tupper gave a short laugh. "Only the ones fool enough to stand in front of my pistol." She took a pull on her pipe and stared through the cloud of blue smoke. "You're very good at asking questions. Let's see how you are at answering a few. How is it you're here?"

The memory still seemed to come from deep within a nightmare. "Our ship was captured. The men slaughtered and the women taken." Jocelyn clutched at her chemise. "To be sold."

"Where were you headed?"

"Port Sainte Maria, then *Ile de la Tortue*."

Tupper's head cocked and she narrowed her eyes. "Tortuga?"

"My father is there. He sent for me. I'm to be…I was to be married."

"Your father?" Tupper leaned forward. "You said your name was Beauchamp?"

"*Oui.*"

"Philippe Beauchamp? *Admiral* Philippe Beauchamp?"

Jocelyn's mood lightened. Perhaps she was saved after all. "You know of him?"

"He wears a patch over his left eye."

"Yes," relief flooded her, "you do know him."

"Aye, we know each other well. I am the one who gave him the patch."

Chapter 3

Tupper met Ric in the galley way. "Do you have any idea who you've brought aboard?"

"She told you her name. Joceyl--"

"I heard her name," Tupper snapped. "Philippe Beauchamp is her father."

"*Bâtard de la Mer Beauchamp?*" Ric shook his head. "That's impossible."

"Ask her yourself. Although you might not want to call him the Bastard of the Sea in front of her." Tupper's voice rose. She jabbed a finger back toward her cabin. "She needs to get off this ship."

Ric threw his hands wide. "What should I do with her? Throw her back to those piranhas, or just overboard?"

"Beauchamp is determined to see everyone on this ship hung since we attacked him two years ago. She was on her way to him when her ship was taken. If he finds out we have her, he'll stop at nothing. He'll have the entire French navy scouring the seas for us."

"So what do we do with her?"

"We?" Tupper laughed.

"Come on," he pleaded. "Quinn'll have my hide if he finds her here. There has to be something we can do."

"Let me think..." Tupper ran a hand through her hair.

"Maybe we can keep her hidden somewhere."

Tupper shook her head. "Do you want Gavin to have *my* hide?"

"What if we bring her to the eastern shore of the island? There's bound to be a ship heading toward Port Saint Maria. We could handle the *Scarlet Night* ourselves. Make a quick run, be back before dark. Capt'n wouldn't have to know."

She shot him an incredulous look. "Of course he would have to know." Tupper rubbed her chin. "Fin Willy is probably fixin' to toast his good fortune for hours yet. Who's still aboard?"

"You, me, Bump," He jerked his chin toward the cabin door. "MacTavish, Neo. I think I saw White and Summer. Finch has a comely wife waiting in port, so he's off. Hornbach and Dowd be loading the galley. Could be a few more below."

"The *Scarlet* is easily run with a handful…"

Robbins brightened. This would go a hell of a lot easier if the deed was done before he had to face Captain Quinn. He rushed to convince Tupper. "We can use the east winds, set all the cloth. I bet we could be back by four bells."

She thought for a moment before glaring at him. "Fine. Neo's still nursing the shoulder they pulled a lead shot from last week. I'll send him to The Barnacle. Tell Gavin we be borrowing his ship."

Relief washed over him. "You're the best there be, Tupper."

"Don't be buttering up the goose already in the pan." She pointed a finger into his face. "You owe me."

"Anything." He gave her his most charming smile. "Name it."

"Don't think I won't." Tupper shook her head and waved her finger. "An' keep all your grinnin' to yourself, ya fool. It may work on those empty headed females you like to tumble, but it doesn't work on me." She left him to head deck side.

Malcolm MacTavish, the ship's Master Gunner, exited the Captain's quarters and tossed Ric the empty shackles. "Lass not one of your usual trollops."

"She's no trollop, and she sure as hell ain't mine."

"So ye say," MacTavish grumbled as he moved past. The bearded ox of a Scotsman smelled like sulfur and gun oil and looked like someone'd used him to swab a cannon. His kilt was more black powder than red tartan these days.

Ric knocked on the door before moving back into the Captain's quarters. Jocelyn sat on the side of the bed still holding together the edges of her torn chemise.

No, she wasn't his. Never would be either. But she sure as hell was one of the prettiest women he'd ever seen. He could still smell the sunshine wound into the dark curls of her hair. Memories washed over him of hiding in that alley, pressed against her all close and tight. Bold as new brass touching her like he did. Running his fingers down the girl's thigh to catch the tender back of her knee. Her skin was like nothing he'd ever laid a hand upon. Soft as down. Smooth as a king's satins.

Had there not been a bloodthirsty hoard after them he'd have loved to have dipped his head another inch and had a little taste of her sweet mouth. It might have been worth the slap across his cheek.

But he'd missed his chance.

She was Beauchamp's daughter. If he touched her, he was a dead man. Now he'd never know the feel of her lips. He expected that missed opportunity to haunt him for many nights to come. Fair price, considering he was a damn fool.

"Are you well?" he asked when she remained quiet.

She nodded, blinking up at him.

"We're heading off to find another ship to bring you to your father."

"But he's your enemy," she argued. "You're pirates. Aren't you going to hold me for ransom?"

Why did she sound disappointed? "We don't ransom. We're more of a snatch and grab operation."

Jocelyn pulled her chemise tighter and studied her lap. "You've fought my father before."

"Aye, we've crossed swords a time or two." Ric poured her a finger of brandy from the bottle on Captain Quinn's desk, but when he offered the glass to her, she refused it. "He's a worthy opponent."

"Father enjoys a good fight. Pirates or daughters. It's fair to say he has little tolerance for either. Although, crossing pens and not swords would be more fitting in my case."

Ric debated returning the unwanted brandy to the bottle, but it'd be a sin putting liquor this fine back once it'd been poured. He solved the problem in a single swallow.

Jocelyn continued. "His last visit to the abbey may not have come to swordplay, but it may as well have. His demand to join him now was hardly a request. It was an order. And not one to defy."

Ric choked. "Did you say abbey?"

She nodded. "I've been there since the age of three. My mother passed away suddenly from a fever, and Father couldn't raise me alone. At Sainte-Genevieve we're allowed only four visits a year, but he's always fighting a battle somewhere half a world away. I rarely saw him. In fact, I would argue in the last few years you've probably crossed his path far more than I."

The girl was raised in an abbey?

If being Beauchamp's daughter was not enough to keep his grimy hands off her, this would have been. Innocent with a capital "I." Straight from a virgin vault. Tupper was right, Jocelyn Beauchamp needed to get off this ship.

He contemplated another drink, but he was in enough trouble without adding stealing more of the Capt'n's brandy to the list. "I'm sure he only wanted to keep you safe."

She met his gaze. "You and he seem to agree on that point."

Ric laughed, "I doubt he would see it that way."

"No, he would not." She lifted one delicate shoulder. "And yet, he should be in your debt." She graced him with a small smile sending a warm shaft clear through his chest. "I know I am."

He needed to get out of this cabin. "You may want to hold off before thanking me. I still need to get you out of port."

"I trust you." She dipped her chin and peered up at him.

Ric laughed again to cover his sudden unease. She trusted *him?* Where was her fear? This innocent girl was hardly acting like he'd expect. "Never trust a pirate." He unwound the sash about his waist and pulled his shirt over his head. Jocelyn's eyes went round as portholes. At last, a show of fear. He tossed his shirt to her. "Cover yourself. Stay below until we are well away from the docks. Then it will be safe to come up."

After grabbing another shirt from his gear in the crew's quarters, Ric climbed back into the bright late morning sun on deck. The docking lines were being tossed back over the rails and the lower sails set. Tupper stood at the helm ready to navigate the *Scarlet Night* out of the busy harbor. Once beyond the crowd of ships anchored off shore, they could raise the mainsail and catch the wind.

Bump stood alongside Tupper. Lad looked worried. He held his hands palms up, fingers moving. *"Wait."* He and Tupper over the years had developed their own way of communicating using hand gestures and fingering letters to spell words. Ric learned a few words as well, but Bump and Tupper "spoke" far too fast at times for him to follow.

Tupper patted his shoulder and made a small gesture. "We'll return soon."

Bump frowned and hurried to the back of the ship.

Ric jerked his chin in the boy's direction. "What's his problem?"

"He wants us to wait for Gavin."

"He and Fin Willy could be settling the sale for hours yet."

"More. Neo's gone to tell him to take his time. Even so, every second Beauchamp's daughter is on this ship makes me nervous. Let's do this and get back before Fin Willy runs out of brandy."

"Be a good thing if he does. Capt'n'll be in a fair mood. Else it'll be my tail hangin' from the crow's nest come mornin.'"

"Better yours than mine." Tupper negotiated a final ship anchored on the edge of the harbor. "Give White and Summer a hand hoisting the main."

Once secured, the wide stretch of canvas caught the wind with a snap. Jocelyn appeared at his side. She turned eyes the color of rich dark rum toward the sky.

"Won't be any time at all, and ye'll be back on yer way," Ric reassured her.

She lowered her gaze and fixed it upon him. Twists of dark hair teased across her full lips. The harsh Caribbean sun had pinked the paleness of her skin high across each cheek, down the gentle sweep of her nose, and kissed the tender tops of her shoulders.

His shirt looked a far sight better on her than a torn chemise, but its wide neck still bared those lovely shoulders and revealed a tempting amount of shadowy cleavage as well. She'd caught the voluminous fabric beneath her corset to allow the hems to ride loose over the curve of her modest skirts.

Good thing their time together would be short. She was too tempting, too chaste. Ric Robbins may be a pirate and a confirmed rogue, but he drew the line at an innocent with a father that would disembowel him *before* he hung him should he dare to touch his daughter.

"The sun's strong today. Best you keep to the shade where ye ken." Ric pointed toward the shadowy overhang of the upper deck.

"I--"

A rumble of thunder rolled through the air as the ship trembled beneath them.

"What the....? There ain't a cloud in the sky. Where...?" Ric looked back toward Tupper. She, too, was checking the sky.

All at once, another round of thunder roared louder behind them. The *Scarlet Night* slammed hard into something, tossing everyone off their feet. Ric and Jocelyn both flew forward and landed in a heap together against the bulkhead. Once more Ric's body shielded hers, but he was too shaken to pause long enough to enjoy it. He pushed away from her.

"What the hell did we hit?" Ric shouted.

White and Summer rushed to the bow and looked over the rails. There were no rocks or reefs on this side of the island.

Before he could scramble to his feet, a fierce rush of water past the hull seemed to pull them farther out toward open water as if the ship were being sucked away from the land and spit into the ocean. It tossed Ric and Jocelyn in the opposite direction as the thundering roar continued behind them. From where they fell, Ric could see the others on deck hanging on to rigging, bracing themselves against the jerking motion of the ship.

But then Ric heard them. Screams. Reaching out toward the *Scarlet Night* across the waves. He had little time to think before a great swell of water heading back toward the land caught the bow of the ship and tossed her about as if she were a child's toy.

Around him, everyone struggled to get to their feet. Tupper stood clutching at her forehead. Blood ran between her fingers and down her arm.

Ric looked back in horror at the swollen swell of seawater that grew into a monstrous wave as it reached the shallower waters of the harbor. Beyond, an ominous red cloud rose above Port Royal.

He grabbed for the closest eyeglass, and with shaking hands held it to his eye. It wouldn't focus. Where was the city? He couldn't see anything through the rusted mist. Turning the glass in the direction of the tallest buildings, he couldn't find them. The screams suddenly silenced as a wall of seawater obliterated his view and seemed to swallow Port Royal whole.

Ric couldn't believe what was happening. The vision before him punched all the air from his lungs. He lowered the glass and covered his eyes with a hand hoping to blot the scene from his mind. It couldn't be.

Tupper wrenched the glass from his hands. "What's happening? Oh dear God...."

They all rushed into the stern. Hornbach and Dowd emerged from below. Everyone spoke at once. MacTavish was the last to arrive. "Bloody hell, what the fuk?"

"Earthquake..." someone muttered. "Must have been an earthquake. Triggered the wave."

Tupper dropped the brass. "I can't see anything. We have to go back."

Ric lifted the glass to take another look. The gruesome images he could make out through the cloud of debris defied description. Everything that had once been was no more. Buildings, shops, ships in the harbor.... It was all gone. The city seemed to have vanished. In a matter of minutes, Port Royal had been wiped away.

"Turn about," Tupper screamed. "Someone turn this damn ship around."

"Tupper, no." Ric grabbed her arm. "There's no use. It's not safe. We can't help them. I...it's too late." A deep heaviness had settled in his chest as he looked into her panicked face.

"What are you talking about? Turn this ship around!" She glared at them before shoving past Ric. "Bloody hell, I'll do it myself." She raced back to the ship's large oak wheel and pulled it with all her might to one side.

Ric caught up to her and righted the ship. "Tupper. Stop."

"We're going back." She yanked again pulling it out of his grasp.

"There's nothing to go back to!" He pointed behind them. "Look for yourself. The city isn't there. Pulled down or flooded, there's nothing left. Even if we could make it back, we can't change what's happened. It's too late. If I thought there was a chance they survived…"

She grabbed his shirt in her fists. "Gavin is there. Neo. Finch. The rest of the bloody crew. We're going *back.*"

"To what?" he yelled. "Where they were isn't there anymore." He stared into her wild eyes. Blood mixed with her tears and ran down her cheek. He gave her a shake. She had to listen to sense. "Tupper…they're gone."

"No," She screamed and shoved him back before she returned to the wheel and forced the ship to begin its wide turn.

"Stop!" Ric pulled at her hands. "We can't risk getting caught in another tidal wave in the harbor."

Tupper wrenched away from him and straightened before pulling her pistol. She pointed the barrel at Ric's face and cocked the hammer. Her chest rose and fell in shaky pants. "I said, we're going *back*!"

Chapter 4

White and Summer pulled at the oars. MacTavish and Ric sat like stones in the rear of the skiff. The sights surrounding them defied description.

It was MacTavish who had convinced Tupper the *Scarlet Night* wouldn't be able to get through the debris and carnage in the harbor, or what had been the harbor not an hour before. Tupper was past consolable. She would have dived off the fantail and swum back into the harbor had he not assured her the four of them would return to Port Royal--or where it had been to see if they could find Captain Quinn and the rest.

They all knew it was a fool's mission before they even got close. Gavin Quinn and those members of the crew unfortunate enough to be in the city when the earthquake hit, were dead. There was no chance they survived. What had been now sat beneath what must be forty feet of seawater judging by what was visible. Ships sitting at anchor now lay at the bottom of the sea. Mast tips and hulls beached like bloated whales along the surface of the water.

Bodies. Dozens of bodies floated silent among the debris. The sky still burned red.

"In all me years, I ain't bloody well seen the like of this," mumbled MacTavish.

"They never had a chance." Ric looked for any signs of life among the victims in the water.

Soon the harbor became too choked with wreckage to get the skiff any closer. Ric used the eyeglass once more to scan the landscape. Nothing looked familiar. Any sign of buildings remaining looked as if they had simply dropped into the ground. Roofs and chimneys were all he could see.

The Rogue Wave wasn't there. Neither was Auction Square. He couldn't make out where the Barnacle once sat, or any evidence of the White Witch. What he did see were few survivors trying to dig corpses out of the ground. Some buried to their necks. Silent screams frozen on their faces. Limbs stuck out of the sand. Arms reaching for help, which didn't come in time.

"There's no use trying to get closer. Where we sit now is a good two lanes *inland* from where the docks stood." White shook his head. "Any poor bastard closer to the shore is lost."

Ric lowered the glass and rubbed at his eyes. "I can't believe what I'm seeing."

Summer took off his headcloth and held it over his heart. "Capt'n's gone. They've all been swallowed up."

"Bloody hell." MacTavish scrubbed at his beard.

"I ain't never gonna forget this as long as I live," declared Summer.

What Ric would never forget was the look on Bump's face. After Tupper had threatened to kill him on the spot if they didn't turn around, Ric had seen him. The boy stood looking back toward shore. Not moving, not making even the smallest of sounds. His face a mask of pure grief. Tearless eyes stared in wide shock. His chin trembled with the effort of holding his emotions in check. He'd been the only one in the tail of the ship when the earthquake began. Had he seen what happened? Been witness to it all?

Unlike Tupper, Bump was not demanding they return. It was as if he knew. He knew he'd lost the man he loved like a father. The man who'd saved him from the very streets that now sat at the bottom of the sea.

Ric didn't know what to do. He'd wanted to reach out to touch the boy but feared if he did, the lad would shatter like glass to the decking. So he stood with him in his silence. Looking out at a world forever changed until he was called to help the others lower the skiff.

"White, what the fuck ye think yer doin'?" MacTavish swore.

Ric lowered the glass as the skiff tipped to one side. White was leaning out trying to pull a sword from a scabbard. The last owner of said sword still wore the weapon, however.

"He ain't gonna be needing it, and I broke the tip of me blade last tight." Repulsion spread through Ric. "Yer not stealing from a dead man."

"Why the hell not? Wouldn't be the first time." He looked out over the water. "Fact, bet there be lots more to be had fer some enterprising sorts."

"Not from these dead. Leave 'em be." Ric barked.

"Don't see what difference it makes. Dead be dead." White gave another tug on the sword.

"Ye let go of that weapon, or I'll toss yer sorry arse in te join em." MacTavish warned.

White released the sword's hilt and flopped back onto the thwart. "Don't be gettin' yer hems in a flip, MacTavish. I don't be answerin' to you. Not you, either Robbins." He wiped his hand on his britches.

Summer piped up, "Ye know, man's got a point there. What we gonna do now? No Captain. No crew te speak of. Who do we be answering to?"

"Well that sure as hell ain't gonna be settled by four scabs in a skiff. I say we get back to the *Night*, and mourn our dead 'fore we go deciding something like that," insisted Ric.

"Ain't gonna want te be the one te break it te Tupper." Summer shook his head.

White nodded in agreement. "Woman's gonna be wrecked."

"The boy, too," added Summer as they began to slowly turn the skiff back toward the *Scarlet Night*.

"Bump ain't a boy no more." MacTavish grumbled. "Needs te face the truth of this like a man."

They all had to face the truth of this like men. Ric looked back over the horror surrounding him and swallowed the sudden lump in his throat. They'd all lost their captain. Friends. Crewmates. So many so quickly. "Good thing Bump had Captain Quinn to teach him. We were all lucky to serve under such a fine man."

"Aye," the word caught in MacTavish's throat. The Scotsman tugged at the braids in his beard and sniffed.

"Aye," White agreed before running the back of his hand under his nose and turning his attention back to the oar blade.

"None better."

Summer's words hung over them as they rowed in silence away from the devastation of Port Royal and back to their ship.

* * * *

Jocelyn stood stunned. She started to pray for Sister Bernadette but wasn't sure exactly what to pray for. Was Port Royal another Sodom and Gomorrah? Had the Lord smitten it because of its sins? Had the devout Sister been delivered from evil? Did Jocelyn pray for Bernadette's survival, or say a prayer of thanks for the mercy against such a pious woman being forced into her own living hell?

The scene on the deck of the Scarlet Night was surreal. Quiet, as if each remaining member of the crew held their breaths.

Ric and three others had moved quickly to lower a small boat to return to shore in search of any survivors amongst their fellow crewmates. *"You're safe here, I swear,"* he assured her before he left. *"I'll be back as soon as I can."*

The woman, Tupper, after her fit of panic was now urging one of the remaining men to stitch the gash along her forehead.

"Until Briggs comes back, you're the surgeon, Hornbach, get on with it."

The man stood holding a needle and thick thread in his shaky hand. "I be the cook. Only thing I be used to trussing is a turkey."

"Weren't ye assistant to Briggs? Ye had to have stitched a wound before," reminded Tupper.

"Assistin' Briggs meant I poured as much rum down their gullets as they could swallow before holdin' the poor bastards down. He be the one doin' all the cuttin' and sewin.' I just took care of the screamin' end." He pushed a bottle of rum at her.

"Forget the bloody rum. Pretend my head's a blasted turkey, and do something 'fore my stuffin' falls out." Tupper held her "stuffing" in with a bloodied cloth while Hornbach fussed to gather bandages and the other supplies he'd need.

"Dowd," she hollered to the man standing watch at the rear of the ship. "Any sign of them?"

"Not yet. Hard to see."

Next to him, standing like Lot's Wife, was the boy who helped Ric get Jocelyn away from the city. There was something curious about him. She couldn't figure out what. In all the commotion getting back to the ship and the chaos after the earthquake, he hadn't said a word. Hadn't spoken to anyone. And as far as she'd witnessed, none had spoken to him. Come to think of it, she didn't even know his name.

He was a gangly youth, just coming into his shoulders, with hair that more resembled dark twisted fingers and skin the color of rich honey. But it was his eyes that caught her attention. Deep and soulful, as if they could know all with a simple glance.

Jocelyn owed him her thanks as well, but was unsure how to approach him. He seemed removed. Isolated from the rest, somehow. Perhaps when Ric returned, he could make the proper introductions and--

"There they be." Dowd lowered the eyeglass and called back to Tupper.

"Who's with them?" Tupper waited only as long as it took Hornbach to trim the end of his stitch before slipping beneath his ministering hands and rushing to the rail. "How many?"

The expression on Dowd's face said it all. "There be just the four."

"Get out of my way." Tupper pushed him aside and snatched the long brass eyeglass to look for herself. She made a sound as if the air had been punch from her lungs. "A-another boat...behind... There has to be another... There has to be..."

Tupper lowered the glass. Her legs crumbled. Dowd caught her before she could hit the decking. The brass rolled away as a cry wrenched from deep within her.

All at once, she struggled out of Dowd's hold, fury twisting her face. "Get your hands off me!"

"I was only tryin'--"

"The captain will have you flogged! G-Gavin will see you f-flogged!" She straightened. "He'll see..." Tupper stumbled again, and Jocelyn rushed to help, but the woman recovered once more. She took a few shaky steps and stopped. "Bump." The word came out in a rush. She looked over her shoulder to where the boy still stood. "Bump." she raised her voice before stomping on the deck twice with the heel of her boot.

The boy turned. He looked stricken. Pure anguish etched upon his young face. Silent tears wet his cheeks. He said nothing, but shook his head before tucking his chin. He rushed past Tupper's outstretched arms.

Clutching at the neck of her blouse, Tupper's breath caught as she watched the boy run off. "When C-Captain Quinn returns...tell him...tell him I'm waiting for him in our cabin."

Jocelyn's heart broke as she watched Tupper leave the deck clinging to the last fragile thread of hope. Perhaps her last fragile thread of sanity. Such a tragedy.

Each face of the remaining men held the pain of their loss. Jocelyn felt helpless to ease their grief. They'd all lost too much. Life would never be the same. Not for them. Not for her. She sat in the shadow of a lashed barrel and cried for them all.

It wasn't long before the rescue party returned to the Scarlet Night. A solemn shake of MacTavish's head told the rest everything they needed to hear. "Ne'er seen the like. They didn't stand a chance."

Jocelyn waited. Ric was the last of the four to climb over the gunwales and drop onto the deck. A fist seemed to punch behind her ribs at the mere sight of him. Rugged and golden. A rush of gratitude washed over her. He'd saved her. Not once, but twice in a single day. Had he not rescued her from that horrible auction, she, too, would be among the dead of Port Royal.

He may be an unlikely hero, but he was a hero nonetheless. He was her hero. And a pirate, yet. A pirate with the heart, and the face, of an angel.

Chapter 5

Heaviness settled within Ric's chest on the row back to the *Scarlet Night*. He'd been a pirate most of his life. Fought through countless bloody battles, watched men die brutal deaths. Many by his own hand or at the blast of his cannon. Even given all that, he'd not soon wash the images he'd seen today from his memory. The victims of the earthquake would forever haunt him.

Any hope Ric harbored of returning again to Port Royal the next day were dashed as the skiff rumbled beneath them with a strong aftershock. The ground continued to tremble as if the city fought to claw its way back to the surface. It wasn't safe to go back. They needed to get the ship away from this harbor and to open sea. Another tidal wave would swamp them.

Besides, it would be a fool's errand to return. What was done, was done.

Hundreds dead. With the heat this time of year, it wouldn't take long for the bodies to bloat and begin to decompose. It would be gruesome. Those, if any, who managed to survive one hell would be wishing they were dead before long.

"Where be Tupper?" MacTavish asked as they returned to the deck of the *Night*.

Hornbach shook his head. "She be in a bad way. Took to her cabin."

"Says to send Captain Quinn to her when he gets back," added Dowd. "Convinced he's still alive."

Hornbach cuffed the young seaman, "She's wrestling her mind around what's happened, is all. Give her some time, she'll come about."

"What about Bump?" Ric scanned the deck. He didn't see the boy, but found Jocelyn curled tight to a barrel. Her knees drawn, she had tucked herself into a ball. Wide eyes met his. All he could think at that moment was if not for her, they'd all be among the bodies floating in Kingston harbor.

"Took it hard," Dowd said, jerking Ric's attention back to their conversation. "I'll try to find him."

Ric caught his arm. "Best give him a bit of time as well." He searched the faces of those around him. They all needed a chance to come to terms with what had happened. "We all be needing a bit of time."

"Anybody be needin' *me*, I'm heading te me armory and drownin' meself in a barrel o' rum." MacTavish lumbered off. "If I'm blind drunk, maybe I won't remember what I've seen today."

"I'll help ye," mumbled Summer following in his wake.

"Me, as well," agreed White.

Ric would have to join them later. He still had to explain things to Jocelyn. When he approached her, she stood and smoothed her skirts. She'd been crying, but tried to hide it with a quick swipe to her cheeks.

"I'm sorry," he began, "Auction Square is gone. Washed away. I'm afraid your companions are lost."

"They were already lost." She shook her head. "Even before they were washed away. Do you suppose it's a sin to be grateful for such a tragedy?" Worry creased her brow.

Ric let out a tired breath. Given what awaited those other women, he couldn't blame her. "I ain't the person you should be askin' to judge sin."

"No, you're my hero." She reached out to squeeze his arm.

The look in her eye brought him up short. "I ain't that either."

"You are to me." She lifted his hand, kissed its palm, and held it to her chest. "I owe you my life." She smiled at him with shining eyes and stepped closer. "Not only did you save me from a fate more horrible than death, you saved me from the terror of the quake. I'll be forever grateful. Forever in your debt."

Once again, Ric marveled at the silk of her pale skin beneath his touch. Part of him now wanted not to drown himself in a barrel of rum, but in her. Forget the horror of this day. Lose himself in her innocence. Kiss her lips, caress the milky tenderness of her breasts. Run his fingers over the smoothness of her thigh as he'd done back in the alley. The naïve look upon her face told him it would be simple to use her gratitude to woo her into his arms. Into his bed.

What the hell was he thinking? Looking at his hand, the contrast between the rough filth of his skin against the spotless purity of her jolted him back to reality. He jerked his hand from hers as if he'd been scalded. "Ye owe me nothin.' Ye be the one saved the lot of us scurvy bastards."

He shoved his hand through his hair. "An' if yer smart, you'll be keeping a good distance from me. I ain't yer knight in shining armor. I'm a low-life pirate who only stole ye from that auction 'cause I wanted to have ye for myself."

It was a lie, or was it? Ric struggled with what was true. He'd meant only to save her, but once he got close. Held her tight to him. Touched her. Smelled the sweetness of her skin. The black and white of what he'd done and why became blurred. But there was no way he'd be taking Beauchamp's daughter. Neither would he allow her to believe he was better than he was.

He had to find Bump, and he needed to follow his own warning and keep far away from her. "While ye're busy counting yer blessings, be thankful yer last name is Beauchamp, for there ain't a man left aboard that be wanting what's laying beneath them skirts."

Ric heard her gasp as he stormed away.

He'd hit his mark. Innocent fool. How naïve could she be? Looking at him all moony eyed. Hero? Him? Ha! If she had any idea that he wanted to bend her over the rail and toss her skirts over her head, she'd never be calling him a bloody hero.

For the next hour, he searched for Bump. Tupper had locked herself in her cabin. He'd tried to talk to her through the door. Tell her how sorry he was, but she'd thrown something heavy against the wooden planks and ordered him away. The lad couldn't be with her given her state.

Bump had been a small child when he came aboard. He knew every hiding place on this ship. Ric thought he did too, but obviously he was wrong. It wasn't as if the boy could hear Ric calling out to him. After a while, he gave up the search. If Bump didn't want to be found, he wouldn't be found.

Frustrated, Ric returned topside. It was an eerie sight. The decks of the *Scarlet Night* stretched out in empty silence. A deep sense of sadness and abject loneliness reached into his bones. If he closed his eyes, he could still see them all. Gavin Quinn, Neo, Finch… He could hear them. Captain Quinn giving his orders. Sharp and crisp. The image of efficiency. He was a fine Captain. Good and fair. Fierce and ruthless in battle. A defender of his ideals.

Ric had served under this ship's last two Captains. Gavin Quinn and before him Jaxon Steele. He'd been lucky to have been counted among the crew. But now…

The *Scarlet Night* sat dead in the water. With no sail set, she bobbed, noiseless save for the gentle lap of waves against her hull. She floated adrift, awaiting her orders, but without a captain to set her sails and chart a course…

The stillness on deck screamed at him. He needed to find the others. Ric's search found them in the galley. MacTavish, White, and Summer where three sheets in already. Hornbach and Dowd had filled the table to bursting. Roasted meat and fresh fruits and vegetables, crusty loaves of bread. It was a feast fit for a crowd ten times their size.

"Don't know what we're to do from here." Hornbach filled Ric's plate to overflowing. "But we're sure te eat good. Least till all this food starts to rot." He swept a hand to indicate the stack of crates and barrels overflowing with produce and foodstuffs. "Galley was loaded 'fore we left dock, but in this heat, we can't be keeping some of this more than a week or two. Got enough rum and ale for a crew of forty, so doubt if we'll mind. Least not fer a while."

Ric grabbed a bite of ripe rich ackee fruit. He sat at one of the long, rough-hewn galley tables to eat. From here, he could see Jocelyn sitting alone in the corner picking at the pile of food in front of her. He took a swallow of ale. Somehow, he still had to find a way to get her to the northern side of the island. But that was no guarantee there'd be a ship to take her to Tortuga. There was a good possibility the north had suffered the same fate as Port Royal. Although if the wave came from the south, there might be a chance. There had to be a chance. If not, what would he do with her?

"What we do wit that one?" MacTavish jerked his head in Jocelyn's direction as though reading Ric's mind. He dropped his bulk in front of him blocking his view of the girl. His drinking partners followed suit.

"I don't rightly know," Ric confessed.

Summer sniffed. "I couldn't care less about the girl. She shouldn't be aboard. Bad luck an' all. I say we toss her over."

"If it weren't for her, we'd still be tied to the dock. You remember the dock? The one sitting under all that water?" Ric pointed the tip of his knife at Summer. "How'd that be for bad luck?"

"Still don't like the idea of a woman aboard," grumbled Summer.

"Don't let Tupper be hearing ye." MacTavish spoke into his mug.

"Tupper ain't no woman. She's…Tupper," reasoned Summer. "Woman or no, we still be in deep shit. No captain, no crew. Sitting out here like a turd in a puddle."

"Ye should be a poet there, Summer." White scoffed.

Hornbach and Dowd joined the conversation. "Anybody got any ideas?"

Ric pushed away his plate. "How many of us are left?"

"Yer looking at most all of us. Nine if ye count her." MacTavish tipped his head toward Jocelyn again. "We can sail the *Night* with a half dozen, if we don't run up against somebody wanting to blast us out of the water. What we be needin' is a captain."

"I'd vote fer Tupper in a second," piped White. Since the first day she stepped foot on this ship, White had been her champion. At least now he didn't drool when she walked by.

Summer nodded. "Me, too, if she was fit."

"Could be she be fine come mornin,'" argued White.

"An' if she ain't?" fired MacTavish.

Hornbach thumbed to his right. "MacTavish is senior among us. He should be captain."

The burly Scot near choked on his rum. "I can tell ye how much powder to use if ye want to blow a tick off an arse at twenty yards, but I don't know nothin' about navigating a ship."

"Summer?" Ric asked.

"Ye want te be sailing in circles?"

White raised his hands in surrender. "Don't be lookin' te me."

"Ric, you got some navigatin' skill," noted Hornbach.

He shook his head. "I'm a gunner, not a captain."

"Ye be a captain now." MacTavish slapped the table. "Yer all we got ken read a chart."

Ric jerked. "Me? Captain of the Scarlet Night? Yer all daft."

MacTavish leaned in. "It's you or Dowd, here, an' he's barely out of short pants."

"I call fer a vote." Summer raised his hand. The rest followed. "Majority rules. Ricochet Robbins be the new captain."

Ric finally raised his own hand, but added. "Just until Tupper is up to the task."

Nods and shrugs circled the table. "Done."

"Aye."

"Agreed."

Ric Robbins was now Captain of the Scarlet Night.

"Don't be bouncing us off anything, eh, Ricochet?" jibbed Summer.

MacTavish filled all their tankards to the brim. "That's settled. Now I say, we drink to our new captain." They raised their mugs and toasted Ric.

The sun was setting on the day that had begun with such bright promise. Never could Ric have imagined it would end like this. He remembered a few of the last words he'd said to Captain Quinn in jest, *"Ye could always make me captain."*

The thought sent a shaft of pain through Ric. He was no Gavin Quinn. Not even close. But he owed it to his ship and his crewmates to do the best he could. He owed it to Jocelyn Beauchamp to see her delivered safe to her father, and he owed it to his Captain to take care of the *Scarlet Night* and what was left of her crew.

Ric lifted his tankard. "To hell with me," he countered, "tonight, we drink to our dead."

Chapter 6

Jocelyn pushed at the abundance of food upon her plate. She'd never eat all this in a week. Here in the galley, the men had spent the last hours eating and drinking as much rum as they could hold. They swapped stories about their fellow crewmates, lifted their mugs to each of their memory. Laughed, cried, sang. The revelry swirled around her. In their drunken state, they hardly noticed her presence. They toasted everything from one man's mother to another's pet rat.

The large Scotsman, who'd helped remove the heavy iron shackles that bound her wrists when she'd been brought aboard--MacTavish his mates called him--slammed an overflowing mug of rum down in front of her before giving her a good natured pat on the back. The blow jarred her teeth. "Drink up, Lassie."

Jocelyn had never been one to imbibe in spirits. It was strictly forbidden. Alcohol, namely wine was only allowed during Communion and at evening meals, of course, but the Sisters of Sainte-Geneviève served a weak, watered down Boudreaux one could scarcely call wine. One small glass. Never more.

She eyed the tall tankard. Perhaps she could take a little taste. Lift her own glass in salute to those she lost today. Sister Bernadette would turn in her grave should Jocelyn toast to her with such a brew. Curiosity was a powerful thing, however. Temptation, the devil's tool.

When Jocelyn had departed from the Abbey, an odd feeling had enveloped her. For the first time in her life she had felt freedom. Even under the hawk-like stare of Sister Bernadette, she was outside the thick stone walls that had sheltered her, caged her, most of her life.

It was true she was heading to her father only to be locked in another cage of sorts, but the sliver of time between had been exhilarating in a way Jocelyn had never dreamed. Heady. She was no fool, she knew her fate. What little freedom she experienced during their crossing would soon come to an end. But for a brief moment, for her, it breathed new life into her lungs.

Being captured and dragged through the fetid streets of Port Royal had been terrifying. The thought of what might have been...horrifying. Even now, surrounded by pirates not knowing what was to come, frightened her. And yet... If asked, she would have to confess that there lay a tiny spark deep within her that looked upon this night as a continuation of some grand adventure. One for which she was destined.

One she had been longing for her entire life.

The sweet, burnt aroma of the rum reached out to her. She leaned closer for another whiff. The strong fumes stung her nose. She pulled back and looked around at the others. They drank this? Willingly?

Once again, curiosity enticed her. She slid the tankard closer, and glanced around to see if anyone was watching. At the abbey there was always someone watching. Jocelyn gave herself a shake. She wasn't at the abbey, and she wasn't a child. If she wanted a taste of rum, then she would have one. Perhaps she would have two.

She dropped her chin and marveled at her bravado. When had she become so unrefined? When had the fact that she was alone in a room full of men--pirates--not scandalized her?

She'd never been without a chaperone before this morning. Alone with a man, let alone half a dozen was a disgrace. Her reputation lay in tatters at her feet. She should be horrified. Traumatized. Not reckless and wild and contemplating swilling rum like some tavern wench--if that was indeed what tavern wenches swilled.

The men before her lifted their mugs to their uncertain futures. With a cheeky grin, she followed suit.

The liquor blazed a fiery passageway into her belly. Had she swallowed burning treacle? It stole her breath and turned it into that of a dragon. Jocelyn set her drink down then covered her mouth with her hand and choked. Hot fingers unfurled like scorching tentacles through her body as her eyes watered in protest.

MacTavish circled back, staggered, and jostled her table. Rum sloshed from Jocelyn's mug and ran to drip off the edge.

"A thousand pardons, lass." He refilled her drink from the bottle he'd been hoisting.

"How can you drink this?" Jocelyn coughed again and pushed it away. "It's liquid fire."

MacTavish pushed it back. "After the third or fourth swallow, ye not be noticing the flames." He joked. "After the ninth or tenth, ye'll not notice damn near anything."

"Don't force her te drink, ye damn fool." Ric stared down at her with eyelids at half-mast. How many swallows had he had? "Can't be deliverin' Beauchamp's daughter drunk as a Finnish flounder."

Why she took his words as a personal challenge she didn't know. Jocelyn straightened in her seat, pulled the tankard back toward her, and turned the flame in her stomach into an inferno with a large gulp. She put the back of her hand against her lips. Partly to stifle the gasp threatening to escape, partly to keep her stomach from throwing it back.

Ric's expression of disbelief was followed by another good-natured wallop from MacTavish's meaty paw against Jocelyn's shoulder. "See there. None be forcing the lass."

Jocelyn recovered her ability to speak after what seemed like a week. "The nuns drank rum all the time." She lied and took another healthy swallow to prove her point. "L-like mother's milk," she wheezed.

Ric narrowed his eyes at her before turning back to the others. MacTavish once again topped off her mug.

Jocelyn slumped when Ric's back was turned. She was feeling slightly lightheaded. It wasn't an unpleasant sensation. She caught Ric looking back over his shoulder toward her. Now that she had started this game, she was obliged to finish it. She took another drink.

MacTavish was right. After the fourth sip, the burning had lost some of its edge and become more of a bright heated glow. It made her feel flushed. She raised cool hands to her overheated cheeks, the chilled tips of her fingers a blessed feeling against her skin.

Any more of this, and she'd be lifting her skirts and dancing about singing sea shanties like a true pirate. Only pirates didn't wear skirts. Not even women pirates.

As soon as the words slipped through her mind, she thought of Tupper. Fascinating woman. Jocelyn had never met anyone like her. But tonight, her heart went out to her. She'd been dealt such a blow. It was clear that she must have loved Captain Quinn a great deal. Jocelyn wondered how they met. How they fell in love. Was it love at first sight? Had they been pledged in marriage, then came to have feelings for one another? Or had she been one of the pirate's captives? Held against her will only to have her heart softened by a handsome scoundrel?

Jocelyn's maiden imagination got the better of her. She was being far too dreamy. Silly. Sister Bernadette would have called her a flibbertigibbet for getting lost in such a nonsensical daydream. Love. What did Jocelyn know of love? To her it was as foreign as rum.

Ah…rum.

She gave a small laugh, and took another sip. Her head was quite light. Around her things seemed to move in a slow blur. Maybe she would go out on deck and get some air to clear the childish musing of her mind. At the same time, she wondered if Tupper would want something to eat. There was still plenty of food filling the table. Jocelyn found a long wooden trencher and filled it with bread, fruit, and roasted fowl.

Managing the trencher and lantern while navigating the ladder way below proved more complicated than it should have. The effects of the rum were playing havoc with her coordination.

It took her two trips, but Jocelyn managed to get herself, the heavy iron lantern, and the trencher down to the deck below without injury. Making her way through the narrow galley way, she stopped at Tupper's quarters. She placed the lantern at her feet and held the trencher under one arm to knock.

"Tupper? Are you well? I've brought you some food."

No sound came from within. Perhaps she was sleeping.

"Tupper?" Jocelyn tried the latch. It was locked.

Below deck, the movement of the ship was more pronounced than above. It was hot and smelled of tar and fish and bilge. The combination of rum, heat, and sway of the ship was making her slightly nauseous.

"I'll leave this here."

Once back on deck, Jocelyn pulled great gulps of fresh sea air into her lungs. The cooler night air, a blessing. Overhead the stars carpeted the sky and dipped to twinkle in the ripples of the sea. It was as if the ship floated in a glittery bubble.

Jocelyn slid down the inside of the ship's rails to sit. She pulled open the edges of Ric's shirt to allow the chilled air to whisper over her skin and cool her heated cleavage.

"There you are." Ric staggered, then half sat, half dropped alongside her. "Thought we'd lost you, too."

Jocelyn tugged the neckline of the shirt back as best she could. "I needed some air."

"Aye…air." He lifted his bottle, took another drink, and passed it to her. She shook her head. "I think I've had enough for tonight."

He leaned his head back and closed his eyes. For a long minute she thought he'd succumbed to the alcohol and fallen asleep. The lantern's light carved shadows across his handsome face. His legs stretched out long in front of him encased in snug buff homespun ending in tall unpolished boots.

Jocelyn was tempted again, although not for rum. Something much more intoxicating. She simply wanted to touch him. Feel the solid muscle of his chest and arms. Run her fingertips across the scratch of his jaw. Lay them upon the small tender well at the base of his throat where she could see the pulse of his heart. She'd like to kiss him there.

A tremble of remembrance tumbled through her. Jocelyn flushed in the dark. She wanted him to touch her again, too. Feel the rake of his fingers along the back of her thigh. His breath against the side of her neck. What would it be like to have his lips upon hers? She was suddenly curious to find out.

Ric stirred and startled her. He dragged a heel across the deck boards to raise one knee. "I can't be captain," his voice quiet on the night air. "What the bloody hell they be thinkin?'"

"Sounded to me like you're the most qualified."

Ric cranked open one eye to peer at her as if he'd forgotten she was there. "What do you know about it? So I can read a chart. There be more te captaining than knowing which way be north. I'm a two-bit scallywag scraping through this life by the seat of me britches." He turned and looked her over. "You sure are a beauty. Took my breath from me first time I laid eyes on ya."

He reached out to her with the hand that still held the bottle and ran the backs of his knuckles over the edges of the shirt she wore. "In my shirt. So lovely. Damn kissable mouth. Sorry now I didn't kiss you when I had the chance."

Jocelyn held her breath. Each pass of his hand lowered the wide neckline a bit and brushed a careless knuckle across the swell of her breast.

He pulled his hand away to take another swallow from his bottle. "Most beautiful woman ever been in me shirt. Just don't be thinkin' 'bout gettin' in me pants." He stomped his boot. "I'm puttin' my foot down on that one." He scowled at her. "If I'm captain now, there'll be no more sharing my pants with every female we come across." Ric pointed the bottle at her. "That's an order."

Ric closed his eyes again. "My first order." He laughed. "No more women in my pants." A low moan escaped him. "I can't be the bloody captain…"

Chapter 7

The sun burned into his brain through the painful cracks of his eyelids. Ric didn't dare move. *Bloody hell!* How much had he drunk last night? Maybe if he sat perfectly still, he could die right on this spot and never have to fully open his eyes again.

"Well, look what we have here. Captain?"

Knives pierced his skull. Why were they screaming? And why did it feel like his clothes were made of lead?

"Ric?" The screamer kicked his boot. "Captain Ric?"

Captain Ric? He was too hungover for games. Ric tried to kick back, but his leg was pinned.

"Go away," he managed to mumble. Good Lord, his mouth tasted like it was full of dead barnacles. *Captain Ric.* Suddenly it all came rushing back. The horrible events of yesterday weren't a gruesome nightmare. They were real. Gavin Quinn and most of their crew were dead, and by some form of insanity--and a barrel of rum--the rest had made him captain.

Ric groaned. The last thing he remembered was--the weight holding him down shifted and moaned in return. *Jocelyn.*

He peeled open one eye. The woman was spread across his chest like honey on bread. Dark curls hid her face. Her skirts were hitched high allowing a pale bare thigh to rest over his hip, and her knee...well, her knee was precariously placed.

"Don't ya two make fer a cozy couple?"

Damm. Attempting to lift his hand to shield his eyes from the flaming arrows of the sun, he released the grip he still had on his bottle. The glass toppled from his hand and rolled away.

MacTavish stopped it with his boot and bent to pick it up. He tipped it over. Not a drop remained. "Dinna leave a tipple for a tosspot."

"Jocelyn," Ric mumbled. The word blasting through his skull.

"*La lumière. Couper la lumière.*" She moaned, curling tighter into Ric's side, her knee crushing into his balls. "Please turn out the light."

"Jocelyn." He shoved at her hip. "Get off me, woman."

She shifted back and sat up while battling out from under her riotous hair. "What? Where?" She peered at him from beneath a fall of tangled curls. "Oh…" Jocelyn pushed away while tugging her skirt into place, then leapt to her feet. Immediately regretting the sudden movement, she staggered and held the sides of her head. "Oh…*Sacré Bleu,* I'm dying…" She grabbed for the rail to steady herself.

MacTavish chuckled. "What ye be needin' is a hair of te dog. Bit o' te drink wit yer breakfast will fix what ails ya. Hornbach's got another feast laid out. Fried us up some fresh squid."

Jocelyn clamped a hand over her mouth and turned away.

Ric made a slow rise to his feet. If he held tight to his forehead, perhaps his brains wouldn't fall out onto the toes of his boots. He tried to recall what happened last night.

They'd been in the galley. Somebody's mother was a rat? No. That's wrong.

He closed his eyes and pulled in great gulps of fresh sea air hoping to clear his head.

"Ye got any orders fer te men there, Capt'n?"

Ric scrubbed at his eyebrows. "Orders?"

"Don't ya remember? Ye be Capt'n now."

Ric did remember. There wasn't enough rum in all of Jamaica to let him forget. "Aye." He gave a sloppy salute and glanced back at Jocelyn. Rum or no, she'd spent the night in his arms. Had they done anything else? Somewhere in his liquor-soaked mind, he recalled telling her how beautiful she was. He'd wanted to kiss her. Had he been foolish enough to act on his desire? No, he'd not have forgotten the feel of her lips, or the taste of her mouth. He doubted he'd forget that.

His first order of business had to be getting her off this ship and headed back to her bastard father before he did something truly stupid.

"Let's head for the north side of the island," Ric ordered. "We're goin' te need every set of hands to raise the main sail." He rubbed at his aching head again. "Anyone seen Bump?"

"No." MacTavish shook his head. "Tupper, neither."

"I'll see if she won't let me in." Ric frowned.

"I could try again," offered Jocelyn, looking back over one shoulder. "Are you feeling up to it?"

Her face tinted a pale green in the morning light. "Better that than fried squid for breakfast."

"Good point. We'll go together."

Jocelyn followed Ric below deck as the men disbursed to follow his orders. "May I ask a question?"

The dim light below deck was a relief to his swollen head. "Sure."

"My English may be confusing me, but I've heard it spoken a few times now, and I cannot figure it out. What is *bump*? You keep asking for it as if it is missing."

"Bump isn't a what. Bump is the boy."

"The one with the odd hair? His name is Bump?"

"Aye. It's a nickname."

"What is his given name?"

"Don't rightly know for sure. William, I think. Came aboard when he was no more than a babe. Was always getting knocked about. We called him Bump."

"He's very quiet, I've noticed."

"His whole world be quiet. The boy's deaf." Ric explained. "Doesn't speak. Least not with his mouth. Uses his hands to make the words he needs. Capt'n Quinn found a book to teach him how to spell words with his fingers."

"That explains it. Poor thing."

"He does fine and wouldn't want your pity. Works hard. Fights harder. Smarter than all of us. Knows every inch of this here ship. Sometimes it's like he knows things sooner than most." As soon as the words were out of Ric's mouth, he flashed back to yesterday. At the auction. Bump had been tugging on him to leave. His persistence had nothing to do with the auction. And again, when they were on the *Night* he'd been insisting they wait for Quinn before they pulled away from the docks. Had he somehow known--felt--the quake coming? He couldn't have understood what was coming, but maybe he could sense it before the rest of them.

He'd tried to warn them, and they hadn't listened.

Ric's gut twisted. He had to find him. The lad was no doubt carrying a burden that could crush him. It wasn't his fault they were all thick as tar. It wasn't his fault he couldn't get them to understand him. Still, he knew Bump well, the lad would take on the guilt of this, but Ric wouldn't let him. He'd find him today if he had to tear the ship apart.

Standing before Tupper's door, Jocelyn raked her fingers through her hair and smoothed her skirts. "I must look a fright."

Ric shook his head. He'd never figured out some women, and he certainly wasn't going to start with this one. "Ye look fine. You're not going to meet the queen. You're on a bloody pirate ship."

She shot him an irritated glare. "I know perfectly well where I am. You needn't curse at me."

"Aye, I do...I'm a pirate."

"And that means you have no manners?"

"Aye," Ric puffed out his chest. "Tis exactly what that means."

Jocelyn shook her head. "Odd thing to be proud of."

"Ye'd be amazed at what I be proud of." Ric reached past her and knocked on Tupper's door.

"The trencher I left here last night is gone."

"Tupper?" He tried the latch. It was unlocked. "I'm coming in."

Ric was taken aback by the sight before him. The cabin looked as if cannons had blasted through the wall.

The remaining crew hadn't been the only ones mourning the dead and drinking themselves into oblivion last night. Tupper was curled into a tight knot on the floor. Her face concealed by a battered leather hat of Quinn's. From what he could see, she wore nothing save one of Quinn's shirts. Her arms hugged her knees. Clothing, bottles, papers, and what looked like old letters littered the floor around her.

"Tup?" Ric whispered. Tupper Quinn was the toughest, bad-assed woman he'd ever known. Fact is, he barely thought of her as a woman at all. She was one of the men. Yes, she and Quinn did marry, years ago, but he'd never witnessed them behave as anything other than Captain and crew. Hell they fought on a regular basis. Side by side and with each other. Somehow he'd missed seeing the love they obviously had for one another. Kept it to themselves. A bit of treasure they didn't share. The evidence of the depth of what they had lay in tatters at his feet.

Bloody hell, the woman was wrecked.

Jocelyn turned and blocked the sight from Ric, preventing him from moving farther into the room. "She's lost in her grief. I'll stay with her. You go and find the boy, Bump."

"I-I need a few things from Quinn's desk first. The ship's log, charts. Then...I'm not sure what to do here." Ric hated feeling helpless.

"I am. Get what you need and leave us. Maybe send some water?" She lifted the trencher. The food sat cold and congealed. "She hasn't eaten more than a few bites. Perhaps some bread." She reached a hand out and squeezed his arm. "No matter what MacTavish says, do not let him bring her the bloody squid."

Bloody squid? His gaze shot back to her face. She gave him a small smile. She'd cursed. Beautifully. Only Jocelyn could cuss and have it sound cultured and refined with her sweeping, flowery French accent.

Was she trying to shock him? Make him laugh? Ease his distress? It surprised him she had the power to calm him. She'd done it last night, listening to the ramblings of a miserable drunk. Giving him comfort by allowing him to wrap her in his arms. Lying with him. Calling him a hero.

As much as he'd like to bury his face into the soft halo of dark curls and find that solace again, he couldn't. He had no right. She wasn't his, and never would be.

By the time the sun set on this day, she would be gone as well. On a ship back to her father. Who, if he found out how Ric had found comfort last night, would hang him in a gibbet and let the gulls peck out his eyes.

He couldn't help himself. He traced the line of her jaw with the edge of his finger. A dirty smudge marred the pink of her cheek. He brushed at it with his thumb. As long as he was in command of this ship--and himself--that would be the only dirt he'd allow to touch her. She needed to be off this ship.

Ric lost himself for a moment in her eyes, before nodding. "Take care of her. I'll send one of the men to bring fresh water and light fare. No squid."

His gaze followed the curve of her mouth into another gentle smile. The desire to kiss that mouth made him dizzy.

Ric dropped his hand and stepped back. He had no time to dream about kissing those tempting lips. He had a crew to put back together. A ship to sail with six men. A shore to navigate that no longer resembled the shore he'd known his whole life, while keeping the fact the *Scarlet Night* couldn't defend herself from a school of minnows if any of their enemies chose to attack.

And perhaps more important than fighting the growing need to kiss lips that had never been kissed, Ric had a broken boy to find.

Chapter 8

Jocelyn closed the door behind Ric and turned to survey the chaos of Tupper's quarters. She moved to get her off the floor and into the bed.

"Come now. Let's get you somewhere more comfortable." Jocelyn lifted the hat from Tupper's face, and with a gentle hand, smoothed back the woman's hair.

"Leave me." Tupper flung an arm over her eyes.

"I will. Just as soon as I get you into your bed." Jocelyn scooped a hand under Tupper's shoulders. "It's warm and snug."

Tupper resisted rising. "It smells of him."

"Then I shall change the bedding."

"No." Tupper was quick to object. "We...made love in those blankets... yesterday. Before he left. I wouldn't go with him. I'm so damned stubborn. He asked... and I wouldn't go. I argued him straight back to bed. Silenced by his kisses, I cradled him between my thighs." She ran a hand down her throat to rest over her heart. "I can still feel him inside me. Still hear him. He called out my name in his passion."

Jocelyn got her seated and sat next to her. Her cheeks heated at the image she tried to conjure of the lovers resolving their quarrel with kisses and... "If he asked you to join him, why did you stay behind?"

"I hate that blasted island. Haven't set foot on it since it stole my soul."

"I don't understand." Jocelyn turned to look at her.

Tupper's head dropped back. "My life forever changed on Port Royal." She closed her eyes. "I killed my first man there."

Jocelyn's breath caught. She'd been so busy romanticizing this exotic lawless life she found herself visiting, she'd forgotten pirates were thieves and murderers first and foremost. "I-I'm sure if you're repentant--"

Tupper shot her an angry stare. "I repent nothing. The man was pure, dark evil. I had to kill him."

"But it's a sin to--"

"Look here." Tupper pointed to a silvered scar that ran along the inside of her thigh. "Do you know what that is?" She didn't allow Jocelyn to guess. "The start of a 'B.' He wanted to monogram me before he raped me and slit my throat."

Jocelyn gasped and placed a hand against her neck.

"Still a sin to kill him, do you think?" Tupper scoffed.

"I-I…"

Tupper lifted a hand. "Save your holiness. You can't judge what you'll never understand." Her head dropped back again.

"You're correct. I know nothing of what brought you to this place and this life, but I do know you suffered a great loss yesterday, and I only want to help if I can."

"What can you do? You can't bring Gavin back to me."

"No, but I can keep you warm. Feed you. Bathe your face. Listen, if you want to talk. Hold you if you want to cry."

There was a long heavy pause before Tupper spoke again. Her voice was small and belied her words. "I don't need your help."

"I know. And yet, I will give it to you for the short time I am here." Jocelyn stood and offered Tupper her hands. "Come, rest."

Tupper gazed up at her with eyes rimmed in deep sorrow. Her face drawn and pale. She got up without aid, crossed the room on silent feet, and collapsed into her bed with her back toward Jocelyn. "I don't need you."

Jocelyn pulled the bedcovers up over Tupper's shoulders and smoothed her hair away from her cheek. "I know. Sleep now."

While Tupper fell into a soundless sleep, Jocelyn began to tidy the mess about the cabin. The ship creaked and popped around her as it picked up speed. Building clouds had brought rain that turned the sea the color of aged pewter. She stood in the gentle curve of windows at the back of the cabin and got lost in thought watching the ever-widening wake spread across the darkened sea.

Once again, she was on her way. To her father. Toward whatever life he'd planned for her. Would the man he'd betrothed her to still want her after all she'd been through? Father hadn't said in his letter, but she imagined the man to be a good match for her politically. Strategically. A man of great standing. He'd been promised a chaste woman. She'd been spared many times, but would he believe she was arriving as pure as when she left France? More important, did she care?

Tupper was right. There was much she would never understand. Never know. But the last few weeks had only stoked the fire within her to learn. Life was meant to be lived before you died. Yesterday's horrific quake taught her death could arrive at any time. Suddenly. Without warning.

It was always her objection to the teachings of the good Sisters. Their message had been for one to lead a pure holy life in order to reap bountiful rewards in heaven. To Jocelyn, it always seemed odd, backward, to wait until you were dead to start living.

She wanted to experience great adventures. Great passion. Now.

Jocelyn glanced over her shoulder at Tupper's sleeping form. *"He called out my name."* What did that mean? Frustration welled at her ignorance. Did he cry out in ecstasy? Did he shout his love for her? Would anyone ever call out her name in such a way? What if she never reveled in such fervor?

A short time later, Dowd brought water and a simple plate of bread, cheese and fruit. Jocelyn moved the stack of yellowed pages she'd retrieved from the floor to make room on the desk for the food.

"Don't touch those." Tupper scolded, rising suddenly.

"I'm sorry. I was neatening them. They were scattered--"

"He'll kill me if he finds them out of order." Tupper gathered them to her chest and returned to sit on the side of the bed.

Several of the pages fluttered to the floor. Jocelyn followed and picked them up. She read the flowing signature at the bottom of one of the pages.

"I thought your name was Tupper?"

"It is. Alice Tupper Quinn." She crushed the pages in her arms. "Gavin was the only person to still call me Alice." She drew a shaky breath. "I'd always said 'Alice' died on Port Royal all those years ago. At least the Alice I'd been. When I joined this crew, they all called me Tupper. All, except him...when we were...alone. I guess Alice died again on Port Royal...with Gavin."

"That's not true." Jocelyn told her. "You're still her." She watched as Tupper's eyes filled with tears. What she had said earlier all at once made sense to Jocelyn. "Before, when you said he called out your name.... He called you Alice."

* * * *

Back on deck, the rain fell hard. Jocelyn stood under a protected canopy in the bow. She shivered at the damp chill of the air. Her heart still aching for Tupper or Alice, or whichever name she was called. Tupper had begged her to leave and let her grieve in peace. Jocelyn had honored her wish, but promised to check back before she left the ship.

She'd wanted to ask about the letters. Curiosity pricked at her. If Tupper was Alice and the letters belonged to Gavin, then why were they signed, *"Your Beth?"* Perhaps she'd never know.

"How is she?" Ric came to stand beside her.

"She's mourning the man she loves." Jocelyn glanced at him. "But she's no longer on the floor, and I got her to eat a bit of food. How about you? Did you find the boy?"

"Aye." Ric gave a slow nod.

"How is he?"

"Hard to say with Bump, but I've put him to work. It be the best thing for him, and we need all the hands we can get."

"I can help, as well."

Ric snorted and shot her a smirk. "I don't think so. I'm desperate for more crew, but not that desperate."

Her jaw dropped at his condescension. "Why not? I'm smart, strong."

"Pampered," He countered. His eyes made a slow appraisal of her. "Soft."

There was nothing soft about the tension in her jaw. She could easily chew nails--and not the ones tipping her fingers. "Then what would you like me to do?"

"You're not going to be here long enough for me to teach you to do anything. You'd help me best by staying out of my way."

Jocelyn turned her glare back out through the rain. "I have learned one thing even without you. Seems pirates all have special nicknames. Bet I can guess yours. Is it Jack? Short for Jackass?

Ric threw back his head and laughed. The sound rankled. "No. You'll have to guess again."

"Cabbage Head?" She offered. "Impudent Oaf?"

He was still laughing. "All good guesses, but no."

Jocelyn huffed and glared at his broad retreating back. "I have a good name for you," she mumbled under her breath. *"Son of a...Fils de pute!"* she grumbled. "But that is more of an insult to your mother."

"Whose mother ye be insultin'?" MacTavish startled her as he came up behind her. He tugged at a rope.

I'm forever forgetting to look behind... How many times had she been caught at the abbey? Heat flared in her cheeks. "No one. I was muttering to myself."

His bushy brows knit into a solid line above his eyes. "If ye say so." He pulled sharp on the rope once more. "Come hold this line fer me, so I can tie it off."

"Are you sure I'm capable?" Her anger at Ric spilled over onto the Scotsman.

MacTavish gave her a side glance. "Seen ye hold a fork, pretty sure you can curl them fingers round a hank of rope."

"Forgive me. Of course, I can hold it for you." She grabbed the rope above where his wide rough hands held it.

"Hang on tight, it's gonna want to pull away," he warned before he let go. "Just be for a blink whilst I tie her down."

Jocelyn held on with two hands and nodded to tell him she was ready. When MacTavish let go, she was surprised at the strength of the "pull." Following the line up, she saw it connected to the line of the sail. Worry tugged at her stronger than the line. She hoped he wasn't lying about being quick to tie the rope. The last thing she wanted was Ric to be right about her being too soft. The roughness of the rope bit into her palms.

MacTavish threaded the end of the line through an iron ring, looped it back on itself, made a twist, and a second loop, and jerked the knot tight.

"Ye can let go now."

Jocelyn held fast. "You think that little knot will hold?"

"Lass, I been tying bowline knots fer more years than ye've been breathing. Let go." Rain dripped off the ends of his beard.

She opened her hands, poised to grab hold again if it slipped. It held. "I shouldn't have doubted you. You tied it so fast."

"Like I said, 'ave had lots of practice. Not a proper seaman if ye can't tie yer knots blindfolded, one-handed, behind yer back in the dark." He turned to leave.

"Could you teach me?" she blurted.

"Why ye be needin' te know?" He crossed thick arms over the barrel of his chest.

"Why not?" She lifted her shoulder. "Never know when a good knot may come in handy."

Chapter 9

Ric peered through the rain. Was he lost? He pulled the long brass eyeglass and gave another look. They couldn't be lost. He lowered the glass and ran a frustrated hand over his forehead. This was Port St. Maria, but where were the ships?

He scanned the surrounding area. The docks still stood. All looked as it should.

Ric ordered White and Summer to take the skiff into port. "Find out what's happened. The quake hasn't left carnage in the port, but the only ships I can make out are a handful of small fishing boats."

"So maybe they all weighed anchor when the ground started to shake." reasoned White.

"It'd be what I'd done," added Summer. "We don't need to be dragging the skiff through this mess of weather to figure that."

Ric repeated his order and gave Summer's shoulder a shove. "No, but you need to be finding a ship to take one small French woman to her Admiral father at Fort de Rocher on Tortuga."

"I knew we should have tossed her over," White continued to grumble.

It wasn't long before they returned.

"Rain's comin' down harder than horse piss." Summer wrung out his hat.

"I can see that," urged Ric. "What about the ships?"

"Quake started a panic like I figured. Then Judgment Hill took te moving and headed toward the sea," added White.

"Between the shaking and this weather, it ain't a wonder there be a landslide." Summer shook his head. "Least they didn't sink like them poor bastards in Port Royal."

Ric ran a hand through his damp hair. "What do we do now? The whole reason to come here was to put Jocelyn Beauchamp off the *Scarlet*." And out of his mind once and for all. Even given all that had happened, all the worries, pressure, disaster and grief that had filled his hours, somehow his thoughts would circle back to her. As if she were a balm as well as a bane for his tortured mind.

"I told ya. Dump her." White prompted snapping Ric back to the problem at hand.

"We can't dump her," argued Ric. He looked aft. The one small French woman in question huddled under the bulkhead overhang and seemed to be winding a length of rope around her hand. Why had he done little else since meeting her, than fight to protect her? Why her? And why did the possibility of her being hurt tear at his gut?

"Why not?" White wiped his nose with the back of his hand.

"'Cause if her father finds out we have her, he'll hang us by our nuts," explained MacTavish. "If he finds out we had her and dumped her, he'll feed us our nuts before he hangs us."

White's hands moved over his crotch as if to protect his jewels.

"So, where does that leave us?" Ric waved a hand toward White. "Other than nutless."

MacTavish tugged on the braids in his beard and thought. "Ifn' I were capt'n...and I *ain't*, we'd be heading through toward the Windward Passage. I'd dump the wee lass all right, but I'd dump her on dear daddy's doorstep."

"That's days away," Ric sighed. "That's if the weather doesn't churn things up worse than they are now. More than that, seein' we can't raise the main with seven of us. We'll be crawling at less than six knots, fighting against the winds the entire way. I've been going over Quinn's charts. I was thinking after we left here, we could lay low, head up the coast of America. Meet up with the *Raven Wing*, and gather some extra men. By then Tupper would be Captain, and I'd go back to polishing my cannon. Now I'm taking us into Tortuga?"

"Might be we ken pick up more hands in Tortuga. Wouldn't be a wasted trip," added Summer.

"If we could git close 'nuf. Sailin' into Tortuga be like sailin' into the lion's mouth." White whined. "How do we know we ken even get in there? Or better yet get out?"

MacTavish shook his head. "Yer all fergettin' another thing. Windward Passage ain't no stroll on the beach. We cross paths with a few unfriendlies while we're standing here with our willies out, we might as well take turns shooting each other now. Get it over with quicker. Be a might less bloody that way, too."

Ric rubbed at the scruff on his jaw. "Well, we can't sit here doin' nothing."

Jocelyn dashed through the rain to join them. "Are you taking a vote to see who brings me ashore?"

No one answered her. Their gazes passed from one to the other. The sound of rain on the canvas overhead turned to a roar inside Ric's skull. There was no getting away from it. He was the captain. He couldn't wish it away. Drinking it away only gave him the king of all hangovers. Avoiding it until Tupper was ready wasn't an option either.

God help them all. He was truly in charge.

"Luck seems to be on our side, and it's all been bad. Ye won't be going ashore. Looks like we're goin' to have to be the ones to take ye to Tortuga."

No sooner than the words were out of his mouth, something dark and fast hit the foresail and fell to the deck.

MacTavish ducked. "Luck's out te get ye from all directions," He laughed. "Next ye'll be struck by lightning and come down with a case of the pox."

"What is that?" asked Jocelyn, stepping to the edge of the canopy's protection. Rain sheeted past the edge to splash at her hems.

White rushed out to recover the wet lump and brought it back under the canopy. "It be one of them jabberin' crows."

"Ain't jabberin' no more," Summer observed. White flipped in on its back and checked it over.

Jocelyn reached out a hand to touch. "Poor thing."

Her compassion warmed Ric. "They're usually farther inland. Landslide probably forced it off shore. Got confused in the rain."

Worry marred her face. "Is it dead?"

White ran his fingers over the span of the bird's wings. "Not yet. But he be a goner. Bunged one wing when he hit. I'll put him out of his misery and drop him over the side."

"No," Jocelyn's eyes got wide with panic. "You can't." She shot a pleading look toward Ric. "Don't let him do that. Give him to me. I'll tend him. Back at the abbey we nursed a dove back to health after it flew into its reflection in a glass window.

"This ain't no dove. It's a filthy crow," scoffed White.

"It's still a living thing." She took it with great care and cradled it in her skirt. "I'll save you, you'll see. What shall I call you?" She glanced around at the group. "You're all so clever with names, what should we call it?"

"How 'bout Stew?" joked MacTavish.

Summer snorted and slapped MacTavish on the back. "See if Hornbach knows any good recipes fer crow pie."

"Crow a l'orange?" added White.

Jocelyn gasped and turned away shielding the bird. "You can't eat crow or raven. It says so in the bible. Leviticus." She stroked the bird's sleek black head and tipped her face to peer at the sodden creature. "That's what I'll call you. Leviticus." She shot an angry glance back at the jokesters. "That will remind you *not* to eat him."

"Stick with us for much longer, lass," MacTavish jerked his chin toward the galley making his braids dance. "Once all that food starts te spoil, and the only thing left te eat is hardtack and salt cod. That there crow is gonna look mighty tasty. Bible or no."

She whispered to the bird. "Don't listen to him. No one is going to cook you. I won't let them."

"All right, you three," Ric stepped in to end the debate on how best to eat crow. "Turn this ship north and we'll start our crawl toward Tortuga. I'll be lookin' over the charts again. See if I ken find us a better route." To Jocelyn he added. "Follow me."

"I don't know anything about charts and routes." She said to his back.

"Dinna think ye did." He led her down to the galley where he was using one of the long tables as a desk of sorts.

"You're not going to try to cook this poor bird, too?"

"Of course not." He moved to the back where the food was kept and retrieved a wooden box, lined in straw used to store eggs. He removed the last few remaining eggs and gave it to Jocelyn. "Can't be carrying the thing about in your skirts, now ken ya?" He gathered a few bits of fruit and bread and added it to the box. "If he survives the day, you may get him to eat."

She lifted her eyes to his with that look upon her face. The one of adoration he had come to both favor and fear. "Thank you." She laid the bird gently into its new nest. "I'm sorry I called you a jackass earlier. It was unfair of me."

"'Twas yer right." Ric unrolled the charts and looked at them with unseeing eyes. The tenderness in her voice was like a siren's song. Reaching past the noise of his stress and frustration and offering him a soft place to lay his aching head. She couldn't know such kindness only raised a longing in him he didn't dare think about.

"I only wanted to help." Her quiet words reached deeper into his heart. "It's true, I have led a pampered, cloistered life. But it was never my choosing. Now I find myself in a situation where I must be strong and capable, and fight to survive. It's a powerful feeling and I'm confident I'm up to the task. Whatever it shall be."

He lifted his gaze to hers once more. "I understand you want to spread your wings," he gestured to the crate. "Like our sopping friend here. But like him, you're flying blindly into a storm that will kill you. I can't let that happen. I won't. You have no notion of what life is like out here. Every day is a battle of one sort or the other."

"I'm going to have to learn sooner or later."

"You shouldn't have to." Ric opened the logbook. Putting a barrier between him and the pull of her gentle gaze.

"There comes a time when everyone has to, and mine is now. Even you can't save me from that."

"I can do my best."

They sat in quiet for a long moment before Jocelyn stood and gathered her feathered charge. "Is your nickname, The Great Protector?"

"No." Ric lifted his gaze to meet hers.

She gave a small shake to her head. "Exactly."

After Jocelyn left, Ric lit a lantern against the gloom and scribbled into the ship's log. He added the name of one broken bird to their meager roster, and once more tried to figure out how they could make their way from here to Fort de Rocher with five men, two boys, two women, and a one-winged crow.

Why did he feel as if he were sailing them all off the edge of the earth. *The Great Protector?* That was laughable. It was more like The Great Pretender.

Chapter 10

Jocelyn peered into the makeshift nest of straw as she headed down to Tupper's cabin. She remembered seeing rolls of linen strips when she was tidying things yesterday in the Captain's quarters. She would ask for one to bind the poor bird's wing. There was no guarantee the crow would survive, but it should be given a chance.

She tapped lightly on the door, hesitant that she would wake Tupper.

The "Come." from within surprised her. Seeing Tupper up and seated by the window surprised her even more. She was wrapped in a blanket with her knees pulled tight to her chest. Hair in disarray hid half her features.

"I didn't want to disturb you. How are you feeling?"

"How should I feel?" She turned to look at her. Dusty crescent moons shadowed Tupper's eyes, made all the more pronounced by the paleness of her face. She pulled the blanket tighter.

"No one can answer that question. A person's grief is their own."

Tupper turned back toward the windows. "We're leaving Jamaica." It wasn't a question.

"*Oui.*" From the bow of windows, the devastated island pulled farther and farther away. "There were no ships available. Ric promised to return me to my father, however. Without other transport, he means to bring me there himself."

Tupper looked back over her shoulder. Her eyebrows knit in concern. "If the *Scarlet Night* sails into Tortuga, the French will blow us out of the water."

"*The French*, meaning my father." Jocelyn nodded and sighed. "*Oui*, they understand. Ric and the others have been discussing the dangers.

They are working on a plan. You have my word, however, I won't allow them to risk their lives for me."

Turning back to the windows, Tupper spoke to the sea. "So Robbins is captain?"

"For now, I believe." Jocelyn wasn't sure what to say. The way Tupper asked with such a quiet resolve, she wasn't sure if she was angry or hurt or relieved.

Tupper lifted a shoulder. "Someone needed to take charge. Ric will do well. He's smart."

Jocelyn fought the urge to wrap Tupper in a comforting embrace. "He cares a great deal for this ship, and for all of you."

Tupper tucked her chin and hugged her knees. "What's in the box?" She hadn't looked back.

"Oh, this is Leviticus. A Jamaican crow. He flew into one of the sails during the storm and hurt his wing. When I was putting things away here earlier, I noticed some linen strips. I was wondering if I could have one to bind the poor thing. Perhaps it will heal." She set the crate on the desk. "The others don't believe he'll make it, but there's been so much death already, I had to try." As soon as the words were out of her mouth, she regretted them. "I don't mean that a bird compares in any way to--"

"Forget it. I know what you meant. Help yourself to whatever you need."

Jocelyn was grateful for something to do. Not having words to offer comfort made her feel helpless. Binding this small creature's injury at least made her feel like she was doing something to ease someone's pain.

"There is always death and danger surrounding us." Tupper spoke again to the window glass. Her breath fogged the triangle. "It's part of us. We fight it every day. I knew the risks of living this life. Loving Gavin. Once I made the choice to join this crew and become his wife, I never took one day for granted. I always hoped I'd be the one to fall first. Or at least we'd be lucky enough to die together. Amidst some epic battle fighting side by side through a fog of cannon smoke. Or through a hellish storm that would wash us both to our watery graves. I never imagined it would end like this. With him dying first. Not this way. Evening knowing I might lose him one day, I never imagined it would hurt quite this much."

"You love him. From what you've told me, he loved you as much. I can only believe such affection never dies." Jocelyn took care to wrap the bird's wing before winding the bandage loosely around the crow's body to keep the wing still and let it heal. She could feel the flutter of its heart, but it still hadn't opened its eyes. She finished and moved to wash her hands. "I don't know if the Sisters were right in their beliefs, but they always taught us that life goes on. They told me someday I would see my mother again. I've doubted so many of their teachings, but I've held that one tight to my heart. I was but a child when she died. Her face is a soft blur in my memory. But from time to time I still smell her perfume, hear the lullaby she would hum to me when she tucked me in at night. I hold on to the hope in this, the Sisters were right. That one day I will see her again."

Tupper ran a hand over her eyes. "I've heard the same fairy tale. I wasn't a young child, but closer to grown when I lost my mother. Never knew my father. I didn't believe it then, but I would like to believe it now." She gestured toward the crow. "What are you going to do with it now?"

"I don't know. I don't know what I'm to do with myself." Jocelyn raised one shoulder in a shrug as a knock sounded on the door. Two sharp raps followed by two slow.

"*Bump.*" Tupper rose, a flash of worry crossing her face as she rushed to the door and let him in. She held her hands with one finger bent toward her and moved them alternately back and forth in front of her chest. "I was worried. Are you all right?" She grasped his arms and peered into his face before putting a fist to her heart and rubbing it in a circle. "Sorry. I…I'm sorry."

Bump held her gaze with wide unblinking eyes. His mouth pressed to a flat line before he gave Tupper the tiniest tip of a nod. He made a few gestures and pointed toward Jocelyn.

"He's here to show you to your quarters." Tupper's eyes never left the boy. "Ric's set up a bit of space for you. Away from the men." She looked over at her. "I know the space he means. It's small, but you'll have some privacy, and a comfortable place to lie down."

"One night sleeping on the deck was enough for me. I'll be grateful for wherever I can lay my head."

Tupper returned her attention to Bump and gestured over her shoulder. "Come back when you're done?" She put a finger to her lips and tipped it away. "We'll talk?"

Bump nodded in agreement and turned to leave. He shot Jocelyn a glance she quickly translated to mean, "Follow me."

"Leave the bird with me, if you'd like. Your room is barely big enough for you, and it has no windows or light. He may do better to recover here. I can look after him."

"I think that sounds like a fine idea."

Tupper stepped back and checked the crate. "What's his name again?"

"Leviticus. It's from the Bible."

Jocelyn followed the slender back of the young man. She wished she had asked Tupper how to use her hands to say thank you to Bump. She still owed her life in part to the boy.

He stopped and lifted a lantern before opening a narrow rough-hewn door. It swung open a fraction before hitting something within.

Bump handed her the lantern and simply pointed into the darkened space. When he eased past her to leave, she reached out a hand to stop him. "Thank you." She hoped somehow, he would understand.

Instead, he jerked his arm from her grasp and made a few quick gestures. He stood for half a heartbeat staring at his feet before lifting angry eyes to her. She didn't need to know the words his hands spoke. His eyes told her everything. Desolation and fury flittered across his features. His silent mouth pursed in rage as his hands flew at her.

Was he upset they had taken the time to rescue her, when they couldn't save the others? Was he railing at her because he believed he and Ric should have stayed? Tried again to go back? Or was he simply "screaming" at the one person who wouldn't know the pain behind his words.

Jocelyn stood there and "listened" to his rant. She wouldn't deny him his anger. Her heart ached for him. Tears caught in her throat. When it was over, Bump dropped his hands to his sides, his chest rising and falling in rapid breaths. Jocelyn took her fist and made a circle over her heart as she had seen Tupper do a few minutes earlier.

His eyes widened and followed the motion of her hand before meeting her gaze. "I'm sorry, Bump. I really am."

The boy's throat worked as he watched her mouth. He raised those deep, all-seeing eyes to hers once more before turning and hurrying away.

Jocelyn was once again struck by the fact that these men and women... woman...while being fierce, fighting pirates, not only lived in a world larger than life, they lived and loved and suffered as large. Perhaps more so. This wasn't simply a ship. In its own way, it was a village, an army, a family.

Raising her lantern, she inspected her new quarters, if one could call it such. The space was created by walling off a section of the storage hold using a length of sailcloth. Peering past the stiff fabric, Jocelyn could make out barrels and coils of rope.

A narrow cot fit between the door and the curve of the ship's hull. A blanket of rough wool sat folded at its foot. A small table with pitcher and washing cloth, and a small stool were the only other furnishings.

Life at the abbey had prepared her for a life of simplicity. Had she been raised in splendor, she would surely have been horrified at the accommodations, but her room at Sainte-Genevieve had been tiny and stark. Not quite this small, but closing the door, she noticed it afforded her one thing her room at the abbey had not. A lock. Privacy. Suddenly, her sailcloth cabin rivaled a silk bedecked suite.

The first thing she did was rid herself of her sodden skirts and stockings. She paused while removing Ric's shirt. Her thumb rubbing at the rough weave of the fabric. Once again, his generosity surprised her. Touched her. He had a hardened edge like a well-honed ax blade, but there was much more to him. The way he'd taken on the position of captain, stepped up when needed. His caring and consideration, not only for her, but for those around him, was equally laudable.

But standing there in nothing but his shirt, it wasn't his compassion and competency she was contemplating. No. She smoothed the fabric tight across her breasts. The rough weave teased the chilled peaks of her nipples.

Waking up in his arms, feeling the strong curve of his chest beneath her cheek was what filled her thoughts. Her bare thigh slung over his hip. His arms holding her tight. She wanted that again. Dare she admit she wanted more?

Her hand cupped the heaviness of her breast. What would it be like to have him touch her there? Caress the sensitive skin. Her fingers trailed lower, over her belly, down one thigh and back up. She trembled at the thought of his fingers taking the same path.

She shot a glance behind her, making sure the door was indeed locked, then striped out of his shirt and stood naked. Laying the shirt over her front, she took the wide sleeves and draped them over her shoulders as she imagined him taking her in his arms.

Jocelyn closed her eyes and fantasized about pressing against him. Their bodies fitting together perfectly...she'd stand on tiptoe. Run her fingers into his golden hair as his hands would wander down her back, over her behind, drawing her tight to him.

Then he would kiss her. Jocelyn's body trembled at the thought. She remembered some of the country girls at the abbey talking about their stolen kisses behind the hedges. What would Ric's kiss be like? Would he crush his mouth to hers in a blind fit of passion, or would he take her lips slowly in a gentle press? Would he tilt her chin with the touch of a finger? Cup her cheek? Slip the tip of his tongue...

She had to sit down. Her heart raced. Her thighs quivered, and an ache coiled deep within her. She crushed the shirt to her chest and buried a frustrated moan into the fabric.

What had come over her? She was behaving like a starving woman before a loaf of bread. The ache between her thighs spread through her and brought a tingling to her fingers and toes. Moments ago, she'd been cold and chilled, now she was aflame.

Rushing to the pitcher, she dampened the cloth and held it to her throat, her chest, her cheeks. How could the thought of one kiss cause such a heated reaction? Was she so desperate to feel a man's lips on hers? Experience a man's touch?

No, not *a* man, one man...*that* man. Captain Ric Robbins needed to kiss her. And soon.

Chapter 11

"Dowd, I want you in the nest."

The man before him paled visibly. "But...but..."

Ric pointed to the crow's-nest high above the decks. "I need a man up there to keep look out, and you're it."

"I'm beggin' ye, Capt'n. Can't it be somebody else?" Dowd raised his chin and lifted his eyes. "It's so...high."

"Hard having a crow's-nest positioned on the keel. Can't see a damn thing down there between the barnacles and all that water. Of course, if you'd like to give it a try, I'll rig the rope."

"No, no..." He held his hand in surrender. "I'll go...it's just..." Dowd's eyes made the long slow journey up the mast once more. "I'm plum petrified of heights."

Ric pushed an eyeglass into his hands. "Then don't look down." He gave him a shove toward the rigging. "You only need to be up there 'til nightfall. I need to know if there are any ships in the area before they see us. Understand?"

"Aye, I understand." Dowd clutched the brass to his chest and began a slow climb up the main mast muttering, "Don't look down, don't look down."

The rains had passed, and the last of the clouds had given way to the bright blaze of the setting sun that sparkled on the scrubbed decks. Aye, the *Scarlet* was a beauty. Ric stood at her helm a bit taller. Puffed his chest. Pulled in a great breath of sea air, and allowed himself to feel a bit of pride at his new command. Even if it were for a short time, the *Scarlet Night* was his.

He eased the bow to starboard, setting them on a northeastern course. He'd spent the last hours combing over Quinn's maps and charts and made the decision they wouldn't be sailing through the Windward Passage. It was a fool's journey given their lack of speed and men.

They would sail along Hispaniola's southern coast. Instead of fighting the winds, they could circle around the eastern tip and use the trade winds to cut back along the northern shore.

Keeping close to the shallows, there would be more places to slip away should another ship cross their paths. MacTavish had reported that they were in good shape as far as ammunition and readied sacks of black powder, should they need it. Ric prayed they wouldn't.

Once they got close enough to Port de Paix, they could anchor a safe distance away, and he would bring Jocelyn into the city. Then they could cross to Tortuga. Yes, it would take them longer, by a good week, but they weren't in a hurry to be somewhere else. This way would give them time to adjust to operating the ship with so few hands.

Ric watched as Jocelyn came up the ladder way to deck side. She'd pulled her hair up and tied it with a bit of something. He couldn't make it out from this distance, but the effect hit him like a fist. The gentle sweep of her neck and sun kissed shoulders. The soft line of her jaw. His own jaw tensed. She was beautiful.

When he'd decided on this new course, he had to admit, part of him was pleased with the extra bit of time she could be with him, but with the pleasure came the frustration of knowing it would be that much longer fighting his growing attraction to the woman.

His brain repeated the litany of reasons why he needed to keep his hands from her. His body was another matter. It was unused to hearing "No" from his brain. Ric shifted his stance. The sudden tightness in his breeches followed by a pulse of blood to his erection, a clear warning. Yes, the swords were drawn, and the battle between his mind and his need waged.

Seeing him, Jocelyn climbed to the quarterdeck. She moved with a fluid grace, raising her hems to negotiate the stairs. Her delicate ankles reminding him of a single pale thigh which continued to haunt him. A painful ache settled in his crotch. Ric stifled a moan as his body scored a direct hit.

"Captain, it seems I'm to be forever in your debt." She smiled at him. Her hair catching the reds and oranges of the setting sun behind her. His wits suffered another blow. She was stunning. When he stood like a simpleton and forgot how to speak, she continued. "The room? A bed? A place to call my own?"

Ric struggled to get enough blood back to his brain. "A bed?"

"*Oui*, and a door, with a lock." She made it sound as if he'd given her gold and pearls.

He cleared his throat. "Couldn't have you sleeping on the deck another night." As soon as the words were out of his mouth, the image of her draped across him rushed through his mind.

"Might have been the abundance of rum, but I slept quite well on your deck." She touched his sleeve. "Of course, I had you to keep me safe and warm all night."

The battle within him intensified. Another round of fire off his port... his brain returned fire. "A door and a lock will keep you twice as safe."

Jocelyn leaned close and whispered. "But not nearly as warm, no?"

The sudden pulse of blood to Ric's cock had his brain raising the white flag of surrender. All hands were lost. He closed his eyes, gripped the pegs of the ship's wheel and held tight. "I'll see you get an extra blanket." *Retreat! Retreat!* "So...how is the crow?"

"I bound his wing, and now we wait, and hope. I left him with Tupper. Her request. It might do her good to care for him." She smoothed the overturned cuff of his shirt.

Her touch sent more heat to those areas he was desperate to cool. "How is Tupper?"

"A bit better, I think. I didn't find her on the floor. She's a strong woman, and wise. She spoke to me of choosing such a life as this. With all its dangers and risks."

"Some would call her foolish."

Jocelyn gripped one of the pegs of the wheel as if getting a feel for steering the ship. "I wouldn't agree with them. I think she's tenacious and brave."

He noted the way her slender fingers curled around the polished oak pegs. "This is a hard life for a woman."

"How much harder would it be to stand on the docks and watch your husband sail away and never know his fate? I remember my mother crying for days after Father left. At least Tupper got to live her life by her husband's side." She blinked up at him.

"And she's fought and battled, survived storms and all manner of hardships." Part of him reveled in her innocence. She had no idea. She'd not seen the horrors of the world. It hadn't hardened her. Tainted her. "Don't lose sight of the thousand of ways to die aboard this ship."

"That only makes it more incredible having such a woman aboard. I envy her," she sounded wistful.

He shot her a sharp glance. "She just lost her husband. Why would you envy her?"

Jocelyn let go of the ship's wheel to brush a disobedient curl from her cheek. "Because she has lived…" Her rich gaze met and held his. "…and loved. Two things I have waited my whole life to do."

Ric turned his focus back to the horizon. "You still have plenty of time yet."

"I've never been a patient soul." She once more teased the tip of one of the pegs.

He cleared his throat and reminded himself for the thousandth time who she was. "Once you're reunited with your father, you can begin a whole new life."

Jocelyn was quiet for a moment before crossing her arms over her chest. "A whole new life," she reiterated. "Married to a stranger, left standing on a dock. Who would envy me?" She left his side but called over one shoulder. "Thank you again for my room. I think I'll find MacTavish."

Ric watched her walk away. Arms crossed, chin tucked low. She might not be looking forward to what awaited her, but romanticizing what life was like aboard this ship was misguided. If she envied Tupper so much, perhaps she should be the one to try to set the girl straight.

He'd been putting off talking to Tupper, wanting to respect her time of mourning, give her some space and time to come to grips with what had happened. But by Jocelyn's account, she was feeling better.

The sun dropped red into the fire-tipped sea. It was a promise of clear skies ahead. Perhaps it was a sign they had left the worst behind. He'd talk to Tupper tonight. Set things to right. Ask her to do something to quell Jocelyn's starry-eyed notions of life at sea…and him.

* * * *

Tupper bid Ric come in and took the bowl of rich stew and bread he'd brought. "I'm not an invalid. I heard the bell. I could come to the galley on my own. I've no interest in food." She pulled a crystal decanter of brandy off the desk and poured him a glass and refreshed her own.

"Eat anyway." He pointed to the food. "Can't have you becoming weak. We need you."

Tupper ignored his urgings to eat. "I hear they voted you captain." She lifted her glass to him in salute and drank it down.

He followed suit. The brandy warmed his chest. His belly. "What's left of them. I was the lesser evil. Had MacTavish known how to read a chart, we'd all be wearing tartan now and braiding our beards. And I'm only filling in until you say otherwise."

Tupper paused as she refilled their glasses. "Me?"

"It's agreed. We all want you to take Quinn's place." Ric saw the flash of raw pain pass over her face at the mention of his name. He held up on hand in apology. "It's still too soon, but when you're ready there'll be no debate. Already been voted."

Tupper leaned on the edge of the desk and stared into her glass for a moment. "Bump tells me you're doing well. He was here earlier. It's been hard for him, losing Gavin. He feels guilty." She sipped her drink before meeting Ric's gaze. "Said he could feel something wasn't right the moment you all set foot in town, but didn't know what was coming. I think he saw it all happen, but won't say. He holds things so tight inside. He may never tell me."

"Don't push him."

She nodded and took another swallow of her drink. "Thank you for keeping him busy." Tupper frowned into her glass and rubbed a hand over her mouth. "And...thank you for...keeping him safe. I'm glad he was with you when..." She pulled a shuddered breath. "He could have been with Gavin. Had you not been there, he would have stayed with him, and... I can't imagine if I'd lost them both." She lifted pained eyes to his.

"I've had Bump's back since he was four years old. I'll always have his back." Ric swirled the liquor in his glass. "It's been hard for all of us. So many were lost. We're still reeling. I think once we find our feet again, we need to honor them somehow. Do what's right. Proper. Commit them all to the sea with or without a body to slide into the wake. They deserve the honor bestowed as if they'd died in battle. Captain Quinn, especially, deserves nothing less from us.

Tupper nodded and gave him a watery smile. The air in the room seemed to pause and take a breath. Ric waited as Tupper got lost in her own thoughts.

She gave a quick shake to her head then emptied her glass and looked about the room. "I'll get busy and pack up my things. If you'll give me one more night, I can be out of here tomorrow."

"What are you talking about?" Ric frowned.

She waved a hand, sweeping the room. "This is the Captain's quarters. It's only right you have it."

"No. I'm not kicking you out." He glanced around the room. Quinn's presence still filled each corner. They'd occupied this cabin together for years. It was only right Tupper stay here. "You know, the last time I saw

Quinn…I joked with him about wanting to be captain of the *White Witch*. He said I wasn't ready."

"You're ready now. He'd be proud of the way you've stepped up. The others may think I could fill Gavin's boots someday, but maybe when the time comes, the rest of the crew will want you to stay on."

"With White, Summer, and MacTavish leading the charge? I doubt it."

A rustling off to one side of the room brought Tupper to her feet. She placed her glass on the desk and crossed to one of the trunks.

Ric hadn't noticed it when he came in. Frankly, he'd forgotten all about the crow until Tupper pulled a cloth off the crate he'd given Jocelyn for the bird.

"Are you going to keep quiet now?" Tupper fed him a bit of bread.

Ric joined her and was surprised to see the bird awake…and angry by the look of him. "Hey, he's alive."

"So it seems."

The white of the bandage stood out against the bird's sleek black feathers. He fluffed his plumage impatiently and pulled at the linen with his broad beak. "I wouldn't have given him much of a chance."

"Stubborn thing. Came to after Jocelyn left and got to squawking. Got him to eat a bit, and drink. Only way to stop him from making a racket is to cover him. Makes him think it's night. He settles right down."

"Could take him to the galley if he's bothering you."

"No, I don't mind him." Tupper fed the bird another tidbit.

Ric went back to leaning against the side of the wide oak desk filling the space. "Glad you mentioned her. We need to talk about Jocelyn."

Tupper covered the crate again. "I don't mind her either. She's been kind. Not anything like her bastard father."

"Shouldn't we tell her how well we know her father?"

"I will. I haven't had the opportunity." Tupper sat before her meal, pulled a hunk of bread from the loaf Ric brought earlier, and dipped it into the stew but seemed to lose interest after that and set it aside. She brushed her hands and refilled her glass instead.

"She's taken with you." Ric moved the bottle of brandy away from her and pushed the stew closer. She narrowed her eyes at him. "Thinks you've led some fanciful life."

Tupper pushed the bowl away again and flipped a hand. "She's young. Naïve."

"Maybe you can explain things."

"Why?" She leaned back in her chair, tipping onto its two back legs, and crossed her arms over her chest. "Why do you care what she thinks? What are you afraid of?"

"Nothing." He scratched at his chin before pointing to himself and back to her. "But she's looking at the two of us like we're some grand adventure."

Tupper shrugged a shoulder. "To her, I'm sure we are."

"This isn't some fairy tale, Tup, with pirates and mermaids. She's going to get hurt."

Her eyebrow rose as she settled the chair back on all four legs. "Putting a twist in yer britches, is she?"

Ric waved the absurd suggestion away. The fact it was true didn't make it any less ridiculous. "No. It's not like that."

"Really?" Tupper smirked. "So she's attracted to you. Why should she be different from any other woman? Do what you always do. You're still 'love-'em-fast, leave-'em-faster' Ricochet Robbins aren't you? I've known you to hightail it away from a woman before you've finished buttoning yer britches."

"It's different with her." Ric dropped his empty glass on the desk.

Tupper eyebrows rose toward her hairline. "Is it now?"

He pushed away from the desk and began to pace the room. "I can't explain it, but yes."

"You know," Tupper suggested. An amused smile played at her lips. "It might be worth taking her for a quick tumble to see the look on Beauchamp's face when we deliver his less than lilywhite daughter."

Ric looked back at her as if she'd gone mad. "He'd draw and quarter us and use our bits for bait."

Tupper scoffed. "If he catches us, he'll do that anyway."

"I won't use her to get back at him." He shook his head and gave Tupper a hard glare.

"He killed six of our men," she reminded him, anger sharpening her words.

Ric pointed an accusing finger. "*You* took his eye."

Tupper shrugged and filled her glass again. "Just one."

Chapter 12

Ric met Jocelyn in the dark, narrow galley way. He'd been with Tupper more than an hour. He needed to secure things topside before finding his bed for the night.

Jocelyn carried the same hank of rope he'd seen her with before. It made him curious to know what she'd been up to.

"Good night, Captain." She met his eye as she moved to pass him.

"Isn't your door with the lock in the other direction?" He jerked his chin toward the bow of the ship.

In the tight passageway, she needed to press close to pass. "You know it is. I thought I'd stop to bid Tupper a good night and check on Leviticus."

"No need. Just left them both. Tupper's drowning her pain in her cups, and the bird has been eating, drinking, and causing a ruckus, but she got him quieted down to rest."

"I'm sorry about Tupper, but I'm pleased to hear about Leviticus. I won't disturb them. I'll save my visit for morning." She shifted direction, bumped her hip against his and tripped over the toe of his boot.

Ric caught her as she stumbled. His body's reaction to holding her once more in his arms was instantaneous. You'd have thought he was a green lad with no control over such things. Powerless. He pulled the scent of her deep into his lungs. "You've been in the magazine," he whispered.

Jocelyn breath came in quick puffs. "Pardon? H-How can you tell?"

He slid a hand up her arm and smiled at the way his touch caused her to tremble. The blatant admiration from her dissolved into a maiden's timid nerves at his simplest caress. "You smell mildly like MacTavish's lair… black powder and sulfur."

Her eyes widened. "I smell?"

Ric lifted a lock of her hair to his nose. Taking a moment to test the silkiness of its curls between his fingers. He loved her hair. The way the sun caught each wave and separated the rich brown strands from the reddish-gold ones. The wildness of it matched her personality, as did the softness. A potent combination.

"Just a hint." He murmured. "The last time I was this close, you smelled of sunshine and sweet warmth."

"And rum," she reminded him.

"Aye, and rum." Asleep in his arms, that chaos of hair trailing across his chest. A bare thigh cradling his hip. Her stocking had slipped past the bend of her knee. He may have been hung over, but he remembered it well. Each torturous detail. His traitorous body pulsed with the memory.

"I think I learned my lesson last night. No more than three sips." She lowered her gaze to his mouth. "It's not rum you've been drinking tonight."

"Brandy. Quinn's favorite. We were toasting his memory." He wished she would stop watching his mouth. It was if she were silently begging him to kiss her.

"There is a lot of drinking here."

He tipped one corner of his mouth in a grin. "A drunken crew is a happy crew."

"Are you happy?" The gentle lift of her eyes to meet his cooled some of his ardor.

What kind of question was that? When had anyone asked him such a thing? Only an innocent would ask something so ridiculous. Or was she asking if he was in danger of passing out again on the deck? He answered it with a shrug. "I'm not all that drunk." Ric let go of her hair but brushed her cheek with the backs of his fingers and contemplated his happiness. "Just enough, on both counts." He released her and continued on his way toward the ladder leading to the upper deck. "Good night, Jocelyn."

* * * *

The following morning burned bright. Ric had watched its brilliant arrival off their starboard bow hours ago. Last night's close encounter below with Jocelyn had caused a night of questions, restlessness, pacing, and aching frustration.

He'd never encountered a woman who could yank him in twelve directions at once. Perhaps it was due to the fact he'd never given a woman enough time to wind their way into his thoughts the way she had.

Tupper's description of him had been true. Love 'em fast, leave 'em faster. It was a fair motto for him. But none of those women he'd been loving and leaving with reckless abandon had been living in such close quarters. And none of them had ever been so off limits.

Was the thought of her being forbidden driving his sudden insanity? Wanting what he couldn't have? What he shouldn't have. Was that the cause of this irrepressible attraction?

Ric huffed an exasperated breath and cursed at the rigging. "That's such a load of gull crap."

He began to pace the deck once more.

"Talkin' to yerself, are ye?" MacTavish met him coming from the galley with a tall leather mug of ale.

Ric kept walking. "Beats talking to you."

To add to Ric's aggravation, MacTavish fell into step and kept pace with him. "Ye look like shite."

"Always the flatterer," Ric grumbled.

"What's got ye marchin' the boards and shaking yer fist at the sky so early in te morn?"

Ric stopped and pointed an accusing finger at MacTavish's chest. "What's Jocelyn been doing in the magazine? With you?"

MacTavish knocked Ric's finger aside with a sweep of his hand and laughed. "Jealous?"

"Curious."

MacTavish laughed again. "Sounds jealous te me."

Ric narrowed his eyes. "Answer the question."

The Scotsman ran a smoothing hand over his beard and down the stained front of his shirt before hitching the belt securing his kilt. "I ain't one to kiss and tell." He notched his chin and strolled away before doubling over and slapping his bare knee with laughter.

"Bald arsed, son of a cur!" Ric barked at him.

MacTavish only roared louder.

Hornbach and Dowd emerged from the galley. "What's so damn funny?"

Wiping his eyes, MacTavish pointed at Ric and laughed some more.

"Not a damn thing. MacTavish's brain's getting too much air under that skirt," Ric cursed. "Dowd, get your arse back in the nest."

"But I'm not done eatin' me breakfast," the lad whined.

"Can put you on half rations, if it'll help," Ric suggested.

"I'm goin.'" Dowd grumbled and tucked the bread and cheese he'd been eating into his shirt for safekeeping and headed toward the rigging.

"Be on the watch for Isla Vaca. We should be brushing past her sometime today."

Hornbach stood next to Ric and watched Dowd's slow assent up the main mast. "We be stopping there to gather up more men?"

"No."

Hornbach shot a disbelieving stare at Ric. "Why the hell not?"

"Isla Vaca is Captain Morgan's holding. I want to keep our distance. We sail too close and we might as well hand him the *Scarlet Night*. Besides, I'm not bringing any new men to crew until I get Jocelyn away. Don't need to be fighting every bastard who wants a piece of her." Ric shaded his eyes to see Dowd had finally made it into the crow's-nest. He shook his head in disbelief. The lad would cling to the mast for the next hour 'til his knees stopped rattling. "We'll round up more men closer to Port de Paix."

"If we make it that far," Hornbach ran a finger under his nose.

"We'll make it. Keep our eyes open, heads down, and…" Ric's attention diverted to the arrival on deck of a beautiful, dark-haired woman wearing his shirt. "…our wits about us, we'll make it." Try as he might to ignore the gentle sway of her hips, or the way the breeze lifted the curls away from her face, he followed Jocelyn's every step across the deck and into the galley.

Ric cleared his throat and continued. "We'll do our jobs, stay our course, and protect her at all cost." Was he still talking about the *Scarlet Night*?

* * * *

"Look at him all puffed up and full of himself." Jocelyn dropped a bit of fruit into Leviticus's crate.

"Watch your fingers, he bites," warned Tupper.

No sooner had she said it, the bird ruffled its feathers, squawked, and snipped at her. "Of all the ungrateful…" Jocelyn jerked her hand away.

Tupper reached in and stroked the back of her finger down the bird's breastbone. "He doesn't know it was you scooped him off the deck. You're still a stranger."

"He's not biting you." Jocelyn watched in amazement. The bird settled his feathers and made a small rattle sound.

"Knows my face. Crows are smart and loyal like a hound. He'll get used to you."

Jocelyn stepped back and let Tupper feed the bird. "You have magic where all manner of men are concerned it seems." The words came out clipped and sharp.

Tupper brushed off her hands and frowned. "What does that mean?"

"Nothing. It means nothing." Jocelyn pushed the hair away from her face. "I'm sorry, pay no attention to my ugly mood. I didn't sleep well. I'm not myself."

Tupper nodded and pulled a bottle out of a cupboard. She pulled the cork with a pop and splashed a measure into her glass. "A cot is no feathered mattress. You'll grow used to it."

Brandy. She was close enough to smell its strong aroma. Jocelyn recognized it from the warmth of Ric's breath last night. "It wasn't the cot. I'm used to a hard bed."

"Worried about reaching your father?" Tupper perched on the corner of her desk.

"*Oui*...No..." Jocelyn planted her hands on her hips and sighed. "It's difficult to explain."

Tupper leaned forward and braced her elbows on her knees. "Try."

Jocelyn hesitated for a moment before continuing, "Last night, I met Ric--"

"Oh, say no more." Tupper straightened and held up her hands in surrender. "I figured it was just a matter of time. Did he try something? Kiss you?"

"No." The word left Jocelyn's mouth with an indignant rush.

Tupper jerked back. "Then what's the problem?"

Jocelyn wished she'd never started this conversation. It was foolish, but she couldn't help but feel slighted. "He didn't try to kiss me."

"Wait." Tupper cocked her head as if she hadn't heard her correctly. "You wanted him to kiss you?"

"*Oui*." She crossed her arms and curled her shoulders. She hated sounding like a petulant child who'd been denied dessert. "I can't seem to think about anything else. It's maddening." She chewed at her lip. "I don't know about these things. Maybe he favors someone else? Maybe he doesn't even favor women?"

Tupper choked on a laugh. "Not favor women? No...that is definitely not the problem."

"Then I don't understand. I've given him more than one opportunity. Been a hairsbreadth away several times." Her fingertips brushed her lips. "If he'd tilt his head and move a scant inch..."

"This is rich." Tupper smirked and took a swallow of her brandy.

"Ric?"

"No, *rich,* funny, laughable," Tupper clarified. "Ric Robbins needs no lessons in how to kiss."

"So he's not shy?"

Tupper snorted before pressing her lips together. "No, he is far from shy."

"Then it is me." Jocelyn tossed a resigned hand into the air. "It is obvious he is not interested. He finds me repulsive."

Tupper stood and patted Jocelyn's shoulder before helping herself to more brandy. "I think you may have this completely arse-backward."

"I am still not understanding. What do you mean?"

"Oh, honey, he's interested." Tupper spoke into her glass before winking at her.

Chapter 13

Interested, her left foot! Jocelyn didn't care how much Tupper insisted, if Ric Robbins was interested in her, he sure had an odd way of showing it. Days had passed, and she could barely get more than a few words out of him. Let alone find any time to be alone.

Hours stretched into days. They were never out of sight of land now. Ric kept the *Scarlet Night* tight to shore. He believed they'd run into less trouble there. The crew, what few there were, worked from sun up to sunset, trying to do the work of a half dozen each. Jocelyn kept offering to help, but more often than not, she was only in their way. If she didn't have Tupper to talk to and MacTavish teaching her how to tie knots, she'd have surely gone mad.

She'd also learned a few simple hand gestures or signs to communicate with the boy, Bump. Putting her fingertips to her chin and moving her hand forward toward him, said "*Thank you.*" Using the same fingertip maneuver and dropping her hand, palm up, into her other hand was "*Good.*" She was still learning how to sign the words, morning, day, and night.

Tupper had begun to leave her quarters for meals, and to give a helping hand with some of the daily chores aboard, but grief would wash over her at times in unpredictable towering waves. Her only relief seemed to be found at the bottom of a glass.

Yesterday had been one of those waves. Ric gathered the crew for a small ceremony to honor those lost during the earthquake and tidal wave that decimated Port Royal.

The sails were lowered making the *Scarlet Night* seem to stand still upon the water. Flags flew at half-staff. All stood respectfully at the ship's rail.

Ric led them in prayer. "For as much as it hast pleased Almighty God of this great mercy to take unto himself the souls of our brothers here departed, we therefore by marking this spot, commit their memory, if not their bodies, to the deep until that day when the sea shall give up her dead."

MacTavish, White, and Summer had fired off three of the cannons, and Ric read a list of thirty-two names before dropping a black flag tied to a large square of the *Scarlet's* red sailcloth into the sea. The fabric lay atop the water becoming dark as blood before slowly sinking beneath the surface.

No one spoke. All you could hear was the gentle lap of the water against the ship's hull and the low creak of the rigging as if the ship, too, cried for her loss.

Tupper's door stayed locked that night.

Jocelyn found Ric standing in the bow long after the others had gone to bed. A round lemon moon spilled a path across the water.

She approached him on silent feet. "Beautiful night. The sea is so calm."

Ric's face told her she'd surprised him. After a quick glance, he focused his gaze back out to sea. "You should be asleep. It is almost eight bells."

"Eight, four, halves. I fear I'll never get used to your bells. We had bells, too, at the abbey, but they called us to prayer three times a day… the Angelus. After so many years, now I hear a bell peal, and I feel the sudden need to kneel." She was babbling. "It was a lovely ceremony you gave today. Very respectful."

Ric pulled a deep breath into his lungs. "It is the duty of the captain."

"I remember only bits from my mother's funeral. I was barely four. It rained, poured. The mud seeped into my shoes and stained my stockings. I'm not sure whom it was stood by my side, but she held my hand so tightly it hurt my fingers. Father wasn't there, and the smell of the lilies cloyed in my throat. Two days later, I arrived at Saint-Genevieve."

Ric turned to look at her. "You've been there all this time?"

"*Oui.* I received an education most men would wish for, languages, arts, music. I was allowed to see father four times a year, but he always seemed to be a world away when it came time for him to come. I would receive his letter days later apologizing, explaining the importance of his position, how I should be proud to have a father fighting for our country. Other times the days would pass one after the other. I lived a…quiet life." It was her turn to watch the shimmer on the water.

"Quiet?"

Jocelyn smoothed a hand over the polished rail. "Barren. Colorless." She peeked a quick glance in Ric's direction. He watched her. In the dim light she couldn't read his face. She continued, wanting to explain. "Once a year, the Sisters would take us to the beautiful cathedral of Sainte Chapelle. The first time I stepped inside, I wept. The stained glass windows held every color God had ever created. For hours I would sit and wrap myself in the splendor of it all, then we would go back to our stone walls and brown garments." She plucked at her skirt. Holding up a hand, she turned to face him. "I sound ungrateful. I'm not. It was a privileged life. It simply lacked certain very important things."

"Like color," he offered.

"And love. Simple touch. Warmth. Passion. Without such things, a person comes to crave them like a drowning man craves air."

Ric turned back to the sea. "You're to be married soon. Perhaps you will find those things then."

"And if I don't?" she whispered.

"You will."

She hated the final decisiveness of his words. "What if I don't want to wait?" Her voice sounded small. Considering the boldness of her words, you'd have thought she screamed them.

Ric's head snapped to look back at her. "What are you asking?"

Jocelyn was never more grateful for the dark. Her cheeks flared with the heat of embarrassment. What *was* she asking? For him to love her? Hold her? Teach her what it felt like to be kissed? She'd let her mouth run away with her heart. Idiot.

She turned away from the rail and waved a hand as if to brush away her words. "I don't know. Pay no attention. I was talking to the moon."

* * * *

"The moon?" Ric paced the deck for an hour after Jocelyn disappeared into the night. One minute she was talking about mud-stained stockings and the next she was talking about love and passion and…and what?

He'd tried to keep his distance from her, but every time he turned around, there she was carrying ale to a thirsty man, laughing with MacTavish, walking with Tupper, or looking lovelier than she had a right to.

She refused to wear a hat. The sun kissed pink of her cheeks and shoulders turned golden. Shimmering strands wove through her hair. She fairly glowed.

Night before last, he'd been working in the galley, going over the charts, handling the business of the ship's log when she came in to refill a mug of rum.

"Thought you'd learned your lesson about rum."

Jocelyn turned and smiled. His world lightened. "I didn't see you there." She raised the mug. "This isn't for me. It's payment for MacTavish."

"He has you fetching for him, does he?" The big oaf of a Scotsman had accused him of jealousy. Ric couldn't deny the slight greening of his eyes now. Not when it came to her.

"It's part of our agreement." She brought Ric a short mug as well, taking a sip for herself before setting it down before him.

"What agreement have you made?"

Jocelyn pulled out two lengths of rope from a small pouch tied about her waist. "He's teaching me knots."

Ric laughed. "And why would you be needing knots?"

She toyed with the ends of the thin rope. "You said I knew nothing about life aboard a ship such as this. I decided to learn." A prideful grin curved her lips. "MacTavish says I'm a natural born seaman."

Amused, Ric leaned back in his chair. "MacTavish just wants someone to bring him his rum."

Her jaw dropped. "Not true." She sat next to him and tapped the arm of his chair. "Put your arm here, I'll show you."

Ric leaned forward again and returned to his writing. "Do you think I'm daft enough to let you tie me to a chair?"

"What are you afraid I'll do? Draw pictures and scribble in the ship's log?"

Ric set aside his quill. He'd humor her. He pushed up the wide sleeve of his shirt and laid his arm along the curved arm of the chair. "What have you learned?"

"Well every good seaman knows how to tie a bowline knot. I even know the double bowline." She wore an impish grin and tapped her chin with a small loop of rope. "But, I think I need a buntline hitch in this instance."

He couldn't help but smile. "Aye, sounds right."

"So, let me think…" She traced her fingers down his arm and held his wrist as she looped the rope around the arm of the chair. "Around the tree…"

Jocelyn caught her bottom lip between her teeth and dipped her head as she concentrated. Ric had to close his eyes against the attack to his senses. He fought the rush of heat that flooded his limbs. He'd done his best to stay far enough away from her to keep himself from taking her in his arms again, and here she was practically in his lap. He tightened his grip on the chair.

"You're not watching," she scolded.

Ric's eyes snapped open to find her staring at him. He could see the deep brown that rimmed the lighter iris of her eyes. The tips of her hair brushed his thigh. From this angle he could follow the shadowy path of her cleavage past the line where her tanned skin stopped giving way to the pearl white tops of her breasts.

"Sorry," he mumbled, surprised he could form the simple word.

Jocelyn went back to her task. He watched. Deft fingers looped and tied. Her chest rose and fell in a gentle cadence. Ric found himself matching each breath with his own.

"There." She pulled the rope snug. "A perfect buntline hitch." Jocelyn captured his other hand. "I've learned the round turn and two half hitches as well," she announced with pride. "I'm still practicing the last part," she paused as if trying to remember. Her face brightened. "...whipping the end to the main."

"Very good." Sweat crept down his temple. He'd never been so happy to have his hands tied. Kept him from grabbing her, pulling her closer, setting her in his lap.

She turned then as if reading his thoughts. "Still watching?"

"Aye." His voice broke the word in two. The pressure building in his britches caused a low moan in his throat.

Her eyes widened. "Is it too tight?"

Dear God, yes. Ric shook his head, "No..."

She went back to work. "I can't believe you're letting me do this."

Lurid images floated through his brain. He'd never imagined the idea of being her captive would arouse him this much. Giving her complete control. Wanting, needing, to take her in his arms and not being allowed to only added to his frustrations. He tugged against the restraint holding his right arm as the ache in his crotch made him squirm.

"It's lucky I have no evil plan for you, no?" Jocelyn laid a hand on his shoulder and sat back. "For I have now tied you to the dock." She took another sip of his drink. "And I've stolen your rum." She wiped a stray drop from her lip. "I may be a pirate yet."

Ric's left hand tangled into her hair, pulling her to him as the rope fell to the floor. Her gasp giving him the perfect opportunity to ravage her sweet mouth before sanity reigned and he pulled away. "You're no pirate. You've lost your ship," he panted.

Without looking, she reached over and tugged the tail of the rope still holding his right hand, tightening it. She searched his eyes. Her chest rising and falling with each heated breath. Lowering her gaze to his mouth, she tipped her head before moving her lips to his.

"But I still have you."

Chapter 14

Jocelyn relived the kiss. Savored each second. Every detail. The smoothness of his lips in contrast to the rough scratch of his jaw. She could still feel him. The moist heat of his mouth. She could still taste him.

Her heart had been hammering so loud, she was sure he'd hear. Had she still been breathing? When he'd swept his tongue between her teeth to tease hers, all thoughts of hearts and breaths dissolved. All she could think about was how one kiss could hold such power, and render her helpless.

She mirrored each movement of his mouth. Learning. Following his lead. Waves of desire making her bolder than she ever dreamed possible.

Ric cradled the back of her head and held her to him as he sucked her lower lip between his and nipped at it with his teeth. She gasped with pleasure as light raced along her skin and tingled all the way to her toes.

When she slid onto his lap and wrapped her arms about his neck, Ric's strong fingers raked down her back and fisted the fabric of her shirt. He ground her name into her mouth. His hips lifting her as he rolled them upward sending delicious waves of pleasure through her.

It was all at once everything she desired and not nearly enough. It made her greedy for something she couldn't even name. She wanted all of him.

"Untie me." He rumbled against her lips. His free hand moved lower to cup the curve of her bottom and press her tighter to him.

"I'd have to stop kissing you," she breathed tipping her head to the other side, slanting her mouth in another direction.

Ric nipped at her lip again. "Damn it, Jocelyn, untie me."

She never should have stopped. Should have ignored him. For once she slipped the rope from his wrist, he used his hand to hold her away from him. It was as if by releasing that corded hold, she'd somehow broken the spell.

"We can't do this." He was gentle but forceful lifting her off his lap and setting her aside before shoving his chair back to stand. "I'm sorry."

Then, he was gone. She'd sat there trying to catch her breath. Her lips felt swollen. She tested them with her fingertips. Her body thrummed with denied desire. She sat stunned, struggling to understand what happened.

Tears pinched the backs of her eyes. Her fingernails cut into her palms as her hands curled into fists. She would not cry. Wouldn't give him the satisfaction of knowing what happened was anything more than a simple kiss. Nothing more.

Hornbach walked into the galley, and Jocelyn made her escape before he could speak. The tears wouldn't halt. Head down, she slowed her pace. She'd already humiliated herself once today without racing to her quarters in hysterics.

Once there, she flipped the lock, slid down the backside of the door, and let the tears come.

Two days had passed since their kiss in the galley. The next time she saw Ric, he had started to say something about what had happened between them, but she cut him off with some inane comment about the weather. She didn't want to hear what he had to say. Apology or explanation. It didn't matter one way or the other. They kissed, but it meant nothing to him. It was clear. She would treat it as such. It was nothing.

For two days and two long nights, those three words--*It was nothing*--circled around and around in her mind as she tried to convince herself. If only she could convince her body. Their "nothing" of a kiss awakened something in her. Even the thought of it set her limbs trembling. It had heaped dried tinder onto a tiny innocent flame of passion and wonder, and ignited it into a raging fire.

According to MacTavish, another day or so, they'd round the southeastern shore of Hispaniola and catch the trade winds blowing west from Africa. It wouldn't be long before her time aboard the *Scarlet Night* would be over. She'd return to the life of Admiral Beauchamp's daughter, marry the stranger awaiting her, and say goodbye to her foolish thoughts of embarking on some grand adventure.

Perhaps it was for the best to make a clean break of things before they became more complicated. She and Ric could never be together. Not in the way she was imagining. The mere thought of it was ludicrous. She needed to douse the flames of desire building within her and be practical.

Only Tupper noticed anything amiss with her. Jocelyn had asked her to teach her more of the hand language they used to communicate with Bump. Tupper agreed, but as soon as the door closed on her quarters, she began questioning Jocelyn.

Tupper stopped mid cabin and turned a curious eye in Jocelyn's direction. "What's happened?"

"I don't know what you mean." Jocelyn lowered her gaze and made a move around her.

Tupper blocked her and peered into her face. "Yes you do, I see it in your eyes."

Jocelyn studied her hands rather than raise her gaze.

Tupper tipped her chin. "I knew it. Something happened a few days ago. I noticed it then, but was hoping you'd tell me."

Jocelyn brushed off Tupper's hand. "Perhaps I'm tired of life at sea."

"No, that's not it either." Tupper narrowed her eyes. "Has something to do with Ric, too. Both of you've been acting a mite strange."

Jocelyn dodged Tupper once more. She didn't want to talk about it. Perhaps the best idea would be a counter attack. "Who's Beth?"

Tupper jerked as if she'd been slapped. "Beth? How do you know about Beth?"

"The first night. You know, after… I helped you to bed and tidied the cabin. You yelled at me to put down some old letters. Gavin's letters. But then you told me your name was Alice."

Tupper crossed the room and urged Leviticus to perch on her arm. His black toes curling around her wrist. She pet his throat until he chirped at her in contentment.

Jocelyn continued. "But the letters were all signed 'Beth.'"

"Not that it's any of your business, but Beth was Gavin's first wife." Tupper brought the bird to sit with her behind Gavin's impressive oak desk.

Jocelyn found it curious a man would marry one woman and wish to save letters from another. "And he kept her letters?"

"*I* kept her letters." Tupper used one hand to loosen the cork on yet another bottle of brandy. She held it up in offer, as she always did. Jocelyn politely declined once more.

Jocelyn sat on the edge of the bed. "Why?"

Pulling a glass toward her she poured a dram, stopped, then seemed to rethink her actions and poured another. "Beth's letters were one of the reasons I fell in love with Gavin. He thought he should get rid of them after we married, but I refused to let him. You see Gavin is…was," Tupper stopped and frowned.

Jocelyn immediately regretted broaching the subject. "I'm sorry, Tupper, we don't need to talk about this."

"No, I want to. It feels right to talk about him. Someone else should know about him…about us. Tell our tale perhaps." When she sat back in her chair, she lifted her boots to rest on the corner of the desk, Leviticus sidestepped up her arm and plucked at her hair. Tupper paid him little notice. "Gavin was a hard man. Tough. Fair. Brilliant, but closed off. We didn't agree on much of anything, and I couldn't find a way to get past the wall he'd built around himself. Honestly, I wasn't sure I wanted to in the beginning. Then, I found the letters and they explained everything. They showed me who he was and why he'd become the man he'd become."

She took a long swallow before continuing. "They'd had such a love, he and Beth, I saw a side of him he'd spent years hiding from everyone. It was as if she was telling me through those pages not to give up on him. That it was right to love him, and let him love me in return."

The story touched Jocelyn's heart. Who would have imagined such a tale of Tupper and Gavin coming together? "Were you together a long time?"

Tupper gave her a wistful smile. "Seven years."

"You have no children?"

"Do you see children?" Tupper used her glass to sweep the room.

Hadn't Ric mentioned the deaf boy as a small lad? "Bump?"

"Bump is no one's child. But he's the closest I'll ever come to having a son." Tupper gave a short sigh. "Creating a child of our own wasn't meant to be."

Jocelyn could only imagine how she would feel if she were unable to have children. It had always been a dream of hers to build a large loving family. After a life of forced quiet, she wanted a home filled with laughter and joyful noise. "I'm sorry."

Tupper once more shrugged it off. "Don't be. I'm not."

"Did you know right away you loved Gavin?"

"No. Like I said, we argued about everything. He hated the idea of a woman aboard his ship. It was his opinion that pirating wasn't a fit life for a woman. Things for him were black and white. There was a code to follow. Honor among thieves. Rules for everything. Except when life didn't follow the rules. But he loved like he fought. Fiercely. Completely."

Jocelyn could hear the longing in her voice. "Do you think, some day there will come a time when you'll be able to…"

"No. Gavin was everything I never hoped to have. After the things I'd done, I hardly expected to be anyone's wife. Thought for sure there was nothing left for me in this life. I was wrong. Gavin showed me otherwise."

Jocelyn stood, crossed her arms over her chest, and moved to the windows watching the water pass behind the ship. "I've always known I was to be someone's wife. I've been groomed to run a household and be the proper military wife. I never expected to find my true love."

"Is that what's bothering you? Have you found him? Ric perhaps?"

She spun back toward Tupper. "Don't be ridiculous."

Tupper raised one hand. "You brought it up."

"We weren't talking about Ric." Jocelyn lowered her arms and planted her hands on her hips.

Tupper laid a hand on her chest. "I wasn't, but I think perhaps you were." She eyed her closely. "You've been dancing around the subject of Ric Robbins for days. It doesn't take a brilliant mind to figure it out. You have feelings for the man."

Jocelyn pressed her lips together and didn't answer.

"Don't be embarrassed. You wouldn't be the first woman to be charmed by his golden good looks."

"Meaning?" Jocelyn hated the thread of jealousy that ran through her voice.

"Ric loves the ladies, always has. I, myself, am not susceptible to his sweet talk, but I understand he has quite a way about him with the 'skirts.'"

Jocelyn frowned at the floor. Was she just another "skirt?" Was he kissing a different woman in every port? No wonder he cast her aside. What would he need with her? For goodness' sake, she had to tie the man to a chair to get him to kiss her. She rubbed the ache between her eyebrows.

"But if you have feelings for him, I wouldn't fret." Tupper continued. Leviticus even added a squawk of agreement. "You've got as much of a chance as any of them. I mean, no one's tied him down yet."

"They probably used the wrong knot." Jocelyn muttered.

Chapter 15

Ric held tight to the ship's wheel. Winds had picked up over night and the few sails they had furled, bowed against a cloudless sky. The rigging started to sing.

He was tired, but that's what comes from sleepless nights lying in a hammock, listening to MacTavish snore like a wounded bear. When his mind won't still and all he can think about is a kiss.

Jocelyn's kiss.

How many women had he kissed in his lifetime? Try as he might, he couldn't remember one who left him in such a state. He'd never be able to coil a rope or rig a buntline again without thinking of Jocelyn and that singular amazing kiss.

"Captain?"

Ric couldn't get over the softness of her lips, and the quiet little whimper she made when he'd slipped his tong--

"Captain?"

MacTavish bellowed. "Oh, Captain…Ric, hey! He's talkin' to you." He pointed up to Dowd in the crow's-nest.

Ric gave himself a quick shake and raised a hand to shade his eyes. "What is it?"

Dowd pointed off to the starboard. "Ship coming at us."

"Who is it?"

"Can't make her out from here," called Dowd. "Be a frigate flyin' a Dutch flag."

MacTavish handed Ric the captain's eyeglass. "Could be de Graaf."

"Bit too east for him," Ric held the cool brass to his eye. "Whoever it is, she's headed right for us." He lowered the glass. "Shit."

MacTavish took a look for himself. "We could outrun her."

"To where?" Ric swallowed hard. "No. Let's tell her who we are. We need to raise all the red sails we can manage. And the black bones. Show them we're the *Scarlet Night.*" He called up to Dowd. "Get down here, I need you." To MacTavish he ordered, "Find Hornbach and Bump. I need everybody on deck."

"Aye, Capt'n."

Jocelyn, Tupper, and her newly attached feathered friend came on deck. Ric shouted to them. "Tupper, I need you in the riggin,' if you're able. We've got company."

"Right," Tupper stopped long enough to set Leviticus into the well of a coil of rope for safe keeping before obeying his order.

"What can I do?" called Jocelyn.

"Get below." Ric rushed to the rail, loosened a line from one of the belay pins and strung it through the ships wheel to keep the *Scarlet* continuing on due course without a helmsman.

He slid down the ladder to the main deck and ordered White and Summer to help with the mainsail as well.

"You need me." Jocelyn followed him as he raced toward the bow. "I can help."

Ric stopped and caught her by the shoulders. "You can help, by staying out of the way. I don't need to be worrying about you." He turned her and pushed her toward the hatch. "Go below."

Looking to starboard, the oncoming ship was getting larger. If they got close enough to attack, they were all dead.

It was crazy, but he had an idea. "Dowd!" Ric stomped sharply on the deck twice. He got Bump's attention too. He motioned to them. "Hats. Find me all the hats you can. There are more than a dozen still sitting in the crew quarters. Bring them here."

"Hornbach," Ric grabbed the man's sleeve as he descended the rigging and his boots hit the deck. "How many cabbages do you have in the larder?"

"Bout twenty, I guess. Why?"

Ric gave his shoulder a shove. "Go get them."

Hornbach stumbled. "We be makin' them cabbage stew?"

"Go." Ric spun about to find MacTavish. He was right behind him.

"What are you getting to?"

Ric planted his hands on his hips. "We're attacking."

MacTavish's jaw went slack. "Are you out of ye bloody mind?"

"No, in fact...White, lower the black and raise the red. Tell 'em we'll give no quarter. It's a fight to the death."

"It'll be a death, all right, ours." MacTavish pulled at Ric's arm. "We can't be fighting a God damn frigate. It's suicide."

"Swords." Ric pulled MacTavish's hand off his arm. "I need twenty of your longest, broadest swords."

Within minutes all his orders had been carried out--all but one. Jocelyn had defied him and was helping Dowd and Bump carry some of the late crew's hats to him. He didn't have time to argue with her. If she wanted to risk her neck with the rest of them on deck, so be it.

MacTavish dropped an armload of swords at Ric's feet. "They're dull as a deadman's eye, some got more rust than blade."

"Don't worry, we aren't fighting with them." Ric grabbed one of the swords, and stabbed it deep into a head of cabbage.

"We flinging rotting cabbage instead of cannon shot at them?" White asked.

Ric lifted the leafy green head stuck on a pike and shoved a hat on top. "No, we're building a crew."

To Jocelyn he ordered, "If you won't listen to reason and get below, then take your rope training skills and lash each of our new crew members somewhere about the deck."

They all stood in stunned silence. "Go! We're the *Scarlet Night*. We've never run from a fight. We're the attackers. So let's attack. Mac, you and Summer, I need the starboard cannons loaded and primed as fast as you can. I'll man the forward gun and send a shot over their bow to let them know we're coming. We'll only get one round of shot off the starboard side. If they keep on, we won't have time to reload before they return fire, but I'm hoping it doesn't go that far."

"All we have to do is make them think we're the aggressor. Our reputation will hopefully do the rest." Ric stabbed another cabbage. "We haven't got much time. If this is going to work, we can't let them get too close."

The crew scrambled to do Ric's bidding. He headed into the bow and took position at his gun.

* * * *

The sound of her heart rushed in Jocelyn's ears. They were attacking? The memory of their ship being captured by the slave traders swirled about her. The decks had been in chaos then as well. However, their crew had not been made of cabbage, but real men with real blood which ran bright and red over the deck boards. It was as terrifying then as it was now.

She made short work of tying off each sword as quickly as she could. One of the swords hadn't been quite as dull as MacTavish had claimed. The blade sliced into her palm. She hadn't even felt the cut until she saw the blood dripping onto the rope she was attempting to tie. Tearing a strip off the hem of her skirt, she wrapped it around the wound to stop the flow.

"This be the sickliest looking crew I've ever seen," piped Tupper. "I've got another idea." She rushed off to the galley and returned with potatoes, carrots, small turnip and bits of charcoal from the fire. Tupper sent Dowd down into the carpenter's bay for some cut nails. While she waited, she dug shallow holes with her knife into the cabbage and stuffed each one with a lump of charcoal before using the carrot tops for hair. Once the nails arrived, she broke the carrot in half and nailed it to the face.

They all followed suit, giving their vegetable crew crude features. Jocelyn thought to do it one better. Borrowing Tupper's knife, she cut at her hair. Now some of their crew had mustaches and beards and dark curls falling from under their borrowed hats. It may only have bought them a few more feet before their opponents realized it was all a sham, but a few feet could mean the difference between life and death.

Jocelyn finished lashing the last of their makeshift army on to one of the barrels sitting upon the deck when the blast from the forward cannon drove her to her knees. She covered her head with her arms.

Those members of the crew without carrots and turnip for noses set up an ungodly howl. They screamed and pounded on whatever was within their reach. Jocelyn rose from the deck and tried to imagine what an entire ship full of pirates must sound like during their battle cry. It must have been frightening.

"They're not retreating," Tupper came to stand at Jocelyn's side. "This is not going to end well."

"What else can we do?" A cold finger of fear clawed down Jocelyn's spine.

Tupper pulled her cutlass and handed it to Jocelyn. "If they board, start swinging as if your life depends on it--because it will."

Jocelyn tried to hand it back. "I can't take your sword."

"I have my pistols." She pulled them both from her baldric and cocked the hammers. "Trust me, if they overtake us, it won't make a difference. Nine cannot fight more than eighty men. We'll just be buying time before they kill us."

Kill us? Jocelyn's hands began to shake. "W-we could surrender."

Tupper smiled then. A dangerous, chilling smile. "This is the *Scarlet Night.* We never surrender."

* * * *

"Shit," Ric peered through the smoke from his cannon. The shot cleared the other ship's bow as planned, but the Dutch frigate kept coming. He left his position in the front of the ship and moved toward the other swivel gun in the rear.

Passing MacTavish and Summer, Ric bid them, "Light the quick match and be prepared to fire all five cannons on my command as quickly as you can."

In the midst of the chaos and noise. Ric searched the deck for Jocelyn. When he spotted her, he was shocked to see she'd torn her skirts and tucked the flagging hem into her belt. There was blood on her stockings and what had she done to her hair? In one hand she was holding a cutlass and looking for all the world like a pirate poised to fight.

Never in all his imaginings would he have envisioned her swinging a sword in the middle of a battle, but there she was, ready to do just that.

He wasn't going to allow it to happen. She wasn't going to fight, and she wasn't going to die. Not while he still had breath in his body. Even if he had to fight an entire frigate of Dutch pirates singlehanded.

Ric angled the rear cannon and took aim.

A round of cannon fire from the frigate overshot the *Scarlet*. They wouldn't make the same mistake again. Ric lit the fuse and fired a pinpoint shot, which shattered the other ship's bowsprit.

Hollering back to MacTavish and Summer, he order them to level the guns and aim above the frigate's waterline. What should have been one ferocious blast from all five cannon at once, was more a staccato-ed attack. But the effect was no less damaging.

The Dutch ship lurched and angled as seawater poured into great gaping holes in her side. Her speed dragged to a shuddering halt as the hull filled, dragging her over. The full sails continued to pull the sinking ship until the force snapped the main mast like a dried twig. The frigate began its death roll.

A cheer rose amongst the tiny *Scarlet* crew. Ric slumped against the rail. They'd won the day. As a forward gunner, when a battle was won, Ric would ride the wave of invigorated triumph for hours afterward, adrenaline pumping through his veins.

As captain, the weight of responsibility sat heavy on his shoulders. It wasn't enough to win. It was bringing his men--and women--through the fight, and keeping the ship beneath their feet from sinking into the waves or being overtaken by their foes. It wasn't invigorated triumph he was feeling at this moment, it was more akin to blessed relief.

He dropped his head, closed his eyes and pulled in a deep breath. *Damn it.* His first victory as captain and all he could smell was cabbage.

Chapter 16

Jocelyn's hands shook as she raised the lantern's wick. Her tiny sliver of a room being part of the forward hold was dark as night in the middle of the day. Water rushed past the hull as the Scarlet Night seemed to leap with victory. The wooden beast creaked and popped in its race across the waves. Their battle was over, and they were the victors.

She curled into her cot, trembling, weeping. It had been one of the most terrifying experiences of her life--as well as one of the most glorious, exciting things she'd ever done.

The wave of each blast coursed through her entire being when the cannons exploded, turning her legs to porridge, and punching through her heart. Deafening noise and the unexpected thrill of danger--it took her breath away. Had she ever experienced anything as awe inspiring?

"Jocelyn? Are you in there?" Ric pounded on the narrow door. "Jocelyn, let me in."

In one seemingly single motion, she opened the door to him and was swept into his arms. He held her tight to his chest as sobs wracked her body. Before she knew it, they were in a tangle on the floor.

"Are you hurt? When I couldn't find you…Oh God, don't cry." He wiped at her cheeks, ran his hands over her legs. "There's blood on your stockings. Your hand is wounded." His hands cradled her face. "Your hair, what have you done to your beautiful hair?"

"I-I gave it to you." How could she explain that whatever she possessed belonged to him? Her hair, her heart, her body. She gave it all freely. He'd saved her that day in Port Royal. In more ways than one. She'd never be the same. He'd changed her and the course of her life forever.

Lifted her up to fate. Whether he wanted her or not, she was his, and always would be.

He laid a kiss to her forehead and pulled her back against his chest. "Foolish woman, what have you done?"

She'd given him her heart. Fallen in love. How would she find the courage to tell him? Perhaps it would be easier to show him.

Jocelyn brushed the tears from her face as she raised herself to look into his handsome face. She could read the concern in his eyes. Running her fingers over the planes of his face, she traced the outline of his lips before lowering her mouth to his.

She pressed her lips to his. He stiffened beneath her. Still she kissed him until he began to kiss her in return. She trailed her hand down his throat to slip it inside the open front of his shirt to touch him. Feel the strength of his chest. Skip her fingertips across the flat of his nipple. She laid her palm over the steady beat of his heart.

His tongue swept her mouth as he deepened the kiss. The low moan he made in his throat only spurred her on. She wanted to touch all of him, and have him touch her. Make love to her. Claim her.

Jocelyn placed his hand over her breast, holding it there, arching into his hold, urging him on, but it wasn't enough.

Breaking the kiss, she pulled her arms from the sleeves of her shirt and lifted it over her head before tossing it to one side. Naked to her waist, she placed his hand upon her breast once more. The roughness of his palm against the sensitive peak of her tightened nipple made her sigh against his lips before she returned to kissing him.

"Jocelyn…" He ground out her name in warning. "We can't do this."

"Yes, we can. I want you to." She moved her kisses along his jaw. His day's growth of beard tickled her lips.

His breath fanned her cheek. "It's not as simple as that."

"But it is." She arched into his touch again. "I'm not a child. I know what is at stake. But I can't deny it one more moment. I need your touch. I need you to cease this ache in me." She slid her hand over the ridges of his abdomen and skimmed the top of his waistband.

"You're promised to another man. I won't ruin your life by taking what belongs to him."

She kissed the side of his neck. His skin was salty as the sea. "I promised nothing."

"Your father--"

"Won't know. He'll believe whatever I tell him. Please, I cannot speak of my father while my breast is in your hand and all I can think about is how I want you to stop talking and kiss me again."

"God woman, you would tempt a saint." He circled her ribs with his wide hand and brushed a thumb across the hardened tip of her nipple. The sensation of that simple touch sent bolts of heat directly to her sex.

She gasped against his mouth. "You are no saint."

"No, I am not," he growled.

"Do you want me?" Jocelyn whispered. Almost afraid of his answer. Never had she left herself so vulnerable to a simple question. If he said no...

Ric took her hand and ran it over the hard ridge of his erection. "More than I've ever wanted anyone."

"Then take me. I'm yours."

In one fluid move, Ric laid her on her back and stripped his shirt away before covering her body with his. When he bent to suckle at her breast, she didn't think she'd survive the rush of pleasure radiating through her.

"Ric..."

He pushed her ruined skirts out of the way. His hands stroked the inside of her thighs pressing them wide. She opened for him, as if by instinct. Her body somehow knowing what she needed to do to cease her building desire.

Ric moved his mouth and began lavishing equal attention to her other breast. She tangled her hand in his hair, holding him to her, thinking nothing had ever felt quite as wonderful.

But when his fingers parted her, stroked the tender folds of her, she cried out to him again. He pressed two fingers into her, making her writhe with pleasure.

Ric moved to kiss her. "You're wet for me."

"Is that bad?" She panted.

"No... that's good. Very good." As if to prove his point, he spread the slickness over her swollen flesh.

Jocelyn closed her eyes. Her thighs trembled. Lights sparked behind her eyelids.

"The first time..." he began.

"I know." She gasped, past the point of caring. The same country girls who described their kisses had also whispered about this. There'd be pain and a bit of blood. If it all felt this good, how much pain could there be?

"I'll be as gentle as I can." He moved his fingers inside her, preparing her.

"I know...please..."

Ric fumbled with the front of his breeches and positioned himself between her thighs, bracing himself above her balancing with one arm. He continued to stroke her, building the pressure within her, making her ready.

Taking himself in hand, he pressed the head of his penis against her opening and eased into her.

Jocelyn's first thought was there was no way he'd fit, but still he pressed forward. Pleasure and pain collided. She clutched at his hips. Her body trembled and tensed.

"Relax, Jocelyn… you need to breathe." He held himself still. Nipping at her mouth.

"I am breathing." She lied.

"Kiss me," he murmured against her lips.

She did as he asked. Her body pulsing against the push of his.

In one sharp thrust, he broke through her maidenhead. Fire burned inside her. The searing bite of pain bringing tears to her eyes. She shoved at his shoulder and cried out as her body reacted out of instinct and she tried to get away from the pain. She looked at him in panic when he wouldn't move.

"It's done. Shhhh…I'm sorry." Ric panted. He cupped her cheek with one hand and forced her to look at him. "I know it hurts. Be still for a moment, it won't last. I promise. It's only the first time. Lie still." His body seemed to shimmer as he held himself steady. Sweat shone on his brow. "Let me know when it lessens… I'll not hurt you again."

Jocelyn nodded and whimpered. "I know."

"You're so beautiful." He continued to murmur, telling her how lovely he found her skin, how sweet the taste of her breasts, and how tight and heated she was inside. And he waited. His jaw tensed with the effort, but true to his word, he never moved until at last the sharp edge of the pain lessened within her and her body once more pulsed with pleasure.

"It's better," she took a shaky breath.

He withdrew slightly and pushed in again. "Better?"

She needn't answer him. She closed her eyes and let her head fall back. Her hips made a slow roll.

Ric moved again faster this time. Pulling out and thrusting in. Each drive of his body pinning her to the floor and pushing deeper. He dropped his forehead to her neck as he rocked into her over and over.

The pain was gone. In its place, a low fire burned inside her. Jocelyn moved against him matching his rhythm. When he raised her leg to hook her knee around his waist, his thrusts became faster, deeper, reaching a new place within her.

Soon, she couldn't keep up with him. Holding on as he called out to God, he seemed to grind himself into her, as if he wanted to imprint the pattern of his skin upon hers. His body curled over her and he stilled at last. Ric kissed her neck, panting, before finally withdrawing from her and rolling to her side.

Jocelyn was afraid to move. Was he done? Her body hummed with the new sensation. Was that all there was to it? She didn't know what to say. Were there proper words?

She looked over at Ric. His eyes were closed. He was still trying to catch his breath. A sheen of sweat glistened on his chest as he raised one bare knee.

Opening his eyes, he met her gaze. "Are you well?"

She nodded, still unsure what words to speak.

"I never intended this to happen between us, Jocelyn. But I'm not sorry it did."

She lifted herself to balance on her elbow as she pulled her skirt back into place. "Neither am I."

He reached for her shirt and handed it to her before he rose and slipped back into his pants. "I came down here out of concern. After the skirmish, I looked and you'd disappeared."

"I was overwhelmed." She held her top to cover her breasts and watched him dress.

"You were amazing." He crouched next to her and cupped her cheek. "Both above deck...and below."

Jocelyn's cheeks warmed and a flush rose on her chest.

He fingered her hair. "I wish you hadn't done this, however."

She pulled a curl straight and allowed it to spring back. "It will grow again." She shrugged a bare shoulder and smiled. "The cabbage crew needed it more."

"Get dressed. Your hand has bled through the bandage. It needs tending." He tucked her hair behind one of her ears. "And we need to talk about what's happening...between us." Ric stood to his full height. "I'll be waiting for you in the galley."

After he left, Jocelyn rose and cleaned herself as best she could. She wasn't in a hurry to join Ric. Somehow she knew both the tending of her hand, and the discussion to follow wouldn't be painless.

But she hadn't lied to him earlier. She didn't regret a single moment of what happened. And she wasn't as naïve as he believed her to be. Ric may hereafter hold her heart, but he didn't hold her future. He would insist the plan to bring her to her father remain unaltered, and she had no unrealistic notion to believe otherwise.

And yet, everything was changed. In ways she had yet to figure out. She ran her fingers through her newly cropped hair. Smoothed a hand over her chest. A new lightness filled her.

No, she didn't regret a thing.

Chapter 17

Hornbach hauled ten of the "cabbage crew" into the galley and dropped them on the end of Ric's makeshift desk. "What the hell am I to do with these now?"

"Save them," Ric looked over the pile. "Can't tell if we'll need them again." He reached over and pulled a bit of Jocelyn's hair from under a battered hat. The dark spiral curled around his finger and he smoothed the strands with his thumb.

"When you're done there, I'll need you to gather the surgeon's bag. Jocelyn may need a stitch or two in a wound across her palm."

"Maybe you should do the stitching, Capt'n. Other than Tupper's head, last time I sutured a wound, I ended up stitching me own shirt te the man." Hornbach lifted the tail of his shirt and shrugged. "'Blood makes me a wee light headed."

Ric rubbed a weary hand over his forehead. Four men, two women, two lads and a surgeon who faints at the sight of blood. The sooner he remanned this crew the better. "Bring me the supplies, and I'll do it myself."

"Smart decision." The man huffed. Relief crossed his features. "That's why we done made ye the capt'n."

He'd take care of Jocelyn's hand. Clean the wound. Stitch together the skin. Was it his day to do nothing but cause the woman pain? He pushed the ship's logs away and grabbed for his mug of rum.

He rolled his shoulders trying to ease the tension there, but could only imagine the placement of five perfect fingernail crescents marring him where she had dug her fingers into his arm at the first thrust through her maidenhead.

Ric groaned and dropped his head. What had he been thinking? He hadn't. He'd been riding the frenzy of battle and a blinding need to make sure she was all right. Finding her in tears had torn the heart from his chest. Then she'd kissed him. Bared herself to him. Laid his hand upon her breast.

Damn it, he was only human. Even now, the image of her naked to her waist brought a renewed tightening in his breeches.

Ric studied the length of hair about his finger. Her cutting her beautiful locks was not the only thing that couldn't be undone. Yes, he could stitch the wound on her hand, but he couldn't stitch her hair back to where it was, or restore her purity.

He'd ruined her. It was as simple as that. He slammed a fist on the table. Risking his life back on Port Royal, fighting an angry mob to get her away from the auction block, threatening his position on this ship when he'd brought her aboard, and putting what was left of the crew in danger, all to keep her safe and unharmed. He'd vowed not to touch her. Made her forbidden to him. What a joke, he couldn't even save her from himself.

What was wrong with him? He wasn't a man ruled by his cock. Ric had more control than that. The last time he'd lain with a virgin, he'd been a bloody virgin himself. It wasn't as if he made a habit of leaving a trail of deflowered maidens in his wake.

Why couldn't he stay away from this one, small, powder keg of a woman? He needed to end this insanity this second. Nothing, and he meant absolutely nothing good could come of continuing this infatuation.

He ran the silk of her hair across his lip. Except…Ric closed his eyes to the memory. He could still feel her body wrapped around his. The perfume of their joining still clung to his skin. After her initial pain, she had begun to move like the sea beneath him, her hips cresting to meet his thrusts, dipping to begin another sensuous wave as he withdrew. Calling out his name like a seductive siren to pull him beneath the surface.

That's what she was--a siren. An old, crusty, one-legged crewmate he'd first served with on the *Scarlet Night*, Cookie Burrows, had often told him the tale of those watery temptresses. God rest him, Cookie loved to torture him with tales of ghosts and the supernatural. He'd be enjoying all this. Watching Ric get himself into such a mess. And with a skirt, no less.

Hornbach dropped a surgeon's chest on the table before him. Ric slipped the lock of Jocelyn's hair into his pocket before opening the chest. An entire box full of gruesome items to inflict more pain so that the patient might survive.

He lifted an amputation saw. So it would have to be with Jocelyn. Pushing her away and cutting her out of his life for good would cause them both pain, but it was unavoidable if they both wanted to survive.

"It's only a small gash. Surely, I'll still keep my hand."

Ric's head snapped up. Jocelyn stood at the end of the table. He hadn't heard her come in. His body pulsed at the mere sight of her. With her cropped hair, the elegant sweep of her neck and shoulders beguiled him. He stifled a moan. Which of these tools would he need to cut out his own heart? He fit the saw back into its appointed place. "We'll do our best, but if infection sets in, desperate measures may need to be considered," he teased.

Jocelyn sat next to him, her back to the table, giving him better access to her wound. "Desperate measures,"--she unwrap her hand--, "seems a daily occurrence here."

He met her gaze, before lifting her hand and lowering his eyes to inspect the cut across her palm. "They are." All the teasing had fallen away. The cutting had begun. "But there are times when they are the only option."

* * * *

Jocelyn's hand throbbed. It had taken half a dozen stitched to close the deep slice across her palm. She cradled it to her chest as she pulled in cooling air to quell the slight queasiness she was feeling. Only part of it had to do with watching Ric sew up her palm. He'd barely spoken. It was as if they hadn't just left one another's arms. Hadn't made love. How had nothing changed between them?

"There you are. After the cannon fire, I didn't see you." Tupper joined Jocelyn at the rail. Smoke from her pipe smelled sweet. Leviticus rested on her forearm. "You did a fine job during the skirmish, pitching in like you were one of us. I like the hair, too. Quick thinking. It makes me toy with the idea of cutting mine, but Gavin wouldn't be happy if I did."

At Jocelyn's silence, Tupper turned to study her. "Are you well? You look pale."

"I'm fine." Jocelyn wished she'd ignore her. Stop staring at her so intently. Did it show, what she'd done? Jocelyn closed her eyes and prayed. *Please, talk about the weather. Talk about anything else.*

When Jocelyn opened her eyes, Tupper still stared. "Has something happened?"

She gave a quick smile before lowering her gaze. "I see Leviticus is free of his bandage. Are you letting him fly free?"

When Jocelyn dared raise her eyes, Tupper's shrewd green gaze pierced hers. "His wing was too damaged, it seems. He's not able to fly

properly, but I'm growing accustomed to him. He's free to stay with me."
Tupper bit the stem of her pipe in her teeth and petted the bird. Her wide
gold ring caught the sunlight. "You know, you're good at that." She spoke
around the stem.

"At what?" Jocelyn blinked at her.

Tupper pulled the pipe from her mouth and pointed the clay stem at
her. "Diversion."

She feigned innocence. "I'm sorry?"

"When you don't want to talk about something," Tupper narrowed her
eyes. "You deflect the question and change the subject."

Jocelyn's eyebrows pushed higher. Perhaps she wasn't as skilled as
Tupper believed. She caught her hand. "That's a beautiful ring. Is that an
'A' on its face?"

Tupper pulled her hand away and laughed. "I'm wise to you now.
It won't work."

Jocelyn chewed at her lip. Perhaps it would be good to talk to Tupper
about what was weighing on her heart. A confession of sorts. She was
coming to admire Tupper a great deal. Such a strong figure. So worldly.
"May I confide in you? As a friend, *oui*? Talk to you. Woman to woman?"

"Sure." Tupper drew the word long. "Friends."

Jocelyn took a deep breath. "I'm not sure how to start. It's rather a
delicate subject."

A frown drew Tupper's brows together. "I'm not much good with
delicate. Best to spit it out."

Jocelyn leaned closer. "And you won't repeat this to anyone?" Leviticus
flustered at her closeness.

Tupper smoothed the bird's ruffled feathers. "Go ahead. It's only
me and the bird."

It took Jocelyn a moment to gather her words. "Back at the abbey,
some of the others would talk. About their lives before coming to the
abbey. Some about being with…men. *Rapports*…"

"Men?" Tupper's head snapped up. "*Rapports? As in intercourse? Are
we talking about sex?"

"*Oui*, sex." Jocelyn nodded, grateful she didn't have to be the first one
to say the word. "They would sigh and say how it was *magnifique*, ah,
magnificent…and how they would…how did they put it…soar so high
they could touch the stars."

"And…"

"Well," This was more difficult than she thought. Jocelyn worried her
lip. "Perhaps, like Leviticus, my wing is broken too? There was no flying

amongst the stars. It was more like sweaty fumbling, and messier than I imagined. I prepared for it to hurt, but not so much. I'm worried I did it wrong? Or maybe my *wing* is damaged?"

Tupper coughed. Her lips thinned. "So you like my ring. Yes, that is an 'A'…"

Heat flared in Jocelyn's cheeks. She turned away. "Never mind. I'm sorry I brought it up."

Tupper's hand stopped her. She dropped her voice. "You and Ric?"

"*Oui.*" Jocelyn nodded with a whisper.

"And it wasn't…" Tupper gave a slow shake of her head.

"No. No stars." Jocelyn swept the sky with her hand. At Tupper's pitying look she added, "There were some pleasant parts, like when he put his lips…"

Tupper reared back and raised her hand in surrender. "Please don't tell me anymore."

The throbbing in her hand was getting worse as was this conversation. "I thought where you have more experience than I, you would know. Were those other women telling tales? Perhaps there are no stars at all."

"Oh, there are stars…" Tupper gave a wistful sigh and turned to look out to sea. "Gavin could fill the sky…."

"What can I do?" she begged.

Tupper pushed the stem of her pipe through a small loop in her baldric and planted her hand on her waist. She gave Jocelyn a serious look and spoke low. "To begin with, stop worrying. It was your first time. Those are almost always a disaster, but it will get better." She leaned in closer. "And it isn't up to you…to get yourself…to those stars…or…well, that's another conversation, and…my bird needs a bath…."

Jocelyn let out a small sigh and smiled. "I knew I could confide in you. You are a good friend, Tupper." She squeezed her hand.

When Jocelyn released her, Tupper examined her ring once more. She gave a small smile. "It's been a long time since I talked to someone like this. Having you aboard reminds me of a friend I had long ago. I didn't realize how much I missed her." Her thumb twisted the ring about her finger. "Remind me to tell you about my friend, Annalise. She made this ring for me so I wouldn't forget her. Last I remember, she wore its twin. She would have liked you."

Such sadness flitted across Tupper eyes, Jocelyn reached out to her once more. "Has she passed away?"

Tupper's laugh was short, almost bitter. "No, I did."

* * * *

Ric raised his eyes as Tupper stormed into the galley. He'd heard the strong tap of her boots coming across the decking. She had her fool bird on one arm. The other planted firmly on her hip. "Are you out of your mind?"

He nodded and went back to his work. "There is a good chance." He figured he'd catch hell from someone over the decision to attack a fully armed Dutch frigate with only nine hands aboard.

"What the hell happened to 'she's different'?" She waved a hand toward his crotch. "Is it so hard for you to keep your pecker in your pants?"

Shit. How in hell had she found out? He kept his head down. The muscle in his jaw threatened to crush his back teeth. "No. It just happened."

Tupper threw up a hand and gave him a bitter smirk. "And not too well by the conversation I had with Mademoiselle Beauchamp."

The muscle threatening his molars went suddenly slack. "What does *that* mean?" Ric's voice rose as he dropped the quill he was using and crossed his arms over his chest.

"I would have thought the legendary Ricochet Robbins was better at such things." Tupper taunted. "At least those are the rumors around the docks. Having an off day, are ye?"

Ric was on his feet. "What the hell did she tell you?"

Tupper gave him a haughty look. "I'll not break her confidence. She's had enough things broken for one day, don't you think?"

Ric growled and lowered his voice. "I don't know what you're prattling on about. It happened. It won't happen again." He sat back down, dipped his quill and tried to ignore her.

"Aye, but the damage is done. You could still take my advice and use this against her father."

Ink dripped off the tip of his quill ruining Gavin Quinn's pristine logbook. Ric slammed the book closed. "Perhaps you'd be happy if one lapse of sanity on my part planted a pirate bastard in the girl."

Tupper smiled a wicked smile. "There's always a chance."

"I told you, I'll not use her for your revenge." Ric stood again and pushed past Tupper to refill his rum.

"*Our* revenge," Tupper pointed out. "You'd managed to escape his damned prison before the trial. It could have been you as well. And you didn't hear those men screams. The six. After he held them each in the cage, the *little hell* as he called it. Beauchamp held them for weeks. His hatred for Gavin and I always besting him in battle, spurring him to torture our crew members in the most heinous way he could. Sending us a message. Putting a price on all our heads."

Ric swallowed. The rum burned into his belly. "I remember."

"Do you remember the tarring?"

He shook his head as he recalled that grisly day. "I wasn't a witness, no, but I heard."

Tupper thumped her chest with a fist. "I was there. I saw. I still hear those men screaming as they were covered in boiling tar and hung in the gibbets to die. Yes, I took his eye. I'd take the other given the chance. And perhaps his tongue and his hands and roast his innards on a spit."

"But his daughter is an innocent." Ric injected into her rant.

Tupper snorted. "Not any more. I knew you wouldn't be able to keep your hands off her."

She'd not soon let him forget. "Jocelyn isn't going to pay for what he's done to us. She's been half a world away. What does she even know of her father's crimes? I'm not going to use her like some pawn."

"Jocelyn is already a pawn." Tupper spat. "Don't you see? I'm not unfond of her. I like her. She's strong and tenacious, but naïve to the world and especially the vile things her father is capable of. You've heard her tell of her life. He imprisoned her when she was a child. Now when it suits him, he'll use her for his own political aspirations. He's building powerful allies. Marrying her off to the highest bidder, he'll secure his position. Jocelyn is the key to him gaining an advantage. Why shouldn't we use your disappointing tête-à-tête with her to our advantage?"

Ric threw his hands wide sloshing his rum. "Disappointing?" What the hell had Jocelyn told her?

"Forget your tarnished ego for one moment, will you." Tupper pointed behind her. "She is our chance to destroy Philippe Beauchamp once and for all."

"Tupper…" Ric slammed his mug down on top of a barrel. It was then he caught the movement of someone in the doorway. "Shit…" He barked. Leviticus squawked and flapped as he shoved past Tupper. He rushed to the doorway in time to see Jocelyn hurry down the mid-deck ladder way.

"Jocelyn! Wait." Ric called out before he spun back to Tupper. He spoke between gritted teeth. "As long as I'm captain, I'm making the decisions where this ship and Jocelyn are concerned. We are not destroying her. It is my plan to anchor a short distance from Port de Paix, where I alone will take her ashore. We'll travel by foot into the city and secure transport across to Tortuga. I will deliver her to the gates of Fort de Rocher, then it's finished."

Tupper set her chin. "If the French discover who you are, you risk us all."

"Only if they find the *Scarlet Night*." He swept the maps and charts on the table. "I'm finding the perfect hiding spot to make sure that doesn't happen. Twelve hours, I'm back aboard, we weigh anchor and this will all be over."

"And if you're not back?"

"Then you'll leave me to my fate, and save the ship." He slapped a hand against the doorframe. "But now I need to speak with Jocelyn. There's no telling how much she heard. I need to reassure her we won't be using her as a weapon, or subjecting her to another *disappointing* encounter with me."

Chapter 18

"Jocelyn, open the door." Ric tried the latch. It was locked. "Jocelyn. Tupper was wrong. I don't know what you heard but let me in and we can talk." Not a sound came from within. He ran a hand through his hair in frustration and lowered his forehead to the door.

Disappointing tête-à-tête ... "I give you my word, we will just talk." He tried the latch again with no success. "Fine. I realize you're upset, but there are things you don't fully understand." Still no sound could be heard. "Perhaps it's wise to wait until morning. Discuss things in the fresh light of the new day. I'll see your evening meal is brought down to you, but we'll meet on deck at four bells come morning. Understood?" Silence. "Jocelyn?"

* * * *

The sun dropped into an orange sea off the tip of their bow. Ric had tucked the *Scarlet Night* as close to shore as he dared and ordered the anchor dropped for the night. Along this side of the island, the coral reefs were known to reach their sharp claws and catch a ship unawares. It wasn't wise to float adrift here at night.

A few more days like this one, and Ric would gladly throw himself on a reef. Reaching overhead, he hung tight to a tarred rope of rigging and lost himself in watching the last flash of sun before it disappeared and the sky melted gold into blue as the world debated day against night. With too many thoughts sparring in his brain, he pushed them all aside to stand in the gloaming, his favorite hour.

Still in the play of such magnificent color, he couldn't stop thinking about Jocelyn for more than a moment. He was mad. His mind playing the events of the day over and over. His emotions tumbling over one another in a race to nowhere.

During the skirmish, seeing her rushing about the deck, skirts pinned, sword drawn. Hair flying until with a slice of her blade she transformed from a delicate aristocrat into some fighting hellcat. He'd swelled with pride. Ric slipped his hand into the snug pocket of his breeches to make sure he still had the curl of her hair.

Then after, when the cannon smoke began to clear and he couldn't find her. Had he ever known such fear? Racing to her quarters, his heart threatening to beat its way out of his chest. To find her crying. Relief to anguish to raging desire in three beats of his heart.

He'd taken her like a fumbling lad. Only concerned with the first thrust and moving her past the pain so he could find his release. Never thinking about her pleasure. Not once.

And when all his passion flamed out and had turned to shame, he'd become cold to her. Too caught up in his own failings and trying to justify abandoning her after he'd taken what he had no right to take as some misguided way to once again protect her? Utter rubbish. He was the worst kind of rogue. A cad of the highest rank.

He should have himself flogged.

* * * *

"When was the last time you slept?" MacTavish placed a mug of morning ale in front of Ric.

Dawn was burning red. There'd be strong weather moving in before day's end. Ric gave MacTavish a side glance before lifting the mug. "Slept like a babe the night before you idiots voted me in as captain."

MacTavish lifted his mug, "Heavy is the head that wears the crown."

Ric groaned. "What kind of pirate are you? Draped in tartan, quoting Shakespeare. It's too early in the day."

The Scotsman dropped his bulk across the table from Ric and looked over the charts. "What's got you pacing the decks?"

"The reefs along this stretch." He pointed to several areas on the charts. "We need to keep in tight to the shore, otherwise we've got our arse out for the taking. But if we cut in too close, we'll get hung up."

"So, it wouldn't have nothin' to do with a wee dark-haired lass?" MacTavish spoke into his mug before raising a bushy eyebrow in Ric's direction.

"Not you, too." He glared at him. It was coming on four bells, and he'd been going over in his mind exactly what he wanted to say to Jocelyn.

MacTavish leaned across the table. "Heard Tupper's fit yesterday."

Ric began rolling up his maps. "So did a lot of folk. At least Tupper's voice is back in fine working order."

"Then when ye didn't sleep in yer hammock last night…" MacTavish shrugged a meaty shoulder.

"Shut your mouth." Ric snapped.

"Mother and I were so worried." MacTavish laid a hand to his chest and tipped his head before busting out with laughter and slapping the table.

Ric pushed back and was on his feet. "Did you wake up this morning knowing it would be your last?" He headed out of the galley.

MacTavish called after him. "Don't envy you today, laddie. Two women mad as wet hens at ya. Yer gonna wish this mornin' be yer last."

Damn it, he wasn't waiting for the bells, he'd been awake all night, pacing the deck 'til he couldn't take another step. He'd tried to close his eyes stretched out on one of the hard oak benches in the galley, but images of him and Jocelyn kept flashing through his mind. He'd given up, raised the lantern's wick, and studied those damn maps until he knew this coast better than he knew--Ric stopped short at the top of the ladder way. The saying he'd always used was he knew something better than he knew the way between a woman's thighs.

Bloody hell, he rubbed a weary hand over his jaw. He couldn't say *that* anymore.

"Jocelyn?" Ric tapped on her door moments later. "This can't wait any longer. We need to speak now, so please let me in." Once again, his request met with silence. Was she still asleep? He tapped again. "It's early, but this is important."

Anger and frustration flared in him. "I haven't got time to mollycoddle your tender feelings. Let me the hell in, or I'll kick down this bloody door."

Ric grasped the latch to force his way in. To his chagrin, the door opened. It hadn't been locked. She wasn't there. The food he'd sent down last evening was untouched. A thread of concern slithered down his back.

There was no way she got past him. Perhaps she was waiting topside as he'd requested. A quick scan of the deck answered that question. Dowd was making his morning climb into the crow's-nest. White and Summer were polishing the capstan. Bump checked the ropes securing the cannons. Jocelyn wasn't here.

Tupper came up behind him. That blasted crow of hers cawed at her until she fed him a bit of something from her hand.

Ric spun about at the sound. "Is Jocelyn with you?"

Tupper stroked the crow's throat. "Not unless she's black with feathers."

He frowned. *Where the hell could she be?* "Maybe the galley."

"Came from there. Just Hornbach cursing how quick everything's started to go rank." She gave the bird another bite. "Leviticus doesn't mind a bit of spoil on his meat, do you boy?"

"Have you seen her since yesterday?" Ric looked toward the stern.

"No." Tupper shrugged one shoulder. "Figured if she wanted to talk more, she knew where to find me."

"Capt'n?" White stood behind Ric.

Ric ignored him for the moment. To Tupper he continued, "If you see her, find me." Tupper nodded. Ric planted his hands on his hips, "Maybe she's with MacTavish in the armory."

"Capt'n?" White repeated his request.

Ric spun on him. "What is it, man?"

"Seems we've lost our skiff, Capt'n."

For a moment, all Ric could do was stare at the man. "Impossible."

Tupper spoke to the bird as she walked away, "She's flown the coop."

"No." Ric shook his head. "There has to be another explanation. She couldn't have." Ric followed White to investigate. Sure enough, there was no evidence the boat broke away on its own. The ropes were still intact. "It takes two men to lower this skiff."

"Or one determined woman, by the look." Summer joined them. "Can be done, little from one block, little from the other. Took some time, though."

Ric held his forehead. "But when? I was on deck most of the night." He called up to Dowd, "Do you see any sign of our skiff?"

Dowd called back. "Other than it ain't where it should be? No sir."

Ric pushed past the others and grabbed a spyglass. "She couldn't have rowed it by herself. It's too wide for one. Even if she could, her hand is injured, she wouldn't have gotten far. I'd say she'd head straight to shore, but the winds picked up overnight." He lifted the glass to his eye and began a slow sweep of the coastline. "She's not strong enough to fight anything over three knots. If she used them to her advantage, then we'd be behind her."

He gave the order. "Weigh anchor. We're going to come back in as close to the shore as we can. We'll find her."

White looked from Ric to Summer and back shaking his head. "What ya gonna do then, Capt'n, fly te shore?"

Ric began scanning the coastline again. She had to be there. "I was thinking I'd swim."

Summer laughed, "An' ride a shark or two to find a woman who clearly don't want te be found?"

"The sharks are too smart to come in close to the reef." Ric lowered the glass and looked back at the two men gaping at him.

"But we ain't?" Argued White.

"You'll only be there long enough for me to lower myself over the side. Then you can move off, set anchor, and wait for me to bring back both the woman and the skiff." Ric headed for the ship's wheel.

White and Summer followed. Summer continued to argue his point. "I say we bid her an '*au revoir*' and be on our way."

"Right." White pointed to Summer and nodded his approval. "We ain't nursemaids. Should have tossed her long before now. Losing the chit be worth a skiff. We'll steal another. Let's point the *Scarlet* north and go back to theivin' and pillagin' like proper pirates."

Ric stared them down. "Weigh anchor and prepare to head to port then cut in close."

Chapter 19

"There she be." White called out as the *Scarlet Night* made a slow pass several hundred yards off shore. "Mangrove island, west of the clearing."

Ric handed off the wheel to Summer. "Can you see if she's all right?"

White nodded, "Still floatin.'"

"Jocelyn?" His heart dropped in his chest.

White lowered the scope. "No, the skiff."

"Drop anchor. Give me that glass." White handed over the brass and pointed a finger toward shore. Ric pressed the glass to his eye. There it was, but it floated a few feet off the beach. Had she made it to land and not tied off? He thought he could make out tracks in the sand, but from this distance, it was hard to tell.

He pulled off his boots then handed his baldric to White. Lashing a knife to his thigh, he reminded them. "You have your orders. Now lower a rope."

* * * *

Ric was a strong swimmer, but it had been a while since he'd had to swim any fair distance. Worry and anger pushed him past the point of exhaustion. He misjudged his way through a ridge of coral, caught the side of his knee and sliced through his pant leg. The salt water stung the gash. Blood clouded the water red. Short of wearing a fish-head sash about his waist, he couldn't be a bigger target for a shark attack.

He kicked off through the clear aquamarine water with a renewed burst of adrenaline and within a few tense minutes dragged himself gasping and bleeding onto the wide white beach.

Ric peeled back the ragged edges of his breeches to inspect the wound. It wasn't deep, but it hurt like hell when he stood. Blood mixed with seawater and ran down his leg to stain the pale wet sand. He scanned the water for any shark presence before wading back in to retrieve the skiff.

The small lapstreak boat bobbed free about fifty yards down the beach in waist deep water. If all the blood in the water hadn't attracted sharks to his heels, he'd be amazed.

By the time he'd dragged the boat up the beach, his leg was throbbing, but thankfully he still had it attached to his body along with the rest of his limbs. He moved up to the tide line and headed east looking for any sign of Jocelyn. He called out to her, but heard nothing over the crashing of the surf and the breeze through the tops of the mangrove.

The weather he predicted was moving in. A dark line of clouds stretched across the horizon. He hoped to find Jocelyn and make it back to the *Scarlet Night* before the worst of it arrived.

The island wasn't overly large. Wide beach to the north, high land to the south. A shallow rocky channel separated it from the main island, and with the protection of the reef off the northern coast, only a ship half the size of the *Night* could gain access here.

Ric crossed the beach until he found a trail of footprints heading inland. Relief overshadowed his anger. He'd find her. What could she have been thinking to leave the ship? Did she hope to walk to Tortuga? Did she realize she landed herself on the wrong island?

Moving inland, he called out to her once more. The footprints disappeared the deeper Ric traveled. He plucked at his shirt, pulling the cold damp cloth away from his skin. Unaccustomed to traveling without his boots, each twig and rock beneath his feet slowed him down. At least his leg had stopped bleeding.

It was then he saw her. "Jocelyn!" *Damn it!* Where was she going?

Ric took off after her. Cursing his leg, each stone the sole of his feet found along the way…and her.

"Bloody hell, woman, stop!" He caught hold of her sleeve and held tight.

Jocelyn spun on him, tugging against his hand, but he refused to release her. "Let me go. Why did you follow me?"

"You stole my skiff."

She grabbed for his arm then pushed at him. He dropped his hand ready to capture her again should she decide to run. Instead, she stood her ground. Her gaze darted over him, before meeting his. "You're soaked through. Did you swim here?"

Ric plucked at his clinging shirt once more before bending to remove the boulder lodged in the arch of his foot. "I told you, you stole my skiff."

Guilt followed by defiance flitted across her features. "So take it, and leave me. It's on the beach. I tied it up."

"And you still haven't mastered the round turn and two half hitches. Remind me never to ask you to tie up the ship." Images of being lashed to a chair flashed in his memory.

He watched her throat work before she lowered her gaze, was she having the same memory? "What does that matter anymore?"

A rumble of thunder rolled overhead. "What did you think you were doing? These islands aren't safe. You could have rowed yourself into more trouble." He lifted her hand. "You're stitches are bleeding. Let me see." She pulled her hand away and curled it to her chest. "You're lucky it was only me who found you." He took her arm once more and urged her back toward the beach. "Come back to the *Scarlet Night*."

"I'm not going back with you. My hand is fine." She broke away from him, and crossed her arms over her chest. "I heard what you said. I heard Tupper."

"Tupper was wrong." His voice rose with frustration.

"About which," she snapped, "the fact that my father is evil incarnate, or that you laid with me to exact your revenge?"

Ric returned fire. "I didn't lay with you to get back at your father. Hell, I didn't want to lay with you at all."

Jocelyn's jaw went slack before she turned and kept walking.

"Stop. That didn't come out right." The first step he took to go after her reunited foot with boulder. He winced, cursed, and limped to catch up to her again. Ric turned Jocelyn to face him, but she wouldn't meet his eye. "When I first saw you, something inside of me shifted. I can't explain it, but I knew I wanted to take care of you. Even when I learned who you were, those feelings didn't stop. I made a promise. To you, but more important to myself. I wasn't going to give in to the instinct I had to lie with you. I fought my desire every day."

She met his gaze. "Seems you broke your promise."

"And not well, so I'm told. Quite a blow to my pride." Ric ran a hand down her arm and gave it a gentle squeeze. "I was selfish. I'll never make the same mistake again."

Jocelyn studied the center of his chest. "Did my father truly do all those horrible things?"

"Yes, but I bet he never wanted his only daughter to hear about it in such graphic detail. When the fighting starts, we all do horrible things. To win. To survive. I can't explain your father to you. We might as well be talking about two different men."

"Maybe Tupper isn't wrong. Maybe he is the devil. Perhaps he isn't a different man. What if it's a mistake bringing me to him?"

"What else can I do? Drop you to fend for yourself on some remote island?" He teased before lifting her chin. "He won't hurt you. He's only ever wanted a good, safe life for you. It may not be the life you wish for, but it's better than any life I could offer you."

Jocelyn shook her head and laid a hand on his chest. "If he finds out you're the Captain of the *Scarlet Night*…he'll do the same to you as he did to those other men."

He slipped his hand over hers. The worry in her eyes made him want to sweep her into his arms and kiss it away. "Then we'll make sure he doesn't find out."

Her fingers clutched at the fabric. "I couldn't bear it if something were to happen to you, or Tupper, or the rest."

All at once, it made sense. Realization punched him in the chest. "Is that why you ran?"

"He'll kill you," Her eyes lifted to his. Tears shimmered in the dimming light.

"That's a risk I'm willing to take." He cupped her face and brushed a tear from her cheek with a sweep of his thumb.

"Why?" she whispered.

"Foolish woman, haven't you figured that out by now?" He lowered his mouth to kiss her. "For the same reason you ran."

* * * *

Thunder rumbled overhead. Ric heard the rain before he felt it. "We're going to have to find some shelter."

Fat drops fell from the trees. Jocelyn tipped her chin off to her right. "I found a cave not too far from here. It's not very tall inside, but it has a light shaft that spills into a pool. It's over here."

By the time they made it to the cave's narrow entrance, the sky had opened and the rain fell straight as a mast and hard as hail.

Climbing into the cave, Ric was grateful to see the space opened wider past the pool. Without a lantern, Ric hesitated venturing farther into the gloom. But a faint glow beyond the dark hinted there might be another entrance to this cave coming from the island side.

Rain ran into the light shaft and splashed into the pool. The water was clear. Every rock strewn across its bottom could be seen.

"Looks to be a spring." Ric dipped his fingers into the water and tasted it. "Fresh and warm, full of minerals, tastes a bit like a rusty nail, but I've drunk worse." Taking advantage of clean water, he bathed the wound at his knee."

"There's been a fire here, too." Jocelyn pointed to a charred area farther in before turning back to him. "We should--You're bleeding."

"I'm glad you finally noticed."

Jocelyn stripped a length of her skirt and pushed aside what was left of his pant leg to wrap his knee. Ric was afforded a good glimpse of creamy thigh. If Jocelyn tore anymore of her skirt, there'd be nothing left.

Crouching before him, she placed a gentle hand upon the bandage. "Why didn't you tell me you were hurt?"

He pulled her to her feet so he could finish the kiss the rains had interrupted. "I was too busy trying to tell you I'm in love with you."

Jocelyn pulled back, her eyes wide. "Y-you can't be."

"Doesn't seem to be something I have much control over." He tugged her into his arms again and lowered his mouth to hers.

Before his lips could claim her, she pushed away once more. "But... how will I ever leave you now? And how will you let me go?"

He took hold of her arms and gave a small shake of his head. How did he explain it to her when the thought of letting her go made him ache? But she needed to understand. He wouldn't build her hope for something impossible. *Because I'm a thief and a pirate and you deserve a chance for a better life. A better man.* He slipped his hand over her shoulder and beneath her hair to curve about her nape. "Because it's for the best."

"The best for whom?" Within the cave, the only sound came from the water spilling into the pool. Their voices were hushed and intimate.

Ric gaze held hers. "You."

"I thought you were selfish?"

He gave a bitter smile before brushing her lips with his. "I thought so, too."

Jocelyn let out a small sob as Ric slipped his tongue into her waiting mouth and crushed her to him. Aye, he may let her go, but right here and right now, she was his. He was selfish and even if it were only for this one night, he wanted to love her.

His hands slid down the curved of her back and over the swell of her behind. Jocelyn trembled beneath his touch. Between kisses he murmured, "Maybe I should get a fire going. It's getting cold. Looks like we're going to be here all night."

"We should get you out of those wet clothes," she whispered against his lips.

"We should get you out of your wet clothes, as well." Ric grabbed fists full of skirt and pulled her even tighter to him.

"But mine are dry." She tried to laugh, but he was too intent on kissing her.

Ric lowered his forehead to hers. Their breath coming in quick pants. "You could go stand in the rain? Or I could toss you into the spring?"

"Or you could take them off and kiss me again."

Chapter 20

Rain continued to fall through the opening in the roof of the cave to splash gently in the pool adding to the sound of the crackling fire and the beating of Ric's heart. Flames cast dancing shadows upon the walls and across the planes of her beautiful body.

He cradled Jocelyn in his lap. His back leaning against one low rock, the only thing between them and the soft dirt floor was a makeshift blanket made up of their clothing.

The firm curve of her hip rested over the hard shaft of his erection. As the fire pulsed, so did he, but his were not the needs he would meet tonight. Not at first, anyway. His only desire was to bring her as much pleasure as he could. He owed her a night without a hint of "disappointment."

Jocelyn traced her fingertips over his temple and along the line of his jaw. "Have I told you what I thought when I first saw you?"

He shook his head. He was busy with a lazy tracing of his own. One finger circled the rose-tinted tip of her breast until the nipple tightened.

Jocelyn sighed and arched slightly as if lifting her breasts to his touch. "Golden and handsome, I-I thought you looked like an angel."

Ric teased the firm peak, rolling it slowly between his finger and thumb. "How wrong you were."

She ran a hand over his shoulder and down his arm, urging him on. He purposely slowed his touches. Lightened the strokes. Jocelyn whimpered in protest. Her body moving against his. There would be no rushing tonight. No mindless release. Tonight he would make love to her the way he should have the first time.

He bent over her pulling that tightened tip between his lips. Cupping her breast, pressing the rounded flesh higher, he mimicked the motion of his fingers using the tip of his tongue before drawing it deeper with a gentle suck. Jocelyn's fingers raked into his hair to hold him to her.

She gasped, "Tell me…"

Ric ran her sensitive nipple between his teeth before blowing a cool breath over the heated nub. "Tell you what?"

She shivered in response. "Ah… Y-your nickname. I…I've run out of guesses." She clutched as his shoulder.

"You didn't try very hard." He concentrated on lowering his touch. Following the faint line between her breasts and over her stomach. Teasing her navel. Lower to the patch of dark curls protecting her sex. "Wasn't the last guess Cabbage Head? Did you know your insult is what gave me the idea during the attack on the Dutch frigate?"

"I don't want to talk about frigates," she panted lifting her hips. "I want to talk about you."

Ric kissed the crest of her knee before urging it wide. "You already know my nickname." The skin of her inner thighs was soft and warm. Brushing it with his lips, his body pulsed with desire.

"Robbins?"

"No," he nipped at her thigh, "you're getting warmer."

One finger parted her damp curls to dip between. Jocelyn moaned, opening her legs wider. Her hand covered his. "I can't think…not when you're doing…"

"But you're so close." Ric slid his touch over the slick heat. She was wet with anticipation.

"I surrender…" She gasped, rocking against his touch.

He shifted so he could kiss her and still caress her with sweeps of his fingers. "Never surrender." Ric increased the pressure and speed of his strokes. Jocelyn bit at his lip, panting, writhing with a building passion.

When he plunged two fingers into her, she bucked against his hand. Head back she arched her back and cried out his name. "Oh God, Ric!"

Her release bathed his hand. He stayed with her, slowing the touches, prolonging her pleasure, until she lay limp and trembling in his arms.

Ric's own body screamed for its release, yet he gathered her in his arms and kissed her panting mouth. "You guessed it."

"They call you, God?" she gasped, trying to catch her breath. Damp curls clung to her cheek.

Ric brushed them aside. "No, foolish woman. Ric. Short for Ricochet. Some day when we're not so…busy…I'll tell you the tale of how I got it."

"What is your given name?" She caressed his arm, then his chest.

"You ask too many questions." Ric watched her hand move boldly down his abdomen. He looked up to find her gaze on his face.

"I've always been too curious." Her fingers brushed the head of his penis.

Ric closed his eyes against the painful rush to his already swollen cock. When her fingers wrapped around him he jerked his eyes open and pulled her hand away. In one swift move, he had her straddling his thighs, hands on his shoulders, her wet heat hovering over him.

His breath came shallow and quick as if he'd run a fair distance to rest in the heaven between her thighs. "If…if I tell you, will you cry it out, when I make you come again?

"Again?"

"Aye." He held her hips as he pressed slowly into her.

"Oui..oh, oui."

"Henry. My name is Henry." He rocked his hips and plunged into her once more.

"Henri…" she sighed against his mouth. "A strong name, *Henri."*

"Say it again." He reached between them and slid his hand down the flat of her stomach as he continued to thrust upward. The need to reach his release driving him faster and faster. "I want… you to…cry it out."

Ric's thumb searched until he found what he sought. Swirling strokes soon had her clinging to him, matching his rhythm.

"Yes…oh…yes…"

"Say it…Jocelyn, say my name."

"Henri, Henri, Henri!"

Ric dug his fingers into her hips, surging into her. He wrapped his arms around her holding her tight to him pressing her to him tighter still as he pumped into her body.

* * * *

Later they lay entwined listening to the rain, waiting for their breathing to return to normal.

"You broke your promise again." Jocelyn kissed the dip at the base of his neck.

"Broke one…kept one."

She snuggled close, laying her head on his shoulder. "Stars. Lots and lots of stars," she murmured.

"Stars?"

"Mmmmm…"

He wasn't sure what she was talking about, but she felt too good in his arms for him to question.

Before long, the light of the fire had dimmed to coals. He left her side long enough to add the last few remaining sticks. "The fire is dying. We need to find some more dry wood."

Jocelyn sat up, modestly covering her chest with her shirt. "I thought I saw some back toward that stand of stones." She pointed.

Ric frowned as he got closer. In the flickering light of the fire, the rocks didn't look like any he'd ever seen. Reaching out, he discovered what looked like a pile of rocks was actually heavy oiled clothes covering a pile of trunks and barrels. "Damn…"

Jocelyn slid up beside him. She still held her shirt to her chest and tucked in close to his side. "No wood?"

Lifting the lid to one of the chests, light caught the cache of gold, silver and jewels within. The facets of the stones winked in the flicker of the fire as Jocelyn gasped. "Is that…?"

"It ain't wood."

Ric returned to the fire and pulled one of the long sticks to use as a torch to add some light to their discovery. Holding it aloft, the chest of gold and jewels fairly glowed.

"Holy shite," Jocelyn gasped.

Ric's eyebrows pushed toward his hairline. "MacTavish has been a bad influence. Don't let the good sisters hear you talk like that." He pulled a long strand of pearls each as large as a ripe berry. Slipping it over Jocelyn's head the creamy pearls dipped between her breasts and fell past her navel. Her standing naked in nothing but pearls was an image he would carry with him forever.

She slipped a gold and diamond bracelet onto her wrist and a ruby ring onto her hand. The stones flashed in the firelight. "Can you believe this? I've never seen a ruby so large."

Ric handed Jocelyn the torch and pulled back another oilcloth. Two hog's heads of brandy stood beside three of rum. Beyond the chest they'd first opened, there stood others. One held silver pieces--bowls, vases and the like. A small chest held nothing but coin. Gold pressed into eights.

When Ric opened the largest trunk, Jocelyn gasped beside him. Silks. Bolts of gossamer cloth. Rich hues of royal blue and regal purple. There was an embroidered kimono in black and gold. And a gown of red.

Jocelyn handed the makeshift torch back to Ric. She reached out to touch the dress as if in a trance, stopped, and wiped her palms on her thighs before lifting the claret gown out of its silken nest.

"Have you ever seen anything as beautiful in your whole life?"

Ric smiled at the reverence in her voice. "Perhaps one thing."

She held the dress against her body, swinging the skirts, totally enamored. He, however, was not thrilled at their find. "Do you know what this means?"

"I can rid myself of those horrible skirts?"

"Not quite. This is a cache. Booty. Which means whoever left this here will be back." He examined the oilcloths. "No dust. It hasn't been here long."

Jocelyn laid the sleeves of the dress along her arms, and measured the waist against her own. "Doesn't mean they'll be back soon."

"It could mean anything. If they're Spaniards or Dutch riding into French territory, they could have stowed this here instead of risking the French finding it." Ric dropped the cloth he held. "Come first light, we need to be out of here. I'm not taking any chances on unexpected guests.

"Does it mean I can't keep this?" She swished the dresses skirts once more. "What do pirates know about fine dresses anyway? They can keep their heavy pearls. I want this."

"As long as you can wear it while you help row the skiff."

Chapter 21

"Jocelyn, wake up."

Jocelyn ducked her chin and snuggled closer to Ric's warmth. She laid her cheek on the smooth plane of his chest and reveled in the sheer scent of him. His skin smelled faintly of wood smoke and…them.

She smiled as the delicious aches of her body reminded her of their night together. Jocelyn had barely recovered from Ric's initial lovemaking. Or should she say, *Henri's*.

Oh, yes, she'd touched the stars, and somewhere beyond. She never imagined it could be so…so wonderful.

After finding the stash of treasure, Ric had draped her naked body in jewels. Gold and silver with sapphires and emeralds. Strands and strands of pearls. Rings on each finger. Then he had stripped it all from her. Piece by piece, kissing each bit of skin he exposed before lifting her and carrying her into the pool where he made love to her yet again.

The warm water was heaven. Moving to the side of the pool, the shock of the chilled rainwater falling from the shaft sent them both back to the fire and into each other's arms until their touches heated them once more.

Jocelyn sighed. She'd not forget last night even if she lived to be one hundred years old.

"Jocelyn," Ric pushed at her shoulder moving her aside. "Wake up and put your clothes on," he hissed. He shot to his feet and pulled his breeches on. "We've got company."

"What?" She snatched at her clothing.

"As quick as you can," he whispered, shaking the dirt from her skirts and handing them to her. He put a finger to his lips. Drawing his knife from its sheath, he moved toward the opposite end of the cave.

Jocelyn strained to hear anything past the pounding of her heart. Ric was back before she finished slipping into her shoes.

"I count five. Narrow sloop. We haven't much time. Without my pistols, we're no match for them, but there may be a way."

He rushed to the pile of goods, and grabbing handfuls of coins tossed them amongst the scattering of jewelry from last night. Grabbing a short barrel of liquor, he wrenched out the bung from its side with his knife and dumped a good amount of rum near where they had slept.

With an armful of items scooped from several trunks, he headed out of the cave the way they had entered last night. "Follow me. Stay close."

As they moved through, items fell from his arms, and Ric dropped fistfuls of coins as if laying a trail. Once out of the cave he spoke, "Get yourself hidden." He pointed to a crop of bushes. "I'll be right back."

Jocelyn clutched at his sleeve. "Where are you going?"

"Need to give our visitors a wild goose to chase. Stay down and keep quiet." He must have sensed the panic she was feeling, because he dipped his head and planted a quick kiss upon her lips before he told her not to worry and nudged her toward the hiding spot.

Jocelyn did what he asked alternating furtive glances back toward the cave and down the path where Ric had disappeared. After what seemed like a year, Ric ducked in next to her panting. Sweat glistened across his chest.

"Now we wait," he huffed. "If they take the bait, they'll be chasing after the skiff."

"Chasing the skiff?" Jocelyn tried to follow his thinking.

"Aye," he whispered. "I cut it loose."

"But, the skiff is the only way to escape."

He shot her an impish grin. "Not the only way."

"I don't under--" Sudden shouts and yelling could be heard coming from the low entrance to the cave. Ric covered her mouth with his hand, pulled her to him and murmured against her ear. "Trust me?"

His voice rumbled through her and settled in her thighs. She nodded behind his hand. His breath tickled the side of her throat before he kissed that tender spot where her neck curved into her shoulder. Her nipples tightened.

"Went this a-way!" The call sounded close.

Jocelyn could only gasp as Ric pulled her lower, crouching out of sight.

"Fire still be warm."

"Drank half a head o' rum."

"Can't be far ahead."

"Looks te be, he left in a hurry."

Squeezing her eyes shut, Jocelyn prayed to become invisible as she heard the men thrash their way through the underbrush.

"Back to the cave," hissed Ric as he stood and pulled her to her feet. "Fast as you can. Don't stop. Don't look back. Go." He gave her a small shove.

She could still hear the other men's voices. If they should see them… Scrambling into the low entrance, she heard the first gun shot.

Ric was right behind her. "Move, move, move."

Once inside, he grabbed her arm. "Go to the far end of the cave and wait for me. I'll be right there." He let her go and rushed to drag the larger of the chests back to block the entrance.

She raced past the pool. The morning sunlight shafted into the water turning it a brilliant aquamarine. Had she not been running for her life, she would have stopped to gaze. Instead, she followed the glow coming from deeper in the cave.

The floor began a steady slope downward. The glow grew brighter until at last she reached the end. This side of the cave was markedly different from the other. Where the north side of this place led in from a wide pale beach, this coast mirrored the mainland with its craggy landscape separated by what looked to be a deep channel.

Below her, a ship sat anchored close to shore, planks lowered from its rails balanced on a slender shelf of flat land. With its white hull, it nearly glowed in the sunlight of the morning.

It was small compared to the *Scarlet Night*. Tiny compared to that Dutch Frigate. With no knowledge of ships, she couldn't begin to guess what kind it was, but with its single mast, the ship sat like a life-saving beacon on the water. Not waiting for Ric, Jocelyn began the steep scramble down to the precarious ramp.

One step onto the wide planks had them tipping beneath her weight. She looked down between the crude boards. Water ebbed and flowed around more rocks. It wasn't a long fall, but it was not one she wanted to make. Closing her eyes and lifting a prayer, she ran.

Jocelyn dropped down onto the cluttered deck. Ropes, wood, and broken barrels were trashed about. A huge cargo bay hatch took up most of the deck area. She shot a glance back hoping to see Ric behind her. He wasn't there. Worry for him choked her, but she didn't have time to dwell on the possibility he'd been captured. He'd be there. She trusted him.

Finding the anchor chain, Jocelyn was stymied for a moment. The device attached to raise and lower the anchor was nothing like the *Scarlet's* capstan. It more resembled a toothed, geared spool. She grabbed the iron handle on the side and pulled before realizing she was working it in reverse.

It took all her strength to push the wheel in the opposite direction. Sweat ran between her shoulder blades as the gear inched forward.

"Jocelyn." Ric called out to her.

She stopped only long enough to shout back. "Get on."

The anchor began to lift. The faster she pushed the mechanism, it seemed to double its effort. Jocelyn could sense the ship starting to move with the wind.

"Hold fast." Ric called as he closed in on the ramp. He threw a wrapped bundle across the span to land on the deck.

"I don't know how to stop?" She cried.

Looking back, Ric had begun to cross the planking, but the ship was sliding away. He jumped as the planks lost their hold and fell to the rocks below.

The ship picked up more speed. Jocelyn locked the gear before rushing to the rail.

Ric hung off the side of the ship.

"Oh God," Jocelyn reached over the rail. "Grab my hand."

Ric shook his head and held tight, shooting an anxious look down the side of the ship. "Find the tiller. Hurry. Steer us to port. Away from the rocks."

"You'll fall." She pulled on his sleeve.

He made another nervous glance forward. "I won't, but if we hit the rocks…"

"I don't know what a tiller is," she cried.

"The stick. In the stern. To steer the rudder. Shove it hard to the right. Damn it, hurry."

Jocelyn raced back to the ship's tiller and swung the bow toward the middle of the channel as she willed Ric to use the strength of those muscled arms of his to pull himself up and over the rail.

Angry shouts sounded from the entrance of the cave followed closely by pistol shots. Splinters from the top of the rail, near where Ric still hung, exploded before showering the deck.

"Get down, Jocelyn!" Ric yelled over the gunfire, but instead she turned the ship to position it away from the firing.

When the pirates at the mouth of the cave could no longer get a clear shot at Ric, they turned their pistols on her. A whistling past her ear had her dropping to the deck with a scream.

The sound must have spurred Ric to a final surge of strength because the next thing she knew he was by her side.

"Are you hit?" His hands tugged at her clothing. Was he looking for blood?

"No, are you?" Jocelyn gripped handfuls of his shirt.

Ric ducked as another shot exploded from shore before chipping the mast. "Stay down 'til we're out of range. He poked his head up only long enough to steer the ship back to starboard.

"Hey! What the fuck ye think yer doin'?" A man sporting a stained headcloth was marching toward them. He wore soiled pants which were torn short at the hems. His bare feet were filthy. An oily leather vest covered his top half. Or most of the top half that wasn't hanging out or decorated with inked markings. A wide leather belt held his scabbard.

"Bloody hell…" Ric looked back at Jocelyn and shrugged. "I missed one."

Standing, Ric spread his arms wide. "Takin' 'er for a ride."

"I don't fuckin' think so." The pirate advancing on him moved to draw his sword, but in the second it took him to lay his hand on the hilt and start to pull the steel from the sheath, Ric rushed him, balled his fist and smashed it into the man's jaw.

The pirate spun, staggered a step and dropped to his knees, cradling his face. Ric kept advancing. Grabbing the man by the shoulder of his vest, Ric dragged him to his feet shoving him viciously toward the rail, and in one swift movement, grabbed the man's breeches at the hip and used his momentum to flip him over the railing.

Jocelyn covered her mouth as she heard the man hit the water. Ric was soon back at her side to help her up.

Behind them, the others still fired and hurled curses at them.

"You can get up. They can't hit us now." He cupped her check. "Are you okay?"

"Did you hurt your hand?" She pulled his hand away to examine it. Her head was spinning. How could he use the same hand that moments ago crushed a man's cheek to hold hers with aching gentleness? "You split your knuckle."

"It's fine. Need to be checkin' below. Make sure no more are hiding. Then we can set all the cloth on this tub and get us back to the *Scarlet Night*."

"We did it." She breathed a shaky sigh. Amazement and adrenaline rushed through her, making her tremble.

Ric threw his head back and crowed. "We bloody well did." He pulled her against his chest and crushed her to him. "You do realize what you've done?"

She shook her head, unable now to control the chattering of her teeth.

Ric smiled down at her. "You stole a blasted boat."

"W-wasn't that the plan?" She could only blink at him.

"*My* plan, yes, but you didn't know that. And I never imagined you'd do the thieving." He kissed her then. Crushed his mouth against hers. Stealing her breath from her. "But next time, love, do me a favor? Wait another minute for me to get my arse on board?"

"I'll do my best."

Chapter 22

"What the hell did ya do wit the skiff?" MacTavish asked as soon as Ric's feet hit the deck of the *Scarlet Night*.

Ric turned and lifted Jocelyn the last few feet of the boarding ladder. "We traded it."

"Building yer fleet already?" piped Summer.

White laughed. "Starting small, are ye?"

"*Devil's Pearl*? That ain't no fit name for a ship." Dowd was looking like he tasted something rank.

MacTavish stood shaking his head. "*Devil's Shite* be more fittin.' She's a bloody mess."

"Bit of scrape, she'll be fit. Good line to her." Hornbach argued.

Dowd brightened, "Ye could call her *Robbins Nest*…get it?" MacTavish cuffed his ear.

"Isn't *my* ship. The *Devil's Pearl* belongs to its rightful owner. The one which takes it, keeps it. And she can name her whatever she wishes." Ric jerked his thumb over his shoulder at Jocelyn.

Had he not already loved the woman, what she did on the island--last night and this morning--endeared her to him forever.

She'd been fearless, daring, loving.

There was no one quite like her. Certainly, there were women in his world who were fierce and courageous, but Jocelyn's bravery came from something inherent, pure. Her upbringing should have made her timid and cautious, but not Jocelyn. In her, he saw a hunger and an honesty, which made her extraordinary.

And when he held her in his arms, that same hunger and honesty translated into a passion he'd never found in another's bed. He gave a small laugh. Could be he'd found the reasoning for such passion. The lack of a mattress. They'd yet to come together in an actual bed after all.

Last night went beyond beds and mattresses and his supposed prowess. He had wanted to satisfy her not to massage his bruised ego, but for her. Last night had been all about her. That thought alone left him amazed. When had he taken a woman and considered her desires ahead of his own? Never.

In turn, she came alive in his arms. Bloomed like a tropical flower after a rain. The way she moved, the taste of her skin, the sweet sounds of pleasure in her sighs, they had awoken something new in him.

But with this re-birth of sorts for Ric, came the crushing reminder of the futility of it all. She couldn't stay with him. Jocelyn deserved a beautiful, stunning future. Not one with him.

A pirate's life was an endless struggle to survive--battles, brutality, starvation, and the perils of a fickle sea. Not to mention the constant threat of being brought to justice for your crimes against crown and country.

Ric watched Jocelyn regale the others with the tale of how they managed to get away. In her torn, dusty skirts and dirt-smudged skin, she looked like a true pirate. Ric was all at once filled with pride and love and a longing for her which refused to be sated. But he also was struck with how wrong it was. She wasn't one of them. Jocelyn was too good for this. He refused to let her sink any further into becoming a watery thief.

Stealing a sloop was as far as Ric wanted to see Jocelyn's life of crime extend. He needed to see all of it come to an end, and soon.

"Another two days we'll be off the coast of Port de Prix." Ric confirmed. "We'll make good use of the sloop whatever her name. The *Scarlet Night* can hold back and Jocelyn and I can sail the *Pearl* through the needle's eye of Tortuga harbor."

"And ye had yer hands on all that treasure, and ye ain't brought us presents?" huffed MacTavish.

"There be ten cases of French wine and four barrels of black powder in the hold of her. Dowd, you and Bump start carrying it over," Ric ordered.

Tupper sided up to him. "See ye made good of yer promise to bring her back."

Ric gave a short laugh before turning away. "Some promises should never be made."

"What happened on the island?" Tupper fell into step with him. "Caught all night in a rain storm. Ye don't look like two drowned cats. Find some shelter from the storm, did ya?"

Ric snapped at her. "Since when did you become my mother? You're not captain yet. I don't have to answer to you."

Tupper stopped walking, "Well, well. So that's te be the way of it."

Ric turned on his heel. "Be the way of what?"

"It doesn't take a blind man to see what's written all over yer face." Tupper pointed a finger at his nose before leaning close. "You've gone and fallen in love with her."

He folded his arms over his chest. "What of it?"

"Falling in love wasn't part of your grand plan, Capt'n."

Ric looked past Tupper's shoulder. Jocelyn, surrounded by his meager crew, raised her dark rum-colored eyes and held his gaze. It didn't take a blind man to see what was written on her face either. And when she smiled... "Nay, this was not the plan at all."

* * * *

"Give me your clothes. If you can call them that. I've seen better rags on a swabber's mop." Tupper tossed Jocelyn a drying cloth and some soap.

Jocelyn was admiring the additions to Leviticus's new home. A stand made from what looked to be old belay pins, and a large cage made from spills. The cage was for sleeping, Tupper informed her. The crow had free rein the rest of the time. Right now, he was happy on his new favorite perch. Tupper's shoulder.

Jocelyn plucked at her skirts. "And what am I to wear?" Her mind flashed back to the image of a certain red silk dress, with the fitted sleeves and the deep neckline dripping into a beaded bodice. She'd never even gotten a chance to try it on. Ric had been too eager to drape her in jewels, and now some ugly angry pirate was probably using her dress to wipe his nose--or something worse.

Tupper pointed to a small stack of clothes on the corner of the desk. "It was only a matter of time before we got you wearing breeches. I never figured it would take this long."

"Men's trousers?" Jocelyn plucked at the pile.

Tupper laughed. "You'll love them." She tossed her a belt. "'Course you're such a spit of a girl, they're bound to be too big. You'll need a way to keep 'em up."

Jocelyn held the breeches to her waist. The long legs trailed out over her feet. "Couldn't I just mend my skirts?"

Tupper tipped her head appraising, "Can't mend parts aren't there." She patted her shoulder. "Trust me. It'll make him crazy."

Jocelyn frowned. "I don't understand."

"Women in men's pants. Makes men a bit mad. It's like they all of a sudden remember we've got legs." She nudged her with her elbow, "and what lies between them."

Jocelyn's cheeks heated.

Tupper continued, "Now I don't know what happened between you and Ric, and I sure as hell don't want to…but…I have to hear…stars?"

Jocelyn smiled, unwilling to share the details of her night with Ric. It was as if she'd been given some delicious secret and wanted to keep it near to her heart. Although a part of her desperately needed to ask Tupper whether this feeling of constant wanting ever subsided, or if she'd ever lose the flutter in her belly every time she caught Ric looking in her direction. Would she be able to explain why her soon-to-be-trousered legs seemed to turn to honey? Or could she ask Tupper to help by giving a name to that place…the one lying between…the one Ric seemed intent on, touching and swirling…the one that drove her a bit mad.

A rush of pleasure shot through her thinking about it. "Aye, stars."

* * * *

Stepping onto the deck a short time later, Jocelyn was struck with the thought of the first time she'd set foot on these boards. She'd lost track of how many days had passed, but it seemed each time she emerged, another small part of who she'd been had somehow fallen away. Today was no exception.

Would the blessed Sister Bernadette have even recognized her? Jocelyn ran her hands down the odd-feeling pants covering her legs. Cropped hair, men's clothing, her sudden passion for rum, using the word "shite" in conversation, and a consuming desire to wrap her legs around a certain man's waist. No, Sister Bernadette wouldn't even know her name.

And yet, with all the change, to Jocelyn's mind, she was becoming more and more the woman she was always meant to be. As if her life had always been a size too small, and now, for the first time, she could finally breathe.

She caught sight of Ric climbing the rigging to help with setting a sail. She pressed a nervous hand to the flurry triggered in her belly at the mere look of him. How had she found such a beautiful man? And when exactly had she lost her heart to him?

Jocelyn knew the answer. It was odd. That morning felt as if it were a lifetime ago. Standing in the heat of the beating sun, shackled like a slave, when she had searched the crowd for a thread of hope. Any hope. There he was.

She was still looking for a thread of hope. But this time it wasn't to find him, more to keep him. There had to be some way she could convince him to change his mind about bringing her to Tortuga. She loved him. And he loved her. Didn't such truths mean they were fated to be together? There had to be a way.

One thing she had learned by fleeing to the island, the thought of never seeing him again had made her heartsick. And now, after the night they'd shared, how could she watch him sail away from her?

She couldn't. How was she going to convince him to let her stay? It wouldn't be easy. Who would imagine stealing a skiff, making her way to an island on her own, being overrun and shot at by yet more pirates, and escaping while stealing yet another ship would be simple by comparison?

Chapter 23

Climbing out of the rigging, Ric saw her. Or better yet, he saw her walking away from him. Gone were the torn and ragged skirts Jocelyn been wearing for the last few weeks. The tan britches she had on in their place covered more, but the fabric hugging close to her behind and slipping past each thigh and calf had him adjusting the sudden tightness in his own britches. By rights, it should be *his* trousers she be in.

Even with her hair shorter and wearing men's trousers there was no mistaking the fact she was a woman. There was something in the gentle sway of a woman's walk--correction, this woman's walk--it reminded him of holding those hips in his hands as he pushed into her.

Glancing around, he noticed he wasn't the only one enjoying the new landscape of the beautiful Jocelyn Beauchamp.

"Get back to work. All of you. Summer, keep a steady course due west, but keep her far enough from shore to skirt--" his voice broke the word in two, but he recovered with a cough. "those reefs."

Jocelyn stopped and bent over to roll the bottom hem of each pant leg. Ric stifled a groan as a rush of blood to his cock had him curling his hands into fists. "I-I'll be below."

Coming up behind Jocelyn, he hooked her elbow as she straightened. "I need to speak with you."

She smoothed the fabric over the front of her thighs, "Yes?"

"In private," he growled as he grasped her arm once more and came close to dragging her below.

"Ric?" She ran to keep up with him.

He didn't answer and he didn't stop until they were in her quarters. As soon as the door closed behind them, he pinned her against the rough wood and took advantage of her surprised gasp to ravage her mouth.

Lifting her arms over her head he grasped her wrists in one hand while he swept the other over her body and cupped the gentle curve of her ass pulling her against his erection.

"Good God, Jocelyn. What have you done to me?" He moved a line of kissed down her throat.

"Whatever it was, please tell me so I can do it again," she whimpered.

He smiled against her collarbone, then gathering control of himself, tipped his head back and huffed like some caged beast.

He released her wrists and guided her arms around his neck before lowering his forehead to hers. "I'm sorry. I can't seem to help myself around you."

She cupped his cheek and placed another small kiss upon his lips. "Do you hear me complaining?"

"You should be. Damn it, you should be treated gently, not manhandled against a wall. Or taken on a floor, in the dust. You should be laid in a featherbed with clean white sheets and a mountain of pillows." He brushed his hand across her breast and held its weight in the cup of his palm. "You deserve so much better."

Jocelyn ran her fingers inside the open neck of his shirt to caress his skin. "I don't care about any of those things. None of it matters as long as I'm with you."

Slipping a hand around her waist, he held her close for a long moment. She rested her cheek on his chest and wrapped her arms about him. He loved how she tucked under his chin as if she'd been made for him. If only he could stay this way forever. Stop time.

Or better yet, turn the clocks back. Erase months and years and find her before his life's path had been decided. He'd have chosen better. For her. He'd have changed his course and become something worthy of her. Something honorable.

"We should be anchoring tomorrow after daybreak," he whispered. "By the time the sun sets on another day, you'll be back where you belong."

"Feels like I'm where I belong right now." She held tight.

The words caught in his throat. He simply shook his head.

"We still have tonight?" Jocelyn pulled back enough to look into his eyes.

Ric fingered the dark curls at her temple before brushing them away from her cheek and tucking their softness behind her ear. "Aye, we still have tonight."

She studied the open neck of his shirt. Laying a hand there again. Over his heart. "I-I don't want to spend my last hours in this room. I'll have an endless future of doors with locks. I'd like to be on deck. Surrounded by the night sky. Sea air. You." She lifted her gaze. "Spend the night with me?"

"And wrap you in stars?"

Jocelyn closed her eyes and pulled in a shuddered breathe as she nodded. A single tear slipped beneath her eyelid and began a silvery path down her cheek.

He caught it with his thumb.

* * * *

Ric spent the rest of the afternoon finishing the entries in the ship's log and trying to put the rest out of his mind. Tomorrow with the raising of a sail and the wave of a quill, he'd return things to their rightful place and go back to being a simple forward gunner.

Jocelyn was leaving. Tupper was ready to take command of the *Scarlet Night* once again. They could get back to life before fate had thrown them into the middle of this storm.

Things wouldn't be as they were, of course. Too much had happened. Gavin and Neo and the rest of the crew were lost, but with a new crew and Tupper at the helm, at least they would go back to doing what they did best. Pirating. Laying siege to prey. Engaging in the fight. Battling for their lives through smoke and cannon fire and blood.

Ric set down his quill and poured himself more rum. He contemplated the way it sat in his mug for a long moment before drinking. An odd feeling washed over him.

At one time, the thought of battling and pirating put a fire in his belly and filled him with a rush of reckless danger. It was exhilarating. Manning his gun, smelling the hot oiled steel of the cannon barrel, watching the flame of the quick match drop into the fuse hole, and feeling the power of each blast rock through his body. Seeing that ball hit its mark and explode the target. Turning wood into slivers. Twisting iron like a screw. It's what drove him. Excited him. It's who he was, and he was one of the best.

But now…the idea of it didn't bring the same thrill. Maybe the haunting images of the earthquake's aftermath were taking their toll. Perhaps the responsibility of being captain was too great. Or it could be deep down he realized he could never go back to how things once were.

He couldn't rush through life with the same naïve, carefree attitude. He wasn't immortal as he'd always believed. Defying death took on a new meaning. It wasn't only him anymore. Jocelyn was part of him now whether she was in his arms, or on the opposite side of the ocean. Or more correctly, he was part of her.

No matter where he went or what he did, she would still hold his heart. The idea brought with it brilliant joy and cavernous, crushing sorrow.

Damn it. The day was almost here, and he still couldn't think past raising the sail on the sloop. The idea of saying good-bye to her. Walking away without looking back. There was a chance he wouldn't survive.

Ric emptied his mug, raised the light in the lamp to finish the logs.

"Still at it?" Hornbach came into the galley rolling a barrel of what appeared to be salted meat.

"Aye." Ric rubbed at his eyes. "Did you manage to gather what I asked for?"

"Ye don't ask for much now, do ya?" he grumbled. "fresh bread, cheese. Surprised ye dinna ask me to bake ye a cake."

"I'll remember a cake for next time," Ric countered. "And the blankets and lanterns?"

"Aye, it's all out there." Hornbach flipped a hand.

"Good, and you've passed the word along to the rest?"

Hornbach rolled his eyes. "Aye, we're all te leave ye to yer tea party."

Ric didn't care for the man making light. "I don't want anyone on deck tonight. You told them?"

"Aye." He threw his hands up and gave Ric an impatient look, "Why all the fuss? Ye'd think ye ne're fucked a bloody chit bef--"

Ric was out of his chair and had his pistol pointed in Hornbach's face before the man could finish his sentence. Ric cocked the hammer. "If you ever talk about her like that again, it will be the last thing to cross your lips."

"Easy, easy!" Hornbach pushed the muzzle of the gun away from his nose. "Ye ken, there be a time when ye could take a blasted joke."

"Does it look like I'm joking? Shut your hole and get back to work." Ric shoved his pistol back into his baldric

Hornbach snorted and lumbered away. "Be glad when ye're done captainin'. Ye been a lot more fun 'fore ye started walkin' round here wit that stick up yer arse."

Ric snapped. "I thought I told you to shut up."

Hornbach flipped him a one-fingered salute with both hands. "Aye, aye, Capt'n."

* * * *

Not long after eight bells, the sun relinquished the sky to the moon. Ric stood in the bow and waited for her.

"I'm going to miss this view."

Ric turned at the sound of her voice and drank in the sight of her profile in the fading light. "As am I."

Jocelyn gave him a coy smile and pointed toward the horizon. "I was talking about out there."

"I wasn't." He took her hand. "Come with me, I have a surprise for you."

Ric led her down the length of the ship and up the stairway to the quarterdeck and past the large oak wheel.

"Ric…" Jocelyn gave a surprised sigh.

At the back rail of the ship, he'd set them a small oasis. A few lanterns scattered the light into a darkened corner where several bottles of the wine they'd scored in stealing the sloop awaited them along with some food, the last of the fresh fruit, bread, and cheese. He'd used more than a dozen blankets to construct a comfortable area for them to relax.

"You wanted to sleep out here. I thought you should have something a bit more comfortable than a coil of rope to rest on."

Jocelyn held a hand over her heart. "I-I don't know what to say."

Ric gathered her in his arms. "Say nothing. Just kiss me."

She threw her hands around his neck and lifted onto her tiptoes to bring her lips to his. Ric took full advantage of the stretch of her body to slip a hand down the back waistband of her trousers.

When his fingers cupped the roundness of her behind, she pulled away and looked past him. "Someone will see us."

"Not if they don't want to be keelhauled come morning." He smiled. "I gave orders for everyone to stay below deck tonight."

She pushed her fingertips into his hair. "So we're alone?"

"Just us and the moon." Ric jerked his chin toward the crescent rising off the bow.

Jocelyn tilted her head back. "And the stars, don't forget the stars."

Ric kissed her throat. "After you explained your conversation with Tupper, I'll never look at stars the same way ever again."

Chapter 24

The sun rose through an apricot sky to begin another day. They hadn't slept. As if neither had wanted to waste even a moment of their last night together on something as frivolous as sleep.

They lay still, wrapped in each other's arms. Jocelyn with her head on Ric's chest, listened to the cadence of his heart. She knew he didn't sleep as his thumb continued to make lazy sweeps across the back of her hand, and every so often, he would kiss the top of her head.

Last night had been magical. The food, the wine. They had made love and wrapped themselves in the night's sky. Choosing denial, they didn't talk about tomorrow...or was it now today.

"Seems the sun refused my request." Ric murmured into her hair. "I'd hoped last night would have lasted forever."

"It can." Jocelyn rose on one elbow and stroked his chest. "All you have to do is turn the *Scarlet Night* around. Forget promises, forget my father and Tortuga, forget everything else except being together."

Ric lifted her hand and kissed the backs of her fingers before gathering their clothes and starting to dress. "I can't do that."

Jocelyn clutched her clothes to her chest. "Why not?"

Ric pulled his shirt over his head. "I love you too much."

"If you love me, then you should want to be with me." Fear and desperation mixed with anger and impatience. Why wouldn't he listen? This was simple. She loved him, he loved her. Didn't that mean a lifetime together?

He swept his arm. "Of course I want to be with you. Don't you realize how impossible it would be? This isn't the life you should have. Battling every day to survive."

Jocelyn stood and wrapped a blanket around her to cover her nakedness. "Then come away with me. We can take the sloop, sail far away from here, and make our own way," she pleaded.

"Our own way to what? I can't give you the life you deserve. Pirating is all I know. I have nothing else. I am nothing else."

"You're everything to me." She clutched at his shirt. "You keep telling me how hard it is to survive. Don't you see, if you put me back into my father's stifling world, I won't want to survive."

He held tight to her arms and looked deep into her eyes. "You say that now, but in time, you'll come to thank me."

"No." Jocelyn held his gaze. Tears choked her and distorted her vision. "In time, I'll come to hate you."

The muscle in his jaw tensed. "I can live with you hating me, as long as you promise to hate me for a long, long time."

"I promise, I'll hate you until the day I die." A sob caught her, "But, I'll still love you forever."

* * * *

Ric left Jocelyn on the quarterdeck. The weight of his heart pushed the air from his lungs. There would be no changing course. The decision had been set in stone that first day. Regardless of what had transpired between them, despite their feelings for one another. There was no choice in this. If there had been, God help him, he would have found it.

Below, he gave the order to raise the anchor, set sail, and travel another hour up the coast. There was a protective cove there, which was a short distance from Port de Prix. The *Scarlet Night* would be safe, and from there he and Jocelyn could navigate the small sloop directly into Tortuga harbor.

The square sails of the *Night* snapped as they rose and caught the wind. She leapt over the waves. Ric had always marveled at the speed and grace of this magnificent ship. Today, her speed was more of a curse.

Gathering the ship's log and the charts, he headed down to Tupper's quarters. It was time to return them to their rightful owner.

This morning Tupper was plaiting her hair while Bump added a shine to her boots. Leviticus sat near the boy and cawed at him loudly. Bump heard none of it, and only paid the slightest bit of attention to the jabbering bird when it refused to be ignored and plucked at his shirtsleeve with its wide, dark beak.

"You've got us off to an early start." Tupper filled a mug from a barrel of weak ale.

Ric raised one shoulder. "No point delaying the inevitable."

She moved the bird away from Bump and lifted him to his perch, quieting his squawking with some bits of bread. Tupper glanced over her shoulder. "How's Jocelyn?"

"She's hating me." Ric ran a hand through his hair. He still didn't have any idea how he could make the situation any clearer to Jocelyn. She had to see reason.

Tupper gave a slow shake of her head. "Hate isn't so far from love, you know."

Ric met her gaze. "Her loving me isn't in question."

Tupper went back to tending the bird. "She's stronger than she imagines. Shown some guts. And she knows her own mind. She's told me how she feels about you. It'll be tough and she might not think so now, but she'll get by this."

"Only hope I will," Ric mumbled as he dropped the items in his arms on Tupper's desk. "Before I head out, I wanted to return these."

Tupper came to stand beside him. "Won't you need them when you get back?"

"Not anymore. The captain holds the log," Ric shot her a glance and nodded. "and you're more than ready to take over."

Tupper lifted the logbook and ran her fingertips over the tooled leather cover. "I'm not sure I am."

"The *Scarlet Night* is yours. It's always been. Hell, I've just been keeping her deck side up for you. Gavin would have wanted you to take his place. The rest of the men agreed to making you captain the first night. We wanted to give you some time, but there's no reason why you can't take the reins back today."

Ric rolled out one of the charts and pointed to a spot on the map. "This is where we'll be anchoring. It's a secluded mooring, tucked away. You'll all be safe there. I want you to give me twelve hours. If things go according to plan, I'll be back in little more than six. But twelve will still give you daylight to negotiate the reefs and make it into the Windward Passage before dark sets in. Even if something goes wrong, it still gives you a head start. Once the *Scarlet's* in the passage, there'll be no catching her.

"I wouldn't go much farther without signing on more men," Ric continued. "You should be able to secure enough crew here or here." He indicated a few areas on the map known for strong pirate activity. "Then we're back in business."

Ric left Tupper to look over the charts while he said good-bye to Bump. Over the last few weeks, the boy had stepped up like the rest, taking on more and more responsibilities. Doing what needed to be done before anyone could ask. Every manner of things from running sail, to packing powder, and tarring rigging. He'd come through when they needed him most.

Losing Quinn had been a crippling blow for the boy. There'd been times when Bump had vanished to wherever it was he went. Ric figured he'd needed to grieve in peace. The first few days after the earthquake, he'd go missing for hours at a time. But gradually, he spent more time with the rest of the crew. He kept watch on Tupper. Bump was turning into a good man to have around.

Ric used the few words he knew using his hands to tell Bump how much he appreciated his help.

"We wait twenty-four." Tupper announce behind him.

He joined her and spanned the distance between where the *Scarlet Night* would be sitting and Tortuga with a narrow spread of his fingers. "It's too dangerous. You'll practically be sitting in Beauchamp's back pocket. If you're spotted, you're dead."

Tupper paused to light her pipe. She blew a cloud of smoke over his head. "Twenty-four and not a second less. If I'm captain, I'm making the decision. Besides, you'll be back in six, right? So call it insurance. Make sure you get your arse back on this ship. You're the best damn gunner we've got, and there's no way I'm leaving you behind."

Ric planted his hands on his hips. "You will if you have to."

Tupper mirrored his stance and angled her head. "Don't make me do something I'll regret."

"Aye, aye, Captain Quinn."

* * * *

Tupper and Ric joined the rest on deck and with lowering sails and skillful maneuvering, they threaded their way between a narrow jut of land and a barrier reef to slide the *Scarlet Night* into her hiding spot.

When Ric announced the transfer of power, and Tupper issued the order to drop anchor, the men cheered. She was back.

The others wasted no time in extending the boarding ladder across to the tethered *Devil's Pearl* before bidding their farewells to Jocelyn then doing what needed to be done to secure the *Night.*

Jocelyn approached Tupper. "I suppose this is it."

"It is indeed."

"I realize given who I am, and your history against my name, we shouldn't have been anything but enemies. But you've never held the sins of my father against me. You've treated me kindly. Been nothing but a friend and a confidant." Jocelyn reached out a hand to clasp Tupper's "I'll never forget you."

"And you could have held what I did to your father against me, and taken advantage of our crew at its weakest. You were sweet and helped many of us through the worst of days. For that, we'll not soon forget you either."

Jocelyn embraced her. "Someday I want to be as strong as you."

Tupper thumped her on the back. "You're already stronger than you think."

"I don't suppose we'll see each other again," Jocelyn took a step back and continued.

Tupper shrugged. "You can't tell. I rarely forget a favor, or a debt. And you do owe me a skiff."

Jocelyn smiled. "Ric will bring back the sloop. You're free to trade it."

"God's speed, Jocelyn." Tupper gave Jocelyn's shoulder another pat.

Jocelyn covered her hand with her own and replied in a small voice. "Calm seas…Alice."

Ric cleared his throat, "It's time we were away."

The two women separated, and Ric offered a hand to Jocelyn to help her over the boarding ladder. She refused and crossed without assistance.

From the deck of the *Devil's Pearl*, Jocelyn waved back at Tupper while Ric hoisted the sail. "Good bye, *Scarlet Night.*"

Tupper called down, "Be sure to give your father our regards."

Jocelyn shook her head. "Not until you are safely half a world away."

Chapter 25

With the sail set, the *Devil's Pearl* sprinted through the water. Steep in the hull, she cut through the water like a blade. The rigging began to sing. To make the sloop ride high and fast, it had been stripped of all but one gun. And that was a fixed stern chaser--a four pounder positioned in the tail to discourage anyone who decided to pursue them.

"Won't be long at this speed." Ric called forward. "The closer we get to Port de Prix, the more ship traffic we'll encounter. Being without any flag to mark our country may not invite attack, but it sure as hell is going to draw some attention."

Silence greeted him from the bow. Jocelyn hadn't spoken since they'd boarded. She'd found a place to settle in behind the long bowsprit and all he'd seen of her was the back of her head with her dark hair lifting off the sweep of her delicious neck.

She was upset. He understood. This wasn't a day basking on the beach for him either. Last night, tasting her delicious neck, he'd been ready to cast everything aside and ask her to run away with him. Lucky for Jocelyn, his sanity returned.

He had no reason to feel guilty, damn it. Let her be angry. He'd explained things until he was blue. He'd not say another word about it. If she chose to hate him, then it was her choice. At least she had one.

"Is it your plan to annoy me by not speaking? Because, it won't work. I'll enjoy the peace and quiet," he insisted feeling the slow burn of impatience.

Nothing.

He gripped the tiller until his knuckles paled. "Do you know how pigheaded you're being?"

She had the audacity to notch her chin.

They sailed on in silence for a time before Ric couldn't stand it anymore. He secured the rudder and moved toward the bow.

Standing over her, he planted his hands on his hips. "So this is how we're to spend our last moments together? Aren't you going to rail at me? Try and change my mind?"

"Why should I waste my breath? You've made your decision."

He grabbed her arm and made her look at him. "At least tell me you understand?"

"I'm not an idiot. I understand." She jerked her arm away.

Ric threw his hands wide. "Then why won't you speak to me?"

"Because," She jerked in a shattered breath and looked away from him. "If I start talking, I'll tell you how I'm sitting here frightened I'll never see you again, and how devastated I will be. I'll tell you how unfair this is. If I were a man, I could fight and make my own way in this world and I wouldn't be left to the whims of my father." She turned back to look at him. "I'd be telling you that you've ruined me--not in the way you believe, but because I will never be able to be with another man and not think of you. I'll forever compare the color of his eyes to yours, the shape of his hands, the way he kisses me, touches me. I will forever judge him beside you."

She lifted tear-filled eyes to his. "I'd be telling you I selfishly hope and pray that I carry your child in my womb, so I'll have a part of you to love for the rest of my days. Because, I will love you whether or not I ever lay eyes upon you again, *Henri* Robbins." Dropping her chin she turned away from him again. "You're a...a bloody thief. You've stolen my heart and robbed me of my soul and I will never be the same after today."

Ric dropped to one knee beside her and stroked her hair. Leaning forward, he whispered, "If I've stolen your heart it was only so you could carry mine. Don't you know how much this kills me as well? You've ruined me as well. I've only loved one woman before you. When I was no more than a lad. Her name was Nell. A mad man took her life. When she died, I thought I would never love again.

"But then you dropped into my life, and it was fate reminding me who was the true captain of my future's course. I fought against loving you, knowing how much it would hurt when I said good-bye to you, because that was the only certainty in weeks of uncertainty. Today was decided the moment we met. I never guessed I'd come to love you this much"

He moved closer gathering her in his arms, making her face him, and laying a hand upon her belly. "How selfish is it for me to hope you might carry my child, as well? I pray it would be a son, and he would grow into a fine man and protect you where I couldn't." Ric lowered his forehead to hers. "But carrying my bastard? Talk about ruining your life. What would become of you then?"

Jocelyn gave a sob and Ric crushed her to him. She buried her face against his chest. "I don't want to leave you."

Ric held her while she cried. His own throat tightening at the raw emotion of losing her. "You're so strong and beautiful. Don't you see what a life you'll have? Your father will have picked a successful man to be your husband. You'll live in a grand house, with room after room and gardens and servants to see to your every need."

He lifted her chin and continued, "And a bed. A dozen beds. Two dozen beds. You can look your husband in the eye and swear to him in all honesty that you've never been bedded by another man."

Despite her upset, she smiled. "I swear to you, you're the only man I'll ever make love to on the floor of a cave, draped in jewels."

Ric ran a thumb under her eye to wipe away the wetness there. "Aye, that is a promise I expect you to keep." He kissed her. "That reminds me, I have another surprise for you."

He rose and retrieved the bundle he'd stashed away inside a rope coil. "I was sorry I only wanted to cover you in gems and gold. You never got a chance to try this on." Ric unwrapped the oilskin and shook out a silk gown the color of claret.

"Ric…" Jocelyn plucked at the crumpled skirts. "You took the dress? Of all the treasure to choose from… You risked your life."

"Well…" He lifted a fat leather pouch stuffed with gold coin from within the dress's bodice and shrugged a shoulder. "I am a pirate."

Jocelyn took the gown from his hands and held it to her chest. "I can't believe you did this. It's even more beautiful than I remembered."

"It was the look on your face when you first saw it. I wanted you to have it."

She held it up in front of her before laying it down gently and tugging at the cuff of her sleeve. One bare shoulder pulled from the wide neck of her shirt. Was she going to try it on right here? Right now? Ric wasn't sure he wanted another perfect image of her to haunt all his nights to come.

An explosion off their starboard side had Ric throwing himself at Jocelyn, knocking her to the decking, and covering her body with his.

The shot across their bow came out of nowhere. He looked into her panicked face. "Are you all right?"

She nodded. "Who?"

Ric raised his head. "Shit." A ship powered toward them. He'd been so blind to everything but Jocelyn he'd let them sail right into the hands of--

"Stop by order of the French!" The demand carried across the water.

"Twenty guns." Ric muttered as he began lowering the square sail on the sloop to come about and slow to a crawl. He moved closer to Jocelyn. "Looks like you're going to get an escort."

The third-class brigantine towered over them before a boarding party of six dropped onto their deck. All poised to draw their weapons should the need arise.

Ric stood with his arms wide. Six to one were steeper odds than he wanted to chance. If he played it calm, there should be no reason to draw his pistol.

"I am Lieutenant Moreau." A tall, spindly man led the way. The brass buttons on his royal blue uniform caught the sunlight. Red breeches reached down into red stockings. He gave them a sharp nod of his head.

"Lieutenant." Ric held the man's gaze. "What can we do for you?"

He looked them both over and waved a finger toward the rear of the ship. "You fly no flag, *Monsieur. Mademoiselle.* You are English, no?"

"Aye." Ric scanned the men behind Moreau. This much French wool was making him itch.

"*Français aussi.*" Jocelyn added.

Moreau's eyebrow pushed up the brim of his hat. "English and French?"

Ric cocked his head. "Aye, couldn't decide which flag should fly on top."

The man's eyes narrowed at his sarcasm. "This is the *Devil's Pearl?*"

"Aye." A feeling of unease circled around Ric.

Moreau looked about. "This is your ship?"

"Aye." Unease was quick to become suspicion. He wished the Lieutenant would get to his point. Jocelyn had moved closer. He shot her a quick glance.

"What of your crew?" Moreau turned his attention back to them.

"Just, us," Ric confirmed. "Out for a sail."

"Is that so? In these dangerous waters?" Lieutenant Moreau scanned the decks once more shaking his head. "The *Devil's Pearl* is wanted for the theft of black powder and ten cases of the Admiral's favorite wine from Fort de Rocher not twenty hours ago."

"Really? Well, you'll be happy to know it wasn't us." Ric hooked an arm and tugged Jocelyn against his side. His body tensed like a spring. If they couldn't talk their way out of this, he wanted her close. His brain raced to formulate a plan.

Moreau's eyes narrowed again and he swept the open deck with his hand. "But this is your ship."

Ric shrugged as he struggled to keep his words light. "We traded a leaky skiff for it. The last owners seemed in a big hurry to get away. No doubt they are the thieves you're looking for."

The Lieutenant paused before giving them a small smile. "Then you will have no objection to my men searching your vessel?" He snapped his fingers without waiting for a response. "*Rechercher sur le navire.*" The three men behind him fanned out and began their investigation.

"Search away." Ric and Jocelyn exchanged quick glances. After the French had issued their warning shot, she'd been quick in bundling the gown and gold back in their oilskin and shoving the bundle back where he'd first hidden it. Ric couldn't see it in his peripheral vision. He didn't dare look in its direction. The gown he could explain, but the stolen gold…

Three of the men went into the large cargo hold below, and the other two started their search at the back of the ship.

"We are actually traveling to Tortuga." Ric offered, keeping his gaze purposefully on the Lieutenant.

"Is that so?" Moreau countered.

"Aye," Ric nodded. The French soldiers moved past them to begin searching the bow. Jocelyn stiffened beside him. "Aye," Ric rushed, hoping to distract them from finding the stolen gold. "We're to see Admiral Beauchamp. I have something he'll enjoy far better than his favorite wine. I have his dau--"

"Lieutenant?" The three men emerged from the hold carrying four bottles of wine.

Shit. "Damn, MacTavish," Ric grumbled under his breath. Man didn't believe in anyone traveling without something to wet their whistle. He's sure if the French looked further, they'd find a stash of rum as well.

Moreau gave the wine a cursory glance. "You're both under arrest." He waved a hand at his men before turning away. "Take them to the brig."

Two men wrenched Jocelyn from his hold. "Ric?"

"Stop. You can't arrest her." The two others held Ric while ridding him of his pistol and cutlass. "You didn't let me finish," Ric called after Moreau. "Beauchamp is going to be bloody furious when he hears you've arrested his daughter."

The Lieutenant stopped. Looking back over one shoulder, he laughed. "Nice try, Englishman, Admiral Beauchamp's daughter is dead."

They twisted Jocelyn's arms behind her back. She struggled to pull away. "Get your hands off me."

"Hey, let go of her you bastards!" Ric shoved one of his abductors aside. "She's his…" Turning he swung on the second man. "…daughter." His fist punctuated the statement, making contact with the man's jaw seconds before a blur to his right caught the butt of the first man's pistol before it made contact with his temple.

Chapter 26

Jocelyn screamed as Ric crumbled at the French soldier's feet after the man issued a viscous blow to Ric's head with the handle of his pistol.

"*Arreter!*" Stop! Don't hurt him. He's telling you the truth. I am Jocelyn Beauchamp and I am very much alive. I demand you bring me to my father."

Lieutenant Moreau snapped his fingers and had the man Ric punched dragged off the deck toward the waiting French ship. Another kneeled on Ric's spine while he bound his hands behind his back. "Throw both the prisoners into the brig."

Ric hadn't moved. Blood ran over his face. He could be dead. Jocelyn screeched after the Lieutenant. "You must listen to me." Behind her, iron bands snapped around her wrists.

Moreau's mouth formed a narrow slash. He gave her a hard stare before issuing the order to his men. "If you have to, gag her."

Jocelyn struggled to keep from falling while she was dragged with bruising hands over the rail of the sloop to the boarding ladder and up to the huge brigantine. On the French ship, the deck teamed with men. More than she could count--not as if she were given the chance. Without ceremony, she was dragged below into the dark belly of the ship, and thrown into a filthy, dank room.

Landing in a heap, she recoiled at the stench. Air fowl with the smells of rotten hay, bilge, tar and human excrement had her pulling at her restraints to cover her nose and mouth. She tried to bury her face into her shoulder, but the painful pull of her shackles stopped her.

Indescribable dampness seeped through the cloth of her breeches to chill and claw at her skin. She scrambled to her feet as Ric was tossed in alongside of her with an "Oof," before the iron door was slammed shut. The sound of the key scrapping in the lock distracted her briefly from the intensity of the darkness.

"Ric, oh my God." She tried to focus. Only the tiny barred window in the door let in any semblance of light. She fumbled toward Ric until she found him. With her hands behind her back, she couldn't lift him out of the muck or even feel to see if he was still alive.

She dropped down next to him, ignoring the filth. He'd landed on his side. With the horrifying thought of his face laying on God knows what, she pushed at him with her shoulder until she'd rolled his body over. Laying her ear to his chest, she almost wept to hear the strong beating of his heart.

"Ric, can you hear me?" When he didn't answer, panic crept up Jocelyn's spine. "Oh, please say something. Please." Her breathing started to race, only pulling more and more of the fetid air into her lungs. What was she going to do?

Then something from the depths of her worst nightmare rustled through the rancid hay and scampered across her ankle. Shrieking, she bolted to her feet. *Rats.* Dear God, there were rats down here.

"Get up, Ric. Please…oh Mother Mary, save us." She stomped her feet hoping it would keep the vermin away from them."

A low groan from the floor was the sweetest sound Jocelyn could ever remembering hearing. "Ric? Oh, please be okay." She kept marching as loudly as she could.

"Jocelyn?" he moaned.

"Yes, I'm here," she gasped. "Thank goodness."

"What are you doing?" he groaned.

"There are rats," she sobbed.

"Marching rats?" he mumbled as he struggled to sit.

Jocelyn didn't stop. "No, I'm keeping them at bay."

"Talking…works just as well." Ric managed to lean against one of the sidewalls of the small cell before groaning again. "Bloody hell, bastard nearly cleaved my skull in two."

Jocelyn moved to sit next to him. "You went down like a sack."

"Did I at least knock out the other guy?" He grumbled.

She pressed close to his side and wished she could hold him. "I won't be surprised if he doesn't wake until next week."

He looked her over. "Did they hurt you?" She doubted he could see any more in the dark than she could.

Jocelyn tipped her head to rest on his shoulder. "Not as much as they hurt you."

"Damn it. MacTavish stowing that bloody wine really put my neck in a noose." He shifted to sit straighter. "Wait 'til Beauchamp finds out they shackled his daughter. Moreau will be on barnacle inspection from here on out."

"He wouldn't listen. I tried telling him again, but he refused to hear me." A worried thought kept circling Jocelyn's mind. "What if they don't take me to see my father?"

Ric snorted then winced. "Oh, you'll be seeing your father."

"How can you be so sure?" She didn't dare hope.

Ric leaned his head back against the wall and closed his eyes. "He'll have to read the charges against us, before he orders us hung."

Jocelyn bumped him with her shoulder. "Saying such things is not funny."

"It wasn't meant to be." He met her gaze in the gloom. "How long has it been since you've seen him? Will he recognize you?"

"It's been a few years, but in filthy men's clothing, with wild, cropped hair, sporting shackles? It may take him a moment. If he can get over the fact I'm not dead."

"He must have received word the ship transporting you from France was captured and you were taken to Port Royal. By now, he's heard reports of the earthquake. No wonder he assumes you're dead."

Jocelyn tried to imagine how her father would have reacted to hearing such news. Would he have suffered? Agonized at the thought of her meeting such a horrific end? Wept for her? Somehow doubting it seemed unkind to him. He was her father after all. While she had lived a life accepting his distance, surely there were feelings there. He was a man not a stone.

Ric continued. "If he can't see his beautiful long-haired daughter standing before him in the finest abbey garb, is there something you can say to him, some bit of private information only you and he would know?"

Jocelyn drew her brows together. "I'd need to think."

"Don't think on it too long." Ric let out a long breath.

"I have to believe it will all be fine. I won't need to convince him. And once he realizes I didn't die in Port Royal, he'll be so overjoyed, we'll be released."

Ric snorted again. "Not if he learns who I am, and that you've been aboard the *Scarlet Night* this whole time."

In the dim light she could see the swelling of Ric's temple. It was already starting to discolor. She wished her hands were free. Leaning over, she kissed the smooth skin above. "I realize my father can be a tyrant. He has always led with an iron fist. With his men and his daughter. But I believe him to be a fair man, as well. Once I tell him it was you who saved me, it won't matter what your name, or which ship I happened to traveled on. He'll be so grateful, he won't care."

"Hope you're right. In my dealings with the man, 'fair' was never how I'd describe him." Ric closed his eyes again.

"I am right, wait and see." Jocelyn didn't know who she was trying to convince more. "Father will be so happy to see me he'll insist you keep the damn wine."

"And maybe he'll be so filled with gratitude he proclaims me the next King of France." Ric scoffed. "Offers me my own fleet of warships."

"And the hand of his only daughter?" Jocelyn suggested with a small sigh. Ric kissed her hair. "Aye, we shall wait and see"

It wasn't to be a lengthy wait. Before too long, the ship slowed. The water rushing past the hull and the creak of wet wood quieted. Jocelyn's jump of nerves made her tremble. She dropped her head to Ric's shoulder.

"We're entering Tortuga harbor." Ric confirmed. "It's shaped like a tight purse. Narrow passage into a small ladle of water, perfect for defending from the fort's guns above. None come in or out without notice."

"I wish I could see."

"Fort de Rocher sits high off the shore. You'll see it soon enough. Two star points on each corner face the sea." Ric shifted to look at her. "I need you to listen to me, Jocelyn. I'm not sure I'll get another chance to speak with you."

"Don't say such things."

"They'll separate us when we dock, and I don't know how long we will wait to be brought before the Admiral or even if we'll be taken there together."

"How will I know what happens to you?"

"You won't. That's what I'm trying to tell you. What happens to me doesn't matter. As soon as you get the chance, reunite with your father. It was the plan all along."

"It wasn't the plan for you. How will you get back to the *Scarlet Night*? What if my father's men won't release you? Tupper will sail off without you."

"My being captured always a chance, one I made willingly. But you can't worry about what's out of our control."

"Do you suppose I can stop loving you, as well?"

"Jocelyn…"

"Do not *Jocelyn* me. I will not cease until I know you are away. Watching you leave will be hard enough. You cannot ask me to turn my back on you. Not know your fate. I won't do it."

"You may not have a choice. "The two were jostled as the ship's anchor was dropped and took hold. "We're here. They'll be coming for us soon. God, I wish I could hold you."

Jocelyn leaned in to kiss him. "I'm not ready. Oh, Ric, I love you."

"No matter what happens to me, I will always love you. These last few weeks...I'll never forget, not a second of it."

"Don't you dare say, good bye, not yet."

Ric's gaze jerked toward the door. Footsteps came closer. Turning back, he crushed his mouth to hers before the door crashed open and strong hands pulled her away from him.

"No!" She was hauled to her feet and shoved toward the door. The men hauling her away made crude remarks and jibes. "Ric." She twisted back for one more look.

"She's the Admiral's daughter, you bloody bastards." He shouted out as two more solders did their best to subdue him. "Joce--"

"Let me loose." She jerked at her jailors. "Don't hurt him. Ric!"

They didn't stop until they dragged her out into the daylight. Jocelyn winced at the brightness above deck. The ship they were on sat moored off shore as the docks were crowded with larger ships.

Just as Ric described, a large square stone fortress stood high and foreboding perched upon a great hill well away from the busy harbor as if it had been carved into the surrounding stone. Its front corners resembling arrows or star points. All the trees had been cleared on two sides giving it an unobstructed view of the harbor and surrounding area. There was only one road to the fort. Carts, mules, horses, soldiers, and townspeople crowded the roadway that wound up toward the forbidding gates. Sitting at the top of the hill, lording over the fort, stood a building balanced on the highest point. Gray and brooding over all it surveyed.

A shiver ran through Jocelyn as the sun dipped behind a cloud. She'd been anticipating this moment, stepping into her father's world and a future of his choosing. One cage to another. How appropriate that she was arriving in chains.

From the brigantine to a small transfer boat, to an open, horse-drawn cart, Jocelyn was dragged from one to the other toward her fate. She kept looking back over her shoulder hoping to see Ric, but there was no sign of him. Her wrists burned as did the muscles along her shoulders, but the pain paled in comparison to the ache in her heart. Please let him be all right. *Please, Mother Mary, keep him safe.*

Leading from the docks, a wide curving road arched higher and higher before cutting back past the first star point and traveling on to end at the second. The layout of the fort was genius. Like the harbor, it had one way in, one way out. Anyone foolish enough to attack would be forced past the guns and never make it to the gates. The surrounding terrain made any other entrance impossible.

Her battered heart sank as she looked up the high sheer walls of the fort. This cage would be the death of her.

Through a labyrinth of gates making up the entry, they finally reached the inner courtyard. There had to be a hundred smartly uniformed men inside. The depth of Jocelyn's dread deepened with each clop of the horse pulling their cart.

They came to a stop in front of a row of low buildings. Jocelyn was jerked from the cart, dragged down a shaded corridor, and thrown into a stone cell.

"Please," she begged her captors. She had to try one more time. "You must believe me. Tell my father I'm here. I swear I am Jocelyn Angelique Beauchamp."

One of the men ignored her. The other only laughed, "And I am King Louis."

A door of thick iron bars slammed behind her. The sound of the lock snapping into place sending a shaft of fear and loathing straight through her chest.

Chapter 27

Jocelyn paced the small cell. In comparison to the brig aboard the ship, this cell was a palace. Clean. She could breathe. No rats. After the heat of the day, the stones were cool. Although, she imagined when the sun went down those same stones would turn icy.

But what did she care about heat or cold? Her mind raced with only one thought. What of Ric? Had they beaten him again? Was he nearby? Perhaps they were keeping them separate because she was a woman. She hadn't seen or heard anyone or anything since they dropped her here. She couldn't even tell if there were other prisoners.

Jocelyn kept pacing. It was the only thing keeping her sanity. If she stopped long enough to think, she'd surely lose the tenuous grip she had on her mind. Her arms and shoulders screamed at being twisted behind her, and the sharp burn of her wrists each time she tried shifting to ease that ache made her eyes sting with unshed tears. The clank of the chain tapped at her spine with each step. Utter panic lay beneath the surface.

After what seemed hours, they came for her again. Two different soldiers stood behind the man unlocking the door. Jocelyn pushed back against the far wall as fear welled in her again.

"Where are you taking me?" She questioned the men in French.

The two flanked her and ushered her out. "You don't get to ask the questions," answered one. His fingers bit into her arm.

"You're to keep your mouth shut," warned the second with a cold sneer. "Or we shall shut it for you."

With a soldier in front and one behind, she followed them through what felt like miles of corridors until they reached an ornately carved door.

The room they entered was opulent in scale and design. Thick carpeting covered the stone floor, velvet covered cushions sat on rich wood chairs. Gilded framed portraits hung on the walls. She could smell the beeswax of the candles.

A jumble of uniformed backs formed a sea of royal blue and red, and blocked the rest of her view--and one dearly familiar set of shoulders. *Ric!*

Jocelyn tried to move in closer, let him know she was here, but her captors held her back.

"Ric," she dared. At the glare of her guard, she flattened her lips together, but she'd succeeded. Ric turned sharply to find her. Jocelyn almost cried out at the sight of his battered face. Oh, God, what had they done to him?

He said not a word, but held her gaze before jerking his chin toward the back of the room. Jocelyn tried to see through the forest of uniforms. She caught a glimpse of Lieutenant Moreau standing off to one side. He was addressing someone in French.

"...and we've captured the *Devil's Pearl*, sir."

"Did you recover my wine from the bastards?"

A flush spread over Jocelyn at the sound of the other man's voice. She shoved forward. "*Père!*" At her cry, a hand clamped over her mouth. She struggled to break free, but her guard held her fast.

Moreau continued. "Naught but four bottles, Admiral. They must have sold the rest, along with the gunpowder."

"The gall of these pirates to think they can steal from our own docks and get away with it. I'll hang the lot of them."

"There were only two, sir. A man and a woman."

"I don't care if she's a woman. She pirates like a man, she'll die like a man."

"But, she claims to be your daughter."

"Impossible. You've been played for a fool, Lieutenant. My daughter is dead. I charge them with crimes against the crown. Hang them both."

Jocelyn squirmed against the guard's hold. Her words trapped by his hand. He only tightened his grip.

Moreau saluted. "I'll see to it at once, Admiral."

She bit into the flesh of the man's hand covering her mouth before stomping with all her might on his toes. He yelped and pulled his hand away long enough for her to cry out. "*Ce n'est pas impossible. Je suis Jocelyn!*"

"Silence her," ordered Moreau.

Chaos erupted around her. Jocelyn dodged one set of hands only to be captured by another. "Father, please! It's me!" She shoved to one side at the same time Ric rammed the back of the soldier in front of him and hurled himself against another as if trying to clear a path for her.

Shouts and curses added to the melee. Jocelyn's sleeve tore from her shoulder. She caught the briefest glance of her father's shocked face before being pinned to the floor beneath two men.

"You incompetent fools. Get the prisoners out of here," screamed Moreau.

"Wait, you idiots." Admiral Beauchamp bellowed louder. "Get off her."

With the crushing weight lifted, Jocelyn was dragged to her feet. Before her stood her father resplendent in his uniform. The crisp blue of his coat trimmed heavy with gold braid was fitted with wide red cuffs and crowned with a neckcloth of brilliant white. Red breeches ended in high black boots trimmed in gold. He looked older than she remembered. Thinner. His face lined and weary. Pale beneath the whiteness of his wig, and against the harsh black straps of the patch he now wore across his eye. The sharp gaze from his remaining eye swept her from head to toe. She held her breath.

He shook his head as if in disbelief. "Jocelyn?"

"*Oui, Père.*" She sobbed.

He swept her into his arms. "Is it really you?" His hands soon discovered she was in restraints. "Why is my daughter in shackles? You brainless oafs, get these off her." When the men around him fumbled to find the proper keys, he snapped. "Damn it all, I'll do it myself." He pulled a ring of iron keys from his desk and came behind her to unlock her chains.

Jocelyn trembled with a mixture of fear and delight at seeing her father. There were many times she doubted this day would ever come.

"Were they wrong?" He fit the key into the lock at her wrist. "I was told you'd been captured and stolen away to Port Royal."

The first cuff released. Jocelyn let out another sob of relief and turned to face her father as he rid her of the other. He ran his hands over the raw skin of her wrists before holding her hands in his. The gesture tugged at her heart. "No, they weren't wrong. It is all true."

He stroked her cheek as if he needed to touch her to make sure his vision wasn't playing a cruel trick on him. "But the earthquake destroyed Port Royal? How did you survive?"

Jocelyn looked over her father's shoulder. His men were hauling Ric to his feet. "Him." Her gaze locked with Ric's. It was time for her to rescue him. "That man. He's saved me again and again. Protected me. He was bringing me here to you when your men seized our sloop."

Her father turned and shoved the keys he held toward the two soldiers holding Ric. "Remove his shackles as well, you incompetent fools." Only when Ric stood free did Jocelyn truly begin to believe their nightmare was over. When her father retrieved his keys, he snapped an order to his men to clear the room. "Leave us."

The door closed behind the last man as he returned to her. He ran his hands up her arms to caress her shoulders. Touched her cheek once more. "I cannot believe my eyes. My dear girl. Look at you." He lifted a lock of her hair. "If you didn't share your sainted mother's lovely face, I would not have recognized you."

She smiled at him through tear-filled eyes. "We worried about the same thing."

"We." Her father repeated the word with a slow breath before turning his attention back toward Ric. "*Monsieur*, it seems I am in your debt, and yet I don't even know who you are or how you came to rescue my daughter." He slipped his arm around Jocelyn's waist holding her to his side.

Ric stood tall and proud. Jocelyn noted the fresh bruises on his jaw. The bleeding at his temple had stopped, but dried blood stained his hair and had run into the collar of his shirt. He held his arm at an odd angle. She wanted to go to him. Nurse his wounds, hold him, but her father held her tight. There was something in his grip that caused her nerves to shudder. As if he were claiming her for himself. "I only know him as Ric," she lied. "Indeed we are in his debt, and I will fill you in on all the details, but we've detained him long enough, don't you think?"

"I asked the man a question, Jocelyn." Her father's voice dripped with disguised honey. Jocelyn captured Ric's gaze and gave the tiniest shake to her head. She feared Ric had been right all along. If her father learned who he truly was--

Ric held her gaze. "My name is Henry Robbins. To most, I'm known as Ric. Short for Ricochet."

"Ricochet Robbins?" Jocelyn's father released his hold on her. He moved behind his desk. He pulled the glass stopper from a bottle of brandy splashing some in a crystal goblet. "I know that name from somewhere." He lifted the glass and studied Ric over the rim before drinking. "The *Devil's Pear*l was not your ship." It wasn't a question.

"No sir." Ric shot her a glance.

Jocelyn stepped in front of the desk, putting herself between the two men, hoping to divert her father's attention. "What does it matter how I got here? Isn't the important thing that I am here alive and well and safe?"

Her father would not be easily distracted. He drained his glass and set it down. "I've remembered where I know you from, *Monsieur* Robbins."

"Actually, sir, it is Captain Robbins now. Of the *Sc--*"

"Ric, no." Jocelyn stopped him. His gaze locked with hers. Panic clutched at her heart. What was he doing? He was practically tying his own noose.

"Captain now, is it? You were a simple gunner the last time we welcomed you to Tortuga. Now you stand before me claiming to be the captain of the *Scarlet Night*? You are aware there is a hefty price on your head and a sizable reward for the capture of your ship."

"Yes, sir." The muscle in Ric's jaw pulsed. He still hadn't taken his eyes of her.

"Last time?" Jocelyn's head began to spin. Tears filled her eyes. "Why are you doing this?" She gripped the edge of the desk. "He'll kill you," she whispered.

Ric never broke her gaze. He placed his fist over his chest and made a small circle. One of Bump's signs. *I'm sorry.*

Her father opened the side drawer of his desk and pulled out a long barreled pistol, which he raised and pointed at Ric's chest. "Where is the *Scarlet Night*?"

"She is safely away."

Jocelyn raced around the end of the desk and tried to grab for the gun. "Father, what are you doing? Have you lost your mind? Haven't you been listening? You owe Ric a huge debt. You can't do this."

He never lowered the pistol as he pushed past Jocelyn. "That was before I learned you'd been duped into believing this man was anything more than a thieving, murdering pirate."

"You're wrong. You don't know what you're talking about. He--"

Ric stood fast and held his hands away from his body. "Your father is right, Jocelyn."

Her father pushed her behind him. "I'm sure you didn't return my daughter out of the goodness of your cold, dark heart. What do you want? Money? Mercy perhaps?"

"Neither."

"And neither is what you're going to get." Jocelyn's father never took his single gaze off Ric as he strode to the door. He opened it and ordered for his guards, "Take this man away."

"No. Stop." Jocelyn watched helplessly as the men took Ric away. She clutched at her father's arm. "Father, please, I'm begging you. Don't do this."

"Jocelyn," Her father snapped as he returned the pistol to his desk and poured himself another glass of brandy. "You're young, inexperienced in the ways of the world. You've been sheltered your entire life. You can't begin to understand. Do you know how lucky you are to have escaped that man unscathed?" He stopped and narrowed his eyes at her. "You are *unscathed*, no?"

Jocelyn started to tremble. If her father ever discovered that Ric was her lover, he'd shoot him himself. "That man...has done *nothing* but care for me since the moment we first met."

Seemingly satisfied with her answer, he dropped into his chair and ran a finger around the rim of his glass. "I wonder what he's after?" he mused. "Perhaps a few days of our *hospitalité* will loosen his tongue."

She slammed a fist onto his desk. "Are you deaf? I insist you release him. Now."

He rose to his feet. "Jocelyn, I am your father, and I am also the reigning commander in this territory. Ric Robbins is a confessed criminal. He's committed countless acts against the crown. I must uphold the law or be tried for treason myself."

When she started to object, he held up his hand to silence her. She remembered that silencing hand. It chafed her now as it had always done. A rush of fury struck her dumb.

"There now," He'd mistaken her silence for obedience. "We'll talk no more about him. You're in need of a bath and proper clothing. I cringe when I look at you in those breeches. Perhaps you can do something more appealing with your hair. I can't imagine what you've been forced to eat at the hands of those barbarians. I'll have my chef prepare you a feast." He sat at his desk again and pulled a sheet of parchment in front of him before he dipped his quill. "But first, I must send word to Vice Admiral Lesauvage."

Jocelyn's head was swimming. "Lesauvage?"

"*Oui*, Andre Lesauvage. Your fiancé."

Chapter 28

Her slippered feet fell silent on the thick carpeting in her father's library. Night had fallen, and each time she passed in front of the large spread of windows overlooking the inky harbor she'd catch her reflection in the glass. Corseted and powdered she barely recognized herself.

After her father had dismissed her, he'd had her escorted to what was called the Dovecote. The huge, formidable building perched high above the center of the fort. Her father's fort within a fort.

A set of stone steps carved into the rock cradling the building led to a flat area facing the sheer face of the cliff. A large iron bell signaled the lowering of a ladder to welcome her to her father's abode.

With every step, the slamming of yet another cage door echoed in Jocelyn's head. How would she ever get out of here and find Ric? She needed to get him away from here and back to the *Scarlet Night* before they sailed off, and she was running out of time.

Her father's men handed her off to a bevy of servants who stripped, bathed, perfumed, powdered, dressed, and left her to wait in the library for her father's return.

The only sounds were the methodic tick from the clock set high on the mantle and the rustle of her skirts as she measured the width of the room again and again and again.

Somewhere a door slammed. Moments later, her father swept into the room. At seeing her, he stopped and smiled. "*Magnifique.* Now you look like the daughter I remember. It's as if I'm looking at your mother. That deep shade of green was her favorite as well. Said it complimented her eyes." His hand cupped her cheek. "You have her eyes. She was the loveliest woman I'd ever seen until this moment. Wait until Lesauvage sees you. I told him you were a beauty, but I'm not sure he quite trusts the impartial words of a father. He's a good man though. Will make you a fine match. He is a bit older, but you'll never want for a thing. Wealthy, if not handsome. He's known a life of service to the crown."

Another cage door slammed in her mind. "Father, we need to talk."

"Can it wait, darling? Lesauvage will be here for dinner in less than an hour and I need to dress."

"No, it can't wait."

"May I, at least, pour myself a brandy?" He removed his stiff, tricorn hat with its smart cockade of blue, white, and red.

"I'll pour it for you." Jocelyn's hands shook with impatience as she poured her father's drink. Visions of showing him just how lovely she was, raced through her mind. Perhaps she should show him her new-found knowledge of knots and lash him to a chair before empting this entire bottle of brandy down his throat and demanding he tell her--She slammed the bottle down and pulled herself together.

She handed him his glass. "What happened to Ric Robbins? Where have you taken him?"

He took a long swallow before answering. "Captain Robbins is no longer your concern."

"You must tell me," she pushed.

"He's being held in a private cell where he'll not escape this time. After a few days, when he has told me where my men can find the *Scarlet Night*, he will hang for his crimes. I thought you understood that."

"You can't hang him," she cried, "What has he done, but return your daughter to you?"

"Jocelyn," he barked, "the man is a pirate. His list of crimes is longer than my leg. Members of the *Scarlet Night's* crew are the worst of the worst. " He rose, setting his empty glass aside, and gathered his hat. "By claiming to be their Captain, I have no choice but to take his life."

Jocelyn caught his sleeve. "You're wrong. The man is a hero. He saved my life. Does that mean nothing to you?"

Her father turned and gave her a sad look as if she were too dim to comprehend. "Of course, but there is more to this than gratitude."

"Indeed there is." She held her father's gaze. "I love him."

He laughed before patting her cheek. "Jocelyn...you can't know anything of love. You're a child. An innocent. You're grateful, nothing more." He had the gall to walk away from her.

"You're wrong," she addressed his back. "I'm no child, nor am I innocent." That had him turning about. "*I stole the Devil's Pearl* out from under the men who stole your precious wine," she confessed. "I fought a skirmish and helped sink a Dutch frigate. For the first time in my life, I felt as if I had a choice. I chose to learn and fight and become a crewmember of the *Scarlet Night*. If you hang Ric Robbins, you'll have to hang me as well."

"Did you sign your name--*my* name--to that blasted ship's Articles?"

"No, but--"

Relief washed over his face. "Then you were *not* a member of her crew." He waved her away as if he were swatting a fly. "I'm not listening to this rubbish. I need to dress for dinner."

She waited until he was halfway through the doorway. "Fine. I can't wait to meet Vice Admiral Lesauvage. I'm sure he'll be interested in hearing what I've done. Certainly he won't wish to marry me when he knows the truth."

Her father spun on her. "You'll do no such thing."

She notched her chin. "Then release Ric Robbins."

"Impossible," his shout echoed into the hallway.

Jocelyn crossed her arms over her chest. "Then once again, you leave me no choice."

Her father pushed back into the room. "You're still the stubborn girl I remember. I'd hoped the good sisters would have cured you of such pigheadedness." He jabbed a finger at her face. "*You* will do as you are told. I forbid you to ruin your future for the sake of that criminal." His face was florid.

Jocelyn cocked her head and stood her ground. "Is it my future your concerned with our your own? What deal have you arranged with Lesauvage?" Beyond the open door, a handful of servants had gathered.

"You'll lower your voice," he hissed.

"I will not," she only got louder.

He slammed the door. "I am still your father, and it is my job to make the decisions for your happiness."

"When has my happiness ever been considered? When have you ever acted like a true father? Shown me any hint of caring or love? I am nothing to you. An inconvenience. How many times have you come to see me? Sent me a note? A gift? You left me there and sailed off to live your life. What kind of a parent abandons their daughter?"

"I provided a safe place for you to grow up," he countered.

Jocelyn drew a shaky breath. "Safe, cold, colorless." She'd waited years to say these words, and now that she had, now that the anger had fallen away, they sounded like the sad whining of the child her father accused her of being.

"I did what I thought was the best for you."

"Again, best for me? Or for you?"

He closed the space between them and cupped her shoulders. "You were still a babe when your mother died. I was an ensign at sea. Sending you to the sisters at Sainte-Genevieve was the best option. What was I supposed to do with a child?"

She held his gaze. "Love her."

"I did," he insisted, holding her cheek, swiping at the tears on her cheeks she hadn't realized she'd shed. "I do."

"Then show me," she whispered. "Release Ric Robbins."

At the mention of Ric's name he released her as if he'd been scalded. "You ask too much." He crossed to pour himself more brandy.

Jocelyn followed. "I've never asked you for anything."

He turned to glare. "And yet when I ask for your loyalty to me, you choose that cutthroat murderer. Do you have any idea what I have suffered at the hands of the crew of the *Scarlet Night?*" His fingers curled into the strap holding the eye patch to his skull. "Would you like to see their handiwork?"

She flinched and pointed a finger toward the sea. "I know everything. The gibbets at the mouth of the harbor? Your handiwork? I know about the six men from their crew you tortured."

"They were barbarians. I treated them as such and left them to rot as a warning."

"And yet those barbarians rescued me--more than once. Fed me, clothed me, treated me with great kindness even after they knew my name was Beauchamp."

He shook his head at her. "You're a fool. You're a pawn in whatever plan they've hatched to get back at me. Don't you see?"

Jocelyn notched her chin again. "I'm asking you one last time. Where is Ric Robbins?"

"He's in hell."

Chapter 29

Three days. Ric's brain struggled to stay alert. Or had it been two? No, counting that first day on the sloop, it had been three days since he had water. Food he could survive without for weeks. Torturous weeks, but he'd known that kind of hunger before. However, water was another matter. Living on the sea, it was a lesson learned early. Without fresh water, ale, or mead to drink, you'd be dead in days.

He imagined a shallow pond filled with water…deep in a cave. The cool fresh rain running from the ceiling into the turquoise pool. Jocelyn in his arms. Her tender body pressed against his. Scooping her into his arms to lay her before the fire. Sipping the water off her skin. His body shook with the strength of his memory. Ric howled her name into the night like the caged beast he was.

The sun had set on yet another day. It brought with it both a blessing and a curse. In the cell known as *"Petit Enfer"* or "Little Hell," the heat of the day turned the box into an oven. Too short to stand, to narrow to lie down, through the daylight hours it felt as if he were being roasted alive.

But after the sun went down, it was a different kind of hell. The cold of the stone on which he sat leached that iciness into his bones. With his clothing soaked through with sweat from the day, the night's chill made his teeth chatter so hard, he was sure they'd crumble in his mouth.

The real hell beyond the heat and the cold, however, was the hours upon sleepless hours thinking of her. Jocelyn. Remembering each moment with her. Every word they'd spoken in love and frustration. Reliving the anguished look on her beautiful face when she realized her pleas to her father were useless. She couldn't save him. It tore at his heart. Not for him, but for her. She'd learned a hard lesson about what kind of man her father truly was. He only hoped the bastard wouldn't make her watch the hanging.

Ric scrubbed a hand over his neck and imagined the rope. The short fall, the quick stop. He supposed there were worst ways to die. At least Tupper and the *Scarlet Night* would get away. He owed them that. He may have only been a captain for a few weeks, but he would defend them with his dying breath if need be. There was some honor in that.

And there was a measure of relief in the thought of swinging at the end of a rope. Now he'd not have to lie in his cot at night and ache with missing Jocelyn. He wouldn't have to wonder where she was or if she were happy. Wouldn't have to know the pain of longing for her for years without ever having her. Shivering as the first chill of the evening settled upon him, he could only hope the man her father chose for her would treat her well. Maybe he would take her back to France and make sure she lived her life away from harm. In time she might even come to love him. Lie with him in his soft bed. Open her pale thighs to him. Take his seed. Give him the gift of children. Her belly growing round with each child.

The pain of imagining her with another man sliced clear through him. He curled into himself and moaned.

Ric said a quick prayer for no more water. Another day without and he'd be dead, and Beauchamp would be denied the pleasure of watching him sway in the wind.

* * * *

Hours later, Ric strained to hear past the chatter of his teeth. Someone was outside. "Thank God, you've come to hang me." His body shuddered. "I won't wait for the trap door to fall. Leave it open, I'll jump willingly."

The key scraped in the lock. When the door released, Ric's body tumbled out onto the hard ground. "Give me a minute, I'll help you tie the rope."

"Ric. Oh, thank God, I found you." Jocelyn dropped to her knees then gathered him to her and cried.

"Jocelyn? What are you doing here?" He had to be hallucinating. "You're supposed to be with him now…in France…" He tugged at the low neckline of her dress. "Where is the babe suckling at your breast?"

"Ric, help me. You're talking like a mad man. Please, we haven't much time. She pulled a wineskin from a bundle she carried. "Here, drink, Ric, please." She poured the wine over his lips until he grasped the skin and drank.

"I brought you bread and cheese as well, but we've no time for a lover's meal. It will be dawn soon. I have to get you away from here." She struggled with his weight as she tried to lift him to his feet.

Ric choked on the flood of rich wine he squeezed from the wineskin with both hands. For a moment, his stomach threatened to refuse it, but the alcohol was beginning to clear his head and take the chill from his bones.

"Jocelyn..."

"Yes, love, it's me. Can you stand?"

"I think so." When he tried, his knees buckled from days of misuse, but Jocelyn caught his arm and steadied him. He stared at her in the pale wash of moonlight. Perhaps he was still dreaming. Dressed in a stunning gown her bare shoulders fairly glowed in the light, with errant spirals of her hair framing her face, she was the most gorgeous creature he had ever seen. "You are so beautiful," he sighed.

"And you are so dead if you do not find your feet and start moving." She tugged at him.

"Where are we going?"

"Not we...you. You're leaving Tortuga. Tonight."

Perhaps he truly was mad. Or perhaps she was. There was only one way he knew to get off Tortuga, and that was feet first and only as far as a gibbet. "How do you suggest I leave?"

She tugged at him to follow her. "First I'm getting you off this rock and away from the fort. There are only so many places they could have moored the *Devil's Pearl*. You'll steal the damn boat for a second time and slip out of the harbor before they discover you're missing. The *Scarlet Night*--"

"Is gone. Tupper's twenty-four hours were over forty-eight hours ago."

"Then you'll find her." When he wouldn't be tugged, Jocelyn got behind him and pushed.

He stumbled ahead. "It's not that simple."

"Then you'll lose yourself in Port de Paix until you can get away."

Ric stopped and halted her by grasping both her shoulders. "Even if we make it off the Dovecote, we'll never make it out of the fort."

Her chest rose and fell with each quick breath. "You'll die if you don't."

Ric cradled her cheek and whispered in the dark. "There are worse things."

Jocelyn's eyes went wide with fear before she gripped the front of his shirt in her two fists and shook him. "I will not watch them hang you, do you understand me? I've spent the past two days and nights searching for you. It was only by chance I heard some of the men laying bets on how long my bastard father would keep you in this horrible cell.

"I figured another day without water and he could save his rope."

She dropped her forehead onto his chest. "You don't have another day. He gave the order for you to be hung at noon unless you told him where the *Scarlet Night* was anchored."

He kissed the sweet softness of her hair. "I wouldn't tell him even if I knew."

Jocelyn raised her head, and ran trembling fingertips across his throat. "And you'll die a few inches taller." Her gaze held his. "For two days I've walked this blasted fort. I discovered another way out."

"And you believe I'll leave you after all that's happened?"

"It was always the plan," she insisted.

Ric gave a short laugh. "To hell with the plan."

Jocelyn shook her head. "No. If I go with you, he will hunt us down. No port would be safe for us. No sea wide enough. If it is just you, yes, he'll lose face, but the fierce crew of the *Scarlet Night* has already taken an eye, what's a bit more?"

He didn't laugh at her jest. "What about you?"

"I'll be the dutiful daughter and do as he wishes. I'll marry the man he has chosen for me, and in time, I'll become one of the richest women in France. Every day, I'll take a little bit more from him." She lifted one shoulder. "Not all pirates steal from a boat, you know."

Ric ran a finger over the bow of her breast. "How do I live knowing another man will have you?"

"Have you seen Vice Admiral Lesauvage?"

He dipped into the shadowed valley between her breasts and made her tremble. "No."

"I promise you, he will never have me." She kissed him then, as if sealing her pledge. "Come, we can't wait any longer."

Ric followed close behind her, trusting she knew the way, ducking into shadows, dodging the patrol. The ladder leading away from the Dovecote had already been lowered. "The guard is lazy bringing supplies up from the fort," Jocelyn explained. "He's lazy, but quick. We need to hurry."

At the base of the stone steps, she headed off to the right. Ric caught her skirt. "The gate is in the other direction," Ric hissed.

"We'll never make it out of the gate." She tugged at his hand. "I found another way."

Instead of fleeing from the depths of the fort, Jocelyn led them deeper into the maze of corridors and hallways. He strained to hear anything other than the sound of the blood rushing in his ears. Any moment he expected to hear the warning bell toll or turn a corner and run into the guard. While he didn't care about his own neck, if they caught Jocelyn, her father would have no option but to charge her with treason.

"On the far side, closest to the mangroves, it looks as if the outer wall took a hit, or the stones shifted. There are several loose rocks. We can get out there without raising an alarm and replace them without anyone knowing. If we stay to the wall at the point, we can get lost in the morning's traffic bringing the daily supplies to the fort." Jocelyn stopped. Her breath coming in short gasps.

"What is it?"

"I can't remember which way we go here. Let me think." She turned and looked back the way they came. "I think we may have come too far."

"Are we lost?"

"No." She pointed before dragging him into an alcove. "Shh."

Ric heard them, the guards, coming down the corridor. Their boot heels rapped on the stones. Jocelyn was holding her breath. Pressed close, he could feel her heart fluttering in her chest. He wished along with the wineskin, and food, Jocelyn had remembered to bring him a blasted weapon. If felt like he was standing naked on the deck of the *Night* waiting to have his arse shot off.

As the men passed, Jocelyn closed her eyes as if by not seeing them, they'd not see her. She waited only long enough for the sounds of boot heels to fade around the next corner before she pulled at him again. "This way, I'm certain."

Looking back over his shoulder, Ric followed close at her heels. "Bloody hell, woman. Where the hell are you taking us?"

"Not far now." Jocelyn rushed a few more yards down the shadowed hallway before stopping at a door. She pointed to a scratch by the floor. "This is it. See there? I marked it. The way out is through here."

They pushed into the darkened room and closed the door. "We made it..." Jocelyn panted. "I found these quarters after discovering the breach in the wall. I haven't seen anyone use these rooms. Perhaps they're waiting until they fix the wall." She raised the wick on the lantern hung next to the door.

"Bonjour, Jocelyn..."

Chapter 30

A wave of ice-cold panic crashed over her as she gasped, "*Père…*"

Her father stood on the far side of the room with a pistol in his hand. "A bit early for you to be scurrying about, don't you think?

"H-how could you have guessed?" She took two strides toward him. Her legs turned to liquid. Ric reached for her arm and pulled her back.

"You're a bright girl. I knew you'd end up here eventually." He used the pistol to indicate Ric. "With him."

Ric still held tight to her arm, but she managed to place her body between him and her father's gun. "You can't stop us. W-we'll fight you if we have to."

One corner of her father's mouth tipped in a smirk. He angled his head as if to see around her. "Did she bother to bring you a weapon when she delivered you from hell?" He directed his question to Ric.

With little effort, Ric moved her behind him as if he was the one to be the shield for them both. "No, sir, she did not."

Her father tsked. "Your second mistake, Jocelyn. The first was imagining I wouldn't notice all those long walks you've taken over the last two days and nights. You've hardly slept since your meeting with Lesauvage."

He laid his pistol on the table next to him. "I thought at first you were trying to escape, but then when you discovered this small chink in the armor of this fort and didn't leave, I guessed at the rest. I issued the order to have Captain Robbins hung to play your hand. Although, you had me worried, Jocelyn, I assumed you knew about my 'Little Hell.'"

"I only found out about it tonight after dinner."

He nodded. "Just in time. Speaking of which, I'll need you to stand against the wall there and be silent for a few moments. We're about to have company. I'd rather they didn't see you."

No sooner had he said it, there came a knock at the door. He waited until she and Ric were in place before he opened it.

"Good evening, sergeant. Is all well?"

Jocelyn could only see her father's back from where she stood. What the hell was he up to? She shot Ric a nervous glance. She didn't understand. If he was going to seize them, why didn't he do it?

"Admiral Beauchamp, I'm sorry to disturb you, sir. I believed this area to be clear. Thought I heard voices."

"No one here save me. Insomnia. I've gotten in the habit of coming here to catch up on my reading. Perhaps you heard an echo."

"Perhaps. Is there anything I can get for you, sir, before I continue my rounds? A brandy? Warm milk?"

"Nothing. Thank you."

"If you think of anything, I'll be making one more pass before my watch ends."

"Thank you, sergeant."

He closed the door. Looking at them, her father held a finger over his lips as he continued to listen at the door. "He's gone."

"What are you playing at?" Jocelyn hissed. "You could have turned us over to the guard. Sounded the alarm. Why didn't you? Is this yet another form of torture for you?"

"I am playing at nothing, Jocelyn. How do I explain this to you? I've been doing a lot of thinking since you dropped back into my life. You're not the only one having sleepless nights." He indicated the chairs along one wall. "Please sit." When they refused, he gave a small shrug and continued. "When I sent for you, I had this grand illusion of what life might be for us. We could be a family again, at least until the wedding. Because regardless of what you believe, Jocelyn, you are my child. My only daughter. In my heart, I truly do love you."

Jocelyn crossed her arms over her chest. He was saying the words she longed to hear her entire life and yet they didn't have the effect she'd always imagined? Perhaps because she didn't believe them. Was he toying with them like a cat tortures a mouse before it pounces?

Father continued. "You were right, however. I did abandon you, and not only because you were a child, and there was no way to care for you and be a soldier at the same time. It was too difficult seeing you. Even as young as you were, you reminded me of her. Lynnette. To look upon you and see your mother in your eyes was too painful." He rubbed a hand over his eyes. If he were lying, he was a master at it. God help her, Jocelyn started to believe him.

"I thought I was doing the best thing by keeping you at the abbey all those years, but in truth, it was cowardly. After your mother's death, I didn't want to remember. I did everything I could to block her from my mind. I poured myself into my work, my career. I stayed away from you thinking it would help me heal. I believed I was over the pain of her loss.

"When I got word that you'd been lost to me, I'm ashamed to admit I felt free. Free from the guilt of not being a proper father I've carried all these years."

Ric said nothing, but reached for her hand.

Her father threw his arms wide. "Then you appeared. A great blessing, and a great curse. Seeing you nearly split me in two. You are the very image of her. Exactly the way I remember her. Young and beautiful. Vibrant." He closed his eyes and held up a hand as if to wipe away her image from this mind. He hung his head. "I can't have you here. You can't possibly imagine how difficult it is. Death by a thousand cuts. I die a little each time I see you.

He turned away from her. "I thought Lesauvage was the perfect answer. He saved my life when we were both midshipmen. I owed him. He comes from wealth, power. I thought I could send you off again. It would be a good life for you. But the man is a vomitous toad. He confirmed that the other night. I can't force you into a lifetime with him." He shook his head.

"I loved your mother as she loved me--with all of her heart." He turned back to her. "We didn't have the perfect life, but I believe we had the perfect love. It created you after all."

Her father swept a hand toward Ric. "You love this man. I saw it the first day when you fought for him. Begged me for his life. I saw you look at him the exact same way I remember Lynnette looking at me. As if there were no other person in the room. As if you carried your heart in your eyes.

"It made me crazy. And to make it worse," he jabbed a finger at Ric, "he is my sworn enemy. I have battled with him and the bastards of the *Scarlet Night* from the first day I landed here." Anger raised his voice as he appraised Ric. The muscle in his jaw tightened as he seemed to struggle against it. He met her gaze and took a long breath. "But you love him. I know if I kill him, I kill any feelings you could ever have for me. I might as well hang you both."

Was that his plan? Jocelyn held tight to Ric's hand. "S-so where does that leave us?"

"You claim I've never gaven you a gift. You're right. So I'm giving you one now. I've decided to bestow upon you something I've never given you before. A choice." He pointed to a small bundle on the table. "Those are the clothes you were wearing when you arrived. You've discovered the weakness in this outer wall. The *Devil's Pearl* sits on the east side of the harbor. You have thirty minutes before the guard returns, and I sound the alarm."

Ric shook his head. "How do we know this isn't some trick to get us out into the harbor and have your guns blow us out of the water?"

"Why would I go to so much trouble? If I wanted to, I could shoot you right here."

Jocelyn was still trying to process what she was hearing. She crossed to the table. True to his word there were her breeches folded neatly atop her shirt and belt. She fingered the fabric before turning back to her father. "If I leave, you will be disgraced."

He held her gaze. "Not so. If you choose to don those clothes and leave with him, I will claim you were an impostor sent to infiltrate and destroy our hold here. My beloved daughter, Jocelyn Angelique Beauchamp died on June seventh in the earthquake that destroyed Port Royal, Jamaica."

"And if I decide to stay?"

Her father lifted one shoulder. "He'll hang, and you'll marry a toad."

He then turned toward Ric, picked his pistol off the table, and handed it to him. "The next time we cross paths, Captain Robbins, you will have a weapon, and be my enemy once more. There will be no leniency for you or the *Scarlet Night* after this moment."

Ric took the pistol and studied it before slipping it into the waistband of his breeches. "I understand."

"We live in dangerous worlds, you and I. Watch out for her the best you can."

"Aye, aye, Admiral."

Jocelyn's thoughts raced at what lay at her fingertips. A chance. Standing before her father, she realized he'd given her a choice, which truly was no choice at all.

"Time is fleeting, Jocelyn. What are you waiting for?"

She shook her head. "I'm trying to decide if I trust you."

"I've given you all my reasons. Neither one of us walks out of this room without risk, but there are no guards waiting to ambush you on the other side of the passage. I promise you."

"Why?"

Her father closed the distance between them and grasped her arms. "Foolish girl, I'm doing what you asked. I'm loving my daughter." He pulled her into his arms and embraced her. "I'm a bitter, hardened old fool who's only sorry it took me so long."

Jocelyn gasped as the truth of those words finally hit her. "I-I love you, too."

He stepped back and held her cheek. "Now go."

Without another word, her father left them. Jocelyn was quick to change.

Ric waited at the exit. "It'll be a squeeze. If I can move this stone, we should be able to get through. I'll leave first. Count to thirty. If you don't hear gunfire, follow me." He pushed at the rock with his foot.

Jocelyn grabbed his sleeve. "You believe he's lying?"

"No." He gave a grunt as he dropped to the floor and used both feet to push at the stubborn stone. "He's told the truth."

"How can you be sure?"

One final shove with his legs and the rock shifted. "The pistol was loaded."

* * * *

Light rain soaked through his shirt as he pressed back against the wall of the fort. Ric was under no illusions. Beauchamp hadn't opened the front gates and bid them *au revoir*. There was no guarantee they would ever make it to the harbor alive, let alone find the *Devil's Pearl*, sail through the narrow neck of the harbor, and flee unscathed.

One pistol. One shot. That's all he had. He'd faced those odds before.

Jocelyn's hand was warm in his. The rain was turning her hair into dark spirals that dipped over wide eyes. How was it whenever he looked into those eyes, he became invincible. He kissed the backs of her fingers, checked to make sure the path was clear, and slipped along the wall to their next hiding spot.

The timing of their moves between passes of the guards worked until they made their way to the furthest concealed point. Somehow, they had to make it to the road leading away from the fort and blend into the early morning foot traffic.

"We have to split up," he whispered. "We'll be less noticeable." Reaching down, he scooped a handful of mud and placed it in her hand. "Put some of this on your face and shirt."

"Where should I wait for you?"

"Do you think you can find the *Devil's Pearl?*"

She nodded. "It's moored. We'll have to swim."

"Don't take any chances, understand? I'm right behind you. Head down, don't look back." He kissed her. Mud and all she was still the most beautiful woman he'd ever seen. Now he had to get her off this damn island.

Chapter 31

Ric flopped over the rail and hit the deck of the *Devil's Pearl* like a hooked tuna. Reaching over he grabbed for Jocelyn and pulled her aboard. He pressed his back against the side of the ship while he examined the pistol. Between the rain and the swim, even with it held on top of his head, he'd bet his last gold piece the powder wasn't dry anymore.

"Are you okay?"

Jocelyn sat panting next to him. "You swim too fast."

"I thought we were in a hurry."

"Right. At least the rain has stopped. The sun will be rising soon." She pushed the dripping hair out of her face and pulled the clinging fabric of her top away from her breasts. "Well, Captain, we've made it this far, now what?"

"Now we get to sneak an entire ship out of a bottleneck harbor under the nose of your father's men."

"You make it sound as if it's a difficult thing to do."

He laughed. "Near impossible."

"We've beaten 'impossible' this far."

"We've been lucky." He peeked over the gunwales. "This is going to take some skill."

"We've already stolen this ship once, we're experts."

"Our best chance is to get lost in the crush of ships coming and going. If we can thread the *Pearl* between two, we might make it. I want you to raise the anchor while I set the sail. The winds in this bowl are tough to read, but the tide's heading out. At least that will work in our favor. The last thing we want to do is try to sail through here at full speed."

Jocelyn nodded. "Tell me what to do."

"Pray your father hasn't set the alarm in motion and when I tell you, I want you tucked down out of sight."

Ric raised the sail and eased it into the wind. He'd keep the *Pearl* quiet and close to the rim of the cove and wait for an opportunity to draft one of the larger ships moving out of the harbor. If he came in close enough, the guns mounted on shore wouldn't fire for fear of hitting one of their own, but there was always the risk of being fired upon by one of the French warships.

A huge forty-gun galleon lumbered at half sail into the sheltered cove. This was their chance. He'd wait until she was midway through the pass, and cut in close to slip by her.

He met Jocelyn's worried gaze before nodding and mouthing, "Now."

Manning the tiller, he lowered the sail and slowed the *Pearl* to a crawl.

Cannon fire erupted overhead. The galleon was close to their starboard and took a direct hit. Splintered wood and rigging rained into the harbor. More blasts sounded, this time from the high banks gating the harbor. The galleons rear guns returned fire.

In the chaos and smoke, Ric strained to see who was attacking. He looked toward the fort, but their huge cannons had yet to fire.

The galleon took another hit close to the water line, then another. Men shouted and scrambled over the decks. Their cannons returned a vicious blast.

Ric was too close. If the galleon went down it would take them down with it. Who the hell was firing? An answering shot clipped the top of the *Pearl's* mast. Rigging snapped and the yardarm pitched to one side.

Ahead the huge warship began to list to port. Whoever was firing had taken out their main mast and crippled the massive beast. Ric needed to get past them before the ship sank and blocked the entrance to the harbor completely.

The air split as the guns from the fort erupted on the hill. Alarm or not, they weren't firing at him. He cut the sloop hard to port. Its sail catching the smallest amount of wind, it scrapped through.

Rounding the high banks, he saw the ship that was attacking the harbor as another full round of cannon fire burst from her deck. Her red sails burned bright in the glare of the rising sun.

"Holy shit, it's the *Scarlet Night*."

"What? They were supposed to be days away." Jocelyn poked her head up to look as another blast rocketed over their heads. She covered her ears and screamed. "Are they trying to kill us?"

Ric shouted over the din. "I bloody well think they're trying to save us."

"They're not doing a very good job of it."

"They can't see us. They're too busy blocking the harbor so no one can give chase." Ric scrambled to bring the small sloop out of range. He searched the deck for an idea. He had to find a way to signal Tupper.

"Jocelyn, come back here and man the tiller," he called.

She rushed to the back of the ship and took hold. "What are you going to do?"

Before answering her, Ric had to make sure the French had only found the hidden wine aboard the *Devil's Pearl*. He reached his hand deep into the forward coil of rope. "You're not going to like it, but I can think of no better way."

Minutes later, Ric joined Jocelyn in the stern of the ship. "You're right, I don't like this at all," she grumbled.

He tossed her a sack of gold coins. "You can buy a thousand red dresses with that."

"But I wanted that one." Her eyes rose to the top of the broken mast where Ric had shoved the splintered wood through the bodice of her beautiful claret gown. Its skirts billowed out in the breeze like a great red flag. If Tupper didn't see the billowing skirts, she was blind.

"I didn't even get to try it on," she sighed.

"I liked you better in green." Ric shielded his eyes and watched for any returning signal from the *Scarlet Night*. He didn't have long to wait. "There. They lowered the black. They've seen us." He pulled Jocelyn into his arms and kissed her. "I'll never use the word impossible around you ever again."

"Remember that when I convince Tupper to let me sign on to her crew."

* * * *

The *Devil's Pearl* came alongside the *Scarlet Night*. A rope ladder dropped and soon Jocelyn and Ric stood in the exact spot they'd left days before. This time, however the decks were full of all manner of men. There had to be twenty new crewmen.

MacTavish, Summer, and White helped them aboard and slapped Ric on the shoulder then shook his hand, welcoming him back.

Tupper shouted the order as Leviticus flapped his wings wildly on her shoulder, "Set every inch of cloth we've got. Let's make her dance across those waves, boys. We're headed for the Windward Passage." She ran a hand over the crow's back to settle him before turning to them. "Good to have ye back."

"I thought we had an agreement." Ric planted his hands on his hips. "You were leaving in twenty-four hours whether I was back aboard or not."

Tupper scoffed at him. "Who's the Captain of this ship? I wasn't about to leave my best forward gunner hanging in a gibbet." She pointed the stem of her pipe at the small welcoming party. "We were set to come get you. Summer and White's been brushing up on their *parlez-vous's*. Then heard word they were gonna make you swing at noon. Had to step things up to save yer sorry arse. Put a cork in that bottle neck of a harbor and cleared them a path. If we hadn't seen your red, they'd be dragging you out of there now. How'd you manage to get away?"

Ric's gaze met and held Jocelyn's "Beauchamp had a change of heart."

"Didn't know he had one." Tupper raised an eyebrow.

"Evidently he did for at least thirty minutes." Ric replied before scanning the deck. Activity hummed as the ship began its leap through the waves. "Where did all these men come from?"

Tupper shrugged. "Here and there. Of course we lost half dozen when I told them we were planning an attack on Fort de Rocher. They thought it was bad enough fighting for a woman captain, but a crazy woman captain was more than they signed on for." She jerked her chin in Jocelyn's direction. "Didn't expect to see the lovely Jocelyn Beauchamp back aboard, however."

Jocelyn shook her head. "I'm glad to be back, but I'm afraid Jocelyn Beauchamp is dead."

Tupper's eyebrows pushed toward her hairline. "Is she now? Then who might you be?"

"You've a name for everyone else on this crew." Jocelyn swept a hand across the deck. "You'll have to come up with one for me."

Tupper folded her arms across her chest. "What makes you think I want another woman on my ship? I hear its bad luck."

"You've been pretty damn lucky today."

"I suppose." Tupper narrowed her gaze and headed back toward the galley.

Jocelyn followed at her heals. "Then how about taking a chance? I know my knots. And I can steal a sloop. Pretend I'm a man. You could call me Jo."

"*If* I was to sign ye on, I'd be taking the cost of a new skiff out of your share. I'll call you Beau."

"What about Jo Beau? I like the sound of that." Jocelyn missed a step. "Wait a minute...a *new* skiff? That leaky thing I took was hardly new, and I brought you back the bloody *Devil's Pearl*."

Tupper spun on her and pointed toward the sloop with her pipe. "She's missing the top of her mast."

Jocelyn gasped. "Whose fault is that?"

"I wasn't shooting at you." The two women squared off. Tupper lit her pipe and puffed a cloud over Jocelyn's head. "Get yourself some breakfast, then report to my quarters. If yer to be a member of this here crew, you'll sign the Articles before eight bells."

"Aye, Captain." When they entered the galley, she called out to MacTavish. "I'm done with knots, but I could use a pistol lesson or two."

Ric and Tupper watched her argue with the Scotsman about fitting her for a sword as well. "There's one more thing I need you to do for me before eight bells. Actually, make it two."

Tupper shot him a glance. "Haven't I done enough for ye today? I saved your bloody fool neck from that one-eyed French bastard."

Ric looked back at Jocelyn. He'd never wanted this life for her, but now that she was here, he was going to do it right. Take care of her the best he could as he'd promised the one-eyed French bastard who gave him the greatest gift he'd ever known. "I'd like you to marry us."

Tupper said nothing. She pulled on her pipe and puffed a perfect smoky ring. "And what's your second request?"

"I'll be needing a bed."

Epilogue

The *Night's Price,* formerly known as the *Devil's Pearl,* set sail and pulled away from the *Scarlet Night* for the last time.

"But they need us. Tupper said it herself. You're her best gunner, and I--"

"--am carrying my child."

"It isn't the plague." Jo Beau Robbins smoothed a hand over the slight swell of her belly. "Thousands of women have had babies before."

Ric positioned the square mainsail to catch the best wind. "Not my babies, and not aboard a pirate ship."

"How would you know? You were a rogue when I met you. You could have children scattered all over the Caribbean." Jo moved to stand in the bow.

"I'd like to think I was more careful than that, but I'm only concerned with one baby right now." Ric set the rudder before joining his wife. Standing behind her, he slipped his arms around her and pushed his hand beneath her waistband to span his fingers across the roundness he found there. "This babe, here."

Jo sighed into his embrace and tipped her head back to lean against his shoulder giving him full access to her lovely neck. "What if we don't like Charlestown?"

He kissed the tender skin behind her ear before he teased the lobe with his tongue. Moving her soft curls aside with the tip of his nose, he nipped his way down to her favorite spot where her neck curved into her shoulder. "Then we'll pack up Henry, Jr. and find somewhere we do like."

She arched, writhing against him as his hand moved lower. "Are you certain it will be a boy?" Her backside played havoc with his growing arousal.

"No…" he growled against her throat. "It doesn't matter as long as the child isn't born in the middle of an ocean."

His fingers parted the heated flesh between her thighs. She whimpered. "Oh, Ric…" Jocelyn guided his other hand upward to cup the heavy fullness of her breast. Her body was changing with her pregnancy. So beautifully rounded and full. More sensitive to his touch. The slightest sweep of a fingertip could produce the most heated response from her now. It was like learning her body all over again.

She trembled beneath his hands as he pinned her tight to his erection. "God, I want you."

"You have me." Jocelyn turned in his arms and kissed him deeply. "You've had me from the beginning. Don't you remember," she gave him a sassy smile. "You bought me at the auction?"

"Aye," he bit at her lip. "But I never did pay for you." He reminded her. "I stole you."

She wound her arms around his neck and pressed her body boldly to his. "Only my heart, ye bloody pirate. The rest, I gave you for free."

Be sure not to miss Lisa A. Olech's sequel to *Within A Captain's Hold*, *Within A Captain's Treasure*, and *Within A Captain's Fate*:

Within A Captain's Power

Read on for a special sneak peek of the next book in the Captains of the Scarlet Night series!

Learn more about Lisa A. Olech
http://www.kensingtonbooks.com/author.aspx/31711

Chapter 1

Arlington, Virginia--1715

Samantha Christian pulled the hood of her black wool cloak low to conceal her face. Ahead of her through the gloom of a murky night, her rescuer tugged at her arm and urged her to hurry. She stumbled upon an upturned root and her guide cursed.

"Damn it, hurry. The tide will be high soon. If we are not away, we won't be able to leave 'till dawn."

"I'm moving as fast as I can. These shoes are too big. They keep slipping from my feet."

Less than an hour had passed since Tupper Quinn alerted Samantha by tossing small pebbles at her window. Now was the time. It was tonight or the opportunity--and her savior might be lost.

She raised the window then caught the knotted rope she was tossed before securing it to the heavy post of her bed. Moments later, Tupper swung over the sill to drop into the room.

The wild-haired woman in the breeches and boots wasted no time with pleasantries. "Put these on and be quick about it. If he catches us, we'll never be away."

In the pack she tossed at her, Samantha found a pair of mud-brown breeches and a shirt of coarse linen together with a long wide strip of muslin. Stockings and buckled shoes finished the outfit along with a wide, thick leather belt.

Stripping off her dressing gown, Samantha heard the sharp intake of breath behind her. She turned to find Tupper's narrowed eyes upon her.

"He put those marks on you?" she hissed.

Samantha nodded clutching her gown to her chest. Tupper reached out and brushed the hair away from her face, before tipping it to the light. Samantha couldn't hide the dark ugly bruise that marred her cheek.

"Lowlife son of a whore, bastard," she grumbled releasing her chin. "Best be quick before I change my mind and choose to end his miserable life."

"I'm tempted to let you."

Tupper nodded to the muslin. "To bind yourself. Make it good and tight."

Samantha began to wrap the fabric about her chest, flattening her breasts fullness as best she could. She donned the strange feeling pants and finally slid her feet into shoes that were two sizes too large.

"Now your hair." Tupper instructed.

Samantha smoothed a hand down its long length. "What about my hair?"

"You're passing as a lad, it will have to go." Tupper pulled a short dagger from her boot.

"All of it?" Clasping a handful, she held it to her heart. She always kept her hair long, but knew the cost of this night. She didn't need to hear Tupper's answer. Samantha closed her eyes, and nodded.

The sharp blade made short work of the task. Tupper began cutting through the thick shanks of hair. The soft brown locks fell in curled fistfuls at her feet. Samantha felt tears prick the backs of her eyes, but as the first bit of hair fell, she knew there would be no turning back for her. She would soon be free from her hellish existence and by the grace of God she would be saved.

Later as she struggled to keep pace with Tupper, the cold dampness of the night's air upon her neck felt strange and only added to the surreal scene in which she found herself. How they found their way through the moonless night, she could not say, but soon her feet hit the sandy soil that harkened their arrival upon the shore.

A small skiff with four large men stood waiting. Tupper helped her into the boat, retrieved the shoe that dropped into the water, and scrambled in with the rest.

"Make haste gentlemen, the tide will not be waiting."

The skiff jerked as each man tugged sharply on the oars. It took only a moment for them to find their synchronized rhythm.

The black outline of the land against the ebony sky was Samantha's last sight of Virginia and hopefully the last she would ever see of Damian Wessler and his evil children.

Samantha held her sodden shoe in her hands. The four men made short work of bringing the skiff out to the tall, three-masted sloop that sat anchored off shore. There had been no conversation. Tupper sat facing her but paid her little attention, concentrating instead on the men behind her. One of them hummed to himself, pulling at his appointed oar in time to the song he sang only in his head.

When they reached the ship, a rope ladder was lowered and soon the small party was climbing swiftly up the side of the dark ship. Samantha struggled to keep her footing on the shifting rope. Her shoes were making it nearly impossible. Once she decided to shove them into her belt and make her way without them, it was much easier going.

Tupper pulled her over the gunwale and called out an order. "All set, Gents, let's weigh anchor and be off."

Shouts and a flurry of activity erupted around them. The ship was dimly lit with only a handful of lanterns, but the crew worked as if by feel alone. Three men circled a pegged wheel of sorts. Its brass cap catching the light as they turned it round and round. As it began to move, the ship creaked and popped. The deck beneath her stocking covered feet began to rock.

The snap of the sails catching the night's breeze sounded over head. Samantha stumbled and grabbed hold of the thick, tarred rigging when the ship seemed to leap across the water.

"You, lad," Tupper called out. Samantha looked behind her, until Tupper jostled her shoulder. "*You*, lad, follow me."

Samantha followed Tupper Quinn across the deck, moving between men of every size and description. Some pulled at ropes, other climbed up wide rigging into the dark of the sky.

She slowed her stride to watch, but a bark from Tupper had her rushing to catch up.

"I'm not a patient soul, boy, move yer arse." Laughter arose around her and someone close to her gave her a mighty shove in Tupper's direction. She didn't dare turn to see who had pushed her. Their laughter followed in her wake.

Tupper disappeared down a stairwell and she hurried to follow. The passage way was dark as a tomb with no light to guide her. She groped her way along the rough wood walls of the corridor. Ahead of her a door opened and a blade of blessed light lit her way to the rear of the ship. She stopped in the doorway of a large windowed cabin.

"If you're waiting for a personal invitation, you'll be standing there quite some time. Get in here and shut the damn door." Behind Tupper a fierce looking black bird squawked from an iron perch.

"Oh, I'm sorry." Samantha scrambled into the room and shut the door.

Tupper removed her hat and tossed it into a chair. A fine-tooled leather baldric soon joined it. Turning to look at her, Tupper ran a hand over her head, smoothing the stray hair from her face. The light from the lanterns caught at the wide, silvered streak that ran through her long dark hair. Piercing eyes of green appraised her as she moved to stand behind a large oak desk.

Tupper opened a drawer and pulled a crystal decanter and two glasses from what looked to be a special carved drawer designed to hold the delicate items. She poured a healthy draught of the liquor into each glass and handed one to her.

Samantha eyed her over her glass as Tupper simply tossed the entire contents of hers back in one swallow. She repeated the action and paused to refill Samantha's glass only to find it still full.

"Drink up."

Samantha mimicked what Tupper had done, and soon realized what a mistake she'd made. The rum burned her throat, and stole her breath. Tears filled her eyes as she coughed and sputtered and tried in vain to breathe. Tupper simply filled her own glass again, smiled, and sat down.

"Have a seat." Samantha did as she was told, wiping the tears from her eyes. "Are you all right?" She couldn't answer, but nodded her head. "Another?" Tupper held up the decanter.

"No," rasped Samantha, "No, thank you."

Tupper tossed back another and poured herself a fourth. She must have a stomach like an iron pot. Pulling a small pipe from another cubby hole, she packed the bowl and lit it before leaning back in her chair. Drink in one hand, pipe in the other, she rested her booted heels on the corner of her desk and locked gazes with Samantha.

"Now, would you explain to me why I've been dragged into the middle of your particular mess in the middle of the night? I get a frantic message from Isabelle Whitmore and fortunately for you, I'm close enough to port to be of some assistance. All I know is I have to get you out of some house and away from a man named Wessler and Virginia as soon as possible."

"I…I will be forever grateful, to you and the Whitmores."

"Isabelle is an old, trusted friend. If she went to all this trouble, the situation must have been dire. Your bruises have already told me as much." Tupper blew a cloud of smoke toward the ceiling. "So can I assume Mr. Wessler is at this moment sailing out with the authorities to meet us?"

"You don't need to worry. I still have two days." Samantha ran her thumb over the intricate carvings on her glass.

"I don't understand, two days?"

"When I got the news you were coming, I picked a fight with him. Openly flirted with an English Naval officer at a party we attended night before last." She shrugged a shoulder. "It cost me another few bruises, but I was guaranteed four days of being locked away as a punishment. Wessler won't even open the door unless his cock decides to work, but I wouldn't count on it."

Tupper gave a snort of laughter. "What about when they bring you your meals?"

"No meals."

Tupper's eyes narrowed. "He doesn't feed you?"

Samantha notched her chin and held Tupper's gaze. The last thing she wanted was her pity. "He believes it will break me, but he's wrong."

"Well, at least I know Isabelle didn't exaggerate the situation."

"I know I put her in a precarious position, but I had little choice and an even smaller chance."

Tupper set her pipe aside. "You're tough, I like tough. A good thing too, because I'm not about to nursemaid you. But you've put me in a rather precarious position myself. With my crew. I've never lied to them before and don't particularly like doing so now, but the situation is quite simple. I'm the only woman currently allowed upon this ship. The fact I've been Captain now for more years than I can count makes it an indisputable fact. Hell, I doubt if many of the crew even notices I am not a man anymore and frankly, that's the way I like it."

She pulled her boots off the desk and sat forward. "You, however, are a different story. From the moment you climbed down the rope at Wessler's estate, until the time we deposit you wherever it is we are to deposit you, you are my new cabin boy. Samantha is now Sam and you will do nothing to raise questions to that fact. Clear?"

She nodded. "Yes, of course."

"You will put your mark to the ship's Articles and follow all the rules. You will be given duties and responsibilities to pay for our hospitality and you shall do nothing to disrupt the running of my ship. Do you understand?"

"Yes, Tupper."

"Nay, you say, 'Aye, Captain.'"

"Aye, Captain."

Tupper gave a smart nod and sat back. "Now, about your final destination...."

"Take me anywhere."

"Back to your family in England, I assume?"

"No…" She turned the glass in her hand. "I don't want them to know about what happened at Wessler's. I'll send word when I'm able telling them I am safe and well. Their lives do not need the shame this would bring them."

"The only shame is Wessler's."

Samantha gave a short bitter laugh. "He doesn't know the meaning of the word." She pushed her glass back across the desk. "Could I get a bit more of whatever this was?"

Tupper grinned as she lifted the bottle out and filled both their glasses again. Her sharp green eyes sparkled adding softness to her weathered face. "I'm beginning to think having you aboard may be all right after all." She pushed Samantha's drink across the desk. "How are you at shooting a pistol?"

Sam tossed back her drink and coughed. "If I were any good at it, would I be here?"

Meet the Author

Lisa A. Olech is an artist/writer living in her dream house nestled among the lakes in New England. She loves getting lost in a steamy book, finding the perfect pair of sexy shoes, and hearing the laughter of her men. Being an estrogen island in a sea of testosterone makes her queen. She believes in ghosts, silver linings, the power of a man in a tuxedo, and happy endings. For more please visit lisaolech.com.